A Share ___ ___

by

Paul Beattie

4·S.

Contents

1. Istanbul, March 1929

Jasper Lewingdon was dead. It had to be true; it was in the paper. 23rd September 1928, Westminster Coroner's Court pronounced that a corpse pulled from the Thames was one Jasper Lewingdon. The coroner's verdict? Accidental death by drowning. The reporter's verdict? Death by Daiquiri, helped by a few whisky chasers. The truth? That was still being written. The cutting from the Daily Chronicle looked a bit tired around the edges. Jasper smiled to himself as he slipped it away; that's precisely how he felt these days. He raised his glass in a silent salute to the reporter that had killed his character, if not his body.

The wail of a cornet cut through his thoughts, and one half of the Sabini Sisters flashed a smile at him from the club's dance floor. He grinned back, turning his salute to a distant journalist into a toast to her. If two girls from Hungary could reinvent themselves as the Dolly Sisters and make a fortune from it, why not two sisters from St Petersburg? Istanbul was the place to do it. East met West, old met new; clichés but true all the same. How many Russians had fled the Bolsheviks seeking shelter in this ancient city? How many Armenians? How many newly created Turks expelled from across the now-defunct Ottoman Empire? In a city of a million people, many were keen to forget, or hide, who they had been. Jasper was no different.

But the crowd in this club was here to see the Sabini Sisters. The band upped the tempo. Cecile and Salome were getting close to their finale, but Cecile still had him in her sights. That wouldn't be a bad thing at any other time, but not tonight. Pretty soon, he had to be somewhere else. The band climaxed in a crescendo of cornets as Cecile and Salome hit their ending with practised perfection. The audience leapt to their feet, cheering and whooping. Cecile and Salome took their well-earned applause. Jasper joined in, but it was time to slip away.

* * *

Jasper pulled his coat tighter around him. The bellhop had said that this was the coldest it had been in Istanbul in living memory. The way the chill cut through him, it might just be true. Snow had fallen, trams had frozen to their tracks, and it was rumoured the Orient Express had become trapped by snowdrifts. Who knows, perhaps there was a story in that somewhere. The backstreets of Beyoğlu, just across the Golden Horn from the city's ancient heart, were quiet. Well, as quiet as they ever got, the bars and clubs of this part of the city never shut. With his hat pulled down and shoulders hunched, he was just one more shadow on the street. Nothing to do but wait. Nothing to do but shiver.

A consumptive cough echoed from the tall walls of the alley. Jasper pulled himself deeper into the doorway and checked his watch. It was still too early for the caretaker to arrive. A shiver vibrated up his back. Was it the cold or something else?

Who the hell had sent him that press cutting? Whoever it was, they knew he was calling himself Max Bolton. Worse than that, they knew he was in Istanbul. The cough sounded a second time, now accompanied by the slow tread of someone approaching. Jasper took a few soft steps back into the cover of the doorway and the staircase leading up. Just another night owl, or had someone followed him from the club?

A hunched shadow slouched into view, the tip of a cigarette glowing unnaturally bright in the backstreet gloom. Jasper's pulse quickened with recognition: the caretaker was early. The figure stopped. The seconds dripped by. Run? Which way? A spasm of coughing cracked the silence as the caretaker doubled over. Several lung-racking moments later, the caretaker flicked the cigarette to the ground, swore, and then moved on.

Jasper breathed out. Turkish tobacco could be strong stuff. The caretaker's slow tread sank into the background buzz of the backstreets. How long until he reached the gate? Thirty seconds? A minute? Was it worth hanging around in the cold for the sake of another couple of minutes? That draught of cold air creeping in said no.

The alley was empty; no consumptive caretaker lurking at the corner. Despite the darkness, the place still had all the allure of a minefield swept with searchlights. Act like you belong. Act like you should be there. Easy to say, but far more difficult to do. It was only a short amble, but it would feel like a thousand miles. For God's sake, pull yourself together and get on with it!

Head down and hands pushed into the pockets of his coat, Jasper left the cover of the doorway and headed up the alley. His fingers brushed the lock picks in his pocket. A pool of light from the only lamp in the passage marked out the target: the entrance to a tall house that backed onto the French Consulate. Most of the house was in darkness, but one light in a high-up window remained stubbornly on. It couldn't be helped. He'd just have to risk it.

The double doors of the entrance were directly on the alley with no convenient recess to hide in. Jasper slipped the slim torsion wrench into the lock, followed by the pick. He raked the lock a few times; nothing. His hands were cold, and he couldn't get a good feel for the lock. Breathe, breathe; panicking won't help. He closed his eyes, slowing his breathing. The background bustle of Beyoğlu started to separate: the wail of a cornet, shouts from a few streets away, the strings of an oud close by. His shoulders loosened, and the lock turned.

The left-hand door swung inward. Jasper stepped inside. The hallway was dark, the streetlight throwing his shadow in front of him. He shut the door, and the darkness seemed total. The slow tick of a clock sounded off the long seconds as a semblance of night vision crept back. Keeping his hand against the wall, Jasper walked forward. Ahead he could make out stairs, and upstairs was where he had to be.

The carpet on the stairs softened his tread, refusing to betray him. Why was that light on somewhere upstairs? Who else was in this building? He'd checked the place out as much as he could. It was still owned by a Greek family; they'd left Istanbul a couple of years before. Now the place was in limbo, empty but not forgotten. That light was probably no more than a sop to any would-be burglar or intruder. Jasper grimaced. You keep telling yourself that, it might just turn out to be true. A distant rattle and clunk of a door being opened echoed in the gloom. What now, smart arse?

Jasper took the last few steps quickly, stopping at the top of the stairs. A long corridor ran the length of the building, a row of windows looking out over the courtyard at the back of the French Consulate. His pulse was galloping as he strained to listen. A slight creak? Another footstep? More moments sloughing by. An uncomfortable trickle ran down his back despite the cold. Yes, the clear tread of someone above. He tracked the invisible footsteps along the ceiling; no doubt there was a corridor directly above this one. The footsteps stopped. His pulse hammered.

Come on, come on! Do something. The clock in the hallway chimed the half-hour. Jasper stared at the spot halfway along the corridor's ceiling where the spectre must be. If only it were a phantom. A small squeak signalled movement. Jasper tensed, then breathed out; the footsteps were heading away. Slow, slow breaths; this was no time to react. It was time to get himself together. Should he carry on with the job? The distant door clunked once more, and then, silence. He glanced at the row of sash windows along the corridor. You've got this far, so why not at least check the route?

Jasper walked to the centre window. The courtyard at the back of the consulate was below, a narrow tiled roof separating it from this building. It was going to be much easier to head along that roof rather than scale tall walls, complete with a liberal helping of razor wire. He twisted the catch on the window; it turned silently. With luck, the window was equally well looked after. With half an ear listening for phantom footsteps above, he lifted the window; it slid like a skate on ice. Things were looking up. He ducked through the open window and placed a foot on the tiles below. They felt solid. Once through, Jasper slid the window shut and set off along the roof towards the main block of the consulate.

The two-storey building had a few low lights glimmering in its upper windows. Nothing to worry about. All the staff had long since left and were either in bed or in the clubs and bars of Beyoğlu. All except one consumptive caretaker. He should be safely asleep with his feet up on his desk in the basement. What could go wrong?

He padded along the narrow roof. The odd tile graunched at his passing but nothing else. At the end, he pulled himself up onto the cornice that ran around the top of the ground floor. Jasper grinned; this ledge was perfect if

8

you wanted something to stand on while breaking into a building. Perhaps the architect had been a burglar in his spare time. He worked his way along the wall stopping at the third window. He peered inside. The office's interior was in shadow, but the light from a corridor picked out the desks and cabinets clearly. Jasper examined the casement window; it was old and needed some attention: perfect.

He probed for the window latch with a thin metal strip, finding it on the second attempt. Now for a bit of patience. A gust of wind whipped against him, his hat threatening to fly off. Suddenly, Jasper was very aware of how cold he was getting. Another probe and the latch popped, and the right-hand leaf of the window swung open. He slipped inside, pulling the window shut. He rubbed his hands together, blowing on them to try and warm them up. Gloves would have been a good idea, but he couldn't pick locks in gloves.

The office door was locked. Jasper rubbed his hands again to try and get some circulation going. Despite the sense that his fingers were not all his own, the lock took less than thirty seconds to give up. He opened the door and peered along the corridor. There wasn't much to be seen, but the thin strains of a gramophone were wafting in from somewhere. Was that the caretaker's, or had someone decided to bring the party back to the office? A muffle of voices, a giggle followed by shushing and more muted laughter echoed along the corridor.

It looked like some Pierre, or Francois was trying to impress a girl he'd picked up by giving her a tour of his office. His office, or would he be exaggerating how important he was? Jasper smirked. Despite the adrenalin pinging around his nervous system, he already knew the answer to that one. Pierre will be in the Consul's office, not in a shared shed like this one, bragging about how

9

indispensable he was to the Consul… perhaps in his version, he was the Consul? Jasper took a deep breath. Here's hoping that Yvette, Nicole or whatever her name was, would keep him busy long enough to complete this job.

Two steps, and he was at the office door across the corridor. Jasper checked it: locked. He knew it would be, but it was always annoying when you've spent minutes picking a lock only to find it's already open. A slightly offended shriek rattled down the corridor. Jasper tensed. Don't blow it now, Pierre; I need more time. More murmurs and then a giggle. That's better. Take your time. Goodness knows I need you to. The lock clicked open.

Jasper stepped inside the office, pushing the door shut. Despite the large window, there wouldn't be enough light for what he needed to do. A wide desk dominated the room, a small filing cabinet to its side. Sat in the centre of the desk was a name plaque. Even though he couldn't see the writing on the plaque, he knew it said: Claude Beaudoin. Jasper walked around the desk and looked outside. The enclosed manicured garden in front of the consulate was quiet. The occasional figure could be seen in the street just beyond its wall. Jasper shut the louvres on the windows. He sat down at the desk and switched on the desk lamp; at least he wouldn't alert anyone outside the building.

He tried the desk drawers. They opened. Unlike you, Claude. You struck me as the type that would lock everything away. A tray of neatly arranged stamps was set in the exact centre of the top drawer. Now that is like you, Claude. Jasper lifted out the tray and a couple of sheets of paper. Two days ago, Jasper had sat on the opposite side of this desk as Claude had carefully explained to him what stamps and paperwork Jasper's 'female friend' would need to enter France. Claude had smirked when he called

10

Adrianna, Jasper's friend; it didn't matter that she didn't exist. It still left a nasty taste in his mouth. Then Claude informed him that she wouldn't be able to get the correct stamps and paperwork; perhaps he should try the British Consulate. Au revoir.

Jasper inked the stamps and made a series of impressions of each on the sheets of paper. Once satisfied, he put them away. Now for the correct paperwork. The strains of the gramophone were now audible. He went to the door and opened it slightly. It sounded like Pierre and Yvette were getting along famously, perhaps too well. He'd have to hope that the consumptive caretaker was a sound sleeper. He walked back to the filing cabinet.

A few moments later, the filing cabinet was open. Jasper grabbed the contents of its top drawer and took them back to the desk. Three files down, he found the papers he wanted; the latest blank visa and permit forms. Claude had felt the need to wave them at him just to underline the point that Adriana wouldn't be getting one. Jasper smiled and flicked to the back of the file; the papers were in numerical order. Half a dozen visas and associated forms from the back of the bundle shouldn't be missed, at least not to start with. Now for a passport or two, maybe three? The bottom file contained a stack of blank passports. Make that four.

Jasper returned the files to the cabinet, making sure they were all neat and tidy. We wouldn't want to arouse Claude's suspicions now, would we? He slid the cabinet drawer shut and set about locking it. Picking a lock was easy, but re-locking it was always a test of his patience. The bloody lock was fighting back, but he couldn't leave it. A hacking cough sounded. He froze. What now? Switch the desk lamp off, you idiot, that's what! The room dropped into darkness.

11

Another cough was followed by the sound of a door handle being rattled. Shit! The caretaker was doing his rounds. The door opposite and this one were unlocked. Think, you bloody fool, think! He looked at the telephone on the desk. A second door rattled, closer this time. Jasper picked up the handset, praying he could remember the number when he'd watched Claude dial it. Distant relays clunked, and then the sound of ringing, not just in his ear, but down the corridor too. Pick up, pick up! A door rattle stopped mid-shake. The ringing stopped.

"Hello?" The voice sounded uncertain in Jasper's ear.

"Get out now! The caretaker is doing his rounds and has a gendarme with him!" Jasper hung up. All he could do now was wait and hope. Silence. Seconds seeming like hours slipped by. Another door rattled; the next would be his.

A shout, a scream followed by clattering. Another cry, followed by coughing. More yells, and the caretaker's silhouette sped past the office window. Jasper counted the seconds. Please let Pierre and Yvette be quick on their feet, at least enough to give him time to get away. The shouts and the occasional cough were getting distant. Jasper opened Claude's office door and looked down the corridor. Distant echoes of quick footsteps on stairs hinted that he was alone for now. A lost women's shoe suggested that tonight's adventure would be remembered by Yvette; that was going to cost Pierre.

Jasper locked the office door. Time to slip away the way he'd come. Did he have time to get back to the club before Cecile left?

2. Mayfair, March 1929

"Istanbul! Why that's...that's fantastic. When are we going?" Elspeth forced the sparkle into her voice; this was an unexpected turn of events.

"It's business. There's no need for you to bore yourself travelling all that way. I'll be spending all my time in dull meetings and even duller dinners."

Cameron sounded casual, his eyes fixed on some slight distraction outside the window. Elspeth kept her smile nailed in place. She had to keep her performance going to match the one he was putting on.

"I certainly wouldn't be bored. While you're decomposing in your dull meetings, I can spend my time getting lost in the souks buying carpets and jewellery. Of course, you wouldn't deny your fiancé the chance to go shopping, would you?"

Cameron turned and looked at her. The matinee idol smile was fractionally too slow to drop into place; he was covering something up. An affair or something far worse?

"Honestly darling, Istanbul wouldn't be your cup of tea at all—"

"Don't be ridiculous!" She beamed at him. "You do remember that I'm the society correspondent on that paper you own, don't you? The Daily Chronicle; big building in the middle of Fleet Street?"

"Of course, but—"

"But nothing. Istanbul has the raciest nightlife outside of Soho, Berlin or New York. I've been dying to sample it and write it up for my column. I owe it to my readers."

She turned up the wattage of her smile; Cameron's was starting to look more like a grimace. This must be a sudden decision. He couldn't have thought this through; any other time, he would have made mincemeat of the feeble arguments she was throwing up to accompany him.

"If you're in Istanbul, who will write the column in your absence?"

"That's not a problem. Michael is always pitching stories to me in the hope that I give him an escape from reporting the goings-on at the magistrates' courts. He'd jump at the chance to look after it for a week or two. Besides, I'll have to give up the column once we're married. This will be a good opportunity to try out some talent."

The smile had evaporated entirely, a frown replacing it. Right now, Cameron was giving a good impression of Heathcliff. Tall, dark and brooding was fine in a romantic novel, but she knew a lot more about his secrets than was good for her. The flutter in her stomach suggested it might be time to back-peddle and give him a way out for now.

"What's happened? Everything is alright, isn't it? You're not in trouble, are you?"

She took a pace closer, her hand finding the crook of his arm, a crease of concern touching the corner of her eyes. Cameron beamed back at her; the smile was almost genuine.

"Of course, darling. Nothing to worry about. An opportunity has come up to purchase some businesses I've had my eye on for a while. I just need to find a decent Turkish partner, so I have to go to Istanbul." He glanced at his wristwatch. "Now then, let's go out and find some fun."

Elspeth smiled. She might have believed him if he

hadn't changed the subject.

* * *

As safe houses go, the back seat of a Rolls Royce wasn't bad. Elspeth looked at K. She'd just finished briefing him about Cameron Lowe's sudden need to visit Istanbul on business. K stared ahead, his hands propped on the handle of his umbrella. The weather was dry, no need for an umbrella, but he always seemed to have it when they met in the Rolls. Almost three years had passed since he had recruited her. Three years as what exactly? She didn't appear on the payroll of MI5, but she reported directly to its head, K. An agent? Perhaps, but what had that made Jasper? K cleared his throat, making her start.

"And you're sure Cameron hasn't any business dealings in Turkey?" he asked.

"As sure as I can be. The only dealings he had in the Middle or the Near East were during the war when he was in Persia. He's never mentioned anything about Turkey, Greece or Palestine, not even in passing."

"What about his time in Tehran?" K shifted in his seat, his gaze swinging onto her. His grey eyes looked all the more intense through the pince-nez perched on his nose. The permanent frown lines arrowed down towards the bridge of his nose.

"He's never volunteered anything. When I ask, he says he spent most of his time loafing around the bars of the European hotels, swapping stories with ex-pats, and playing cards."

"And you've not picked up anything else about what he was doing in Tehran, and who for?" The frown deepened. Her pulse quickened.

"No." Apart from some strong rumours he had been in Baku in 1918, making deals with the Bolsheviks to keep the oil flowing. Just before the Turks rolled in. Her stomach twisted. Until now, she'd never lied directly to K. She just hadn't mentioned it. Why? K's stare held her. Did he believe her? Why hadn't she told him when she'd heard about Cameron Lowe being in Baku? It was just rumours; she hadn't tested it; she hadn't… No, you thought there was a story in it and didn't want to share. Well, you're stuck now, aren't you? She stared back at K; the scrutiny was starting to get uncomfortable.

"Have you heard anything?" she asked. Perhaps the question would give her a breathing space. He shook his head.

"No, I haven't heard anything. It's difficult for me to ask questions. People get suspicious when the head of MI5 starts making polite enquiries about important figures like Cameron Lowe. That's why I engage people like you."

"But you must have some idea as to why he needs to go to Istanbul in such a hurry."

The corner of K's mouth twitched, his moustache bristling.

"I'm sure you must have some ideas. What would be at the top of your list if this was for your gossip column?"

Elspeth scanned his face. A hint of a smile was still there, but that could signify anything or maybe nothing. The Rolls braked sharply. A horn sounded as Elspeth glanced at the clog of traffic around Hyde Park Corner.

16

"An excuse to whisk away a mistress or girlfriend would be at the top of the list." Her reply was half-mumbled to the traffic.

"But you don't believe that?"

If only she could.

"No." She mugged a grimace at him. "At the first sign of anything going on, there'd be a queue of bright young things battering down my door to share the news, or giving it to a rival gossip column."

"You have an alternative hypothesis?"

Of course she did, and he bloody well knew it.

"Jasper's in Istanbul."

K's face hardened.

"Jasper is dead. You identified the body."

"I labelled a corpse dragged from the Thames as Jasper." The words fired themselves at K. If she screwed her eyes shut, she'd probably still see the sparse huddle of people at the edge of a grave. Her tears had added nicely to the atmosphere; she'd played her part to perfection. Had she really believed she was doing it to protect Jasper? No, it was a convenient way to justify it to herself. She stared at the traffic as the Rolls pushed its way forward.

"But Max Bolton is very much alive," she said, "and somewhere in Istanbul if Jasper took your advice."

She turned and glared at K. His grey eyes didn't even flicker. His advice to Jasper had been a lot more than that.

"And you think that Cameron is heading there to find him? To what end?"

Was that a genuine question, or was he goading her for his own amusement?

"Jasper was blackmailing Sir Nicholas Linklater; Cameron's political puppet and figurehead for the far right—"

"And Sir Nicholas is dead."

She stared at K. He was staring directly ahead once more, his hands a little tighter on the umbrella's handle. It was unlike him to interrupt her; was this irritation or something else?

"Yes, he died in suspicious circumstances at the same time that Jasper left for Istanbul, or at least Max Bolton did."

K harrumphed.

"The coroner ruled that Sir Nicholas's death was from natural causes, a stroke or something along those lines," said K.

"Something along those lines."

She didn't try to keep the sarcasm from her voice; it had the desired effect. K breathed out and looked at her.

"I can assure you that Jasper did not kill Sir Nicholas Linklater."

"His sister, Lady Susan, disagrees with you, and she still has Cameron Lowe's ear."

K's eyes narrowed a fraction. His right forefinger was starting to tap out a tattoo on the umbrella's handle. Maybe now she had his attention.

"Go on," he said.

"She covers it well, but one too many Martinis and the act starts to slip. Barbed comments tossed my way, cornering Cameron to demand that he do something, cursing Jasper and swearing she'll get even."

K's drumming stopped.

"That sounds like a sister failing to deal with her grief."

"I managed to get a look at the report from the second post-mortem that she had done." K's hands tightened around the umbrella handle; coincidence or acting out a guilty secret? "It looked rather like Sir Nicholas was smothered in his sleep."

K harrumphed again.

"My, you have been busy." He shifted in his seat, his gaze moving away. "It still doesn't mean that Cameron is going to Istanbul in search of Jasper."

"Cameron still heads the Industrial Intelligence Bureau. I'm pretty sure he's put at least some of his private spy ring at her disposal just to get a quiet life. What do you think they may have dug up?" K cleared his throat to speak, but Elspeth cut him off. "If Lady Susan thinks Jasper's alive, then she knows I lied about the corpse. How long before she drops that into a conversation over tea at Claridge's?" If she hasn't already.

K's fingers were fairly drumming as the Rolls swept along Piccadilly.

"Lady Susan can be known to be bitter, verging on vindictive. With encouragement, I'm sure you could persuade Cameron that this is all borne out of jealousy. They were once an item."

"Cameron's not a fool. He'll check her story; that's what I'm afraid this trip is about. He'll be wondering why I lied, and we both know the answer to that."

The traffic was starting to bunch as the Rolls approached Piccadilly Circus. K's fingers stopped drumming.

"You need to convince Cameron to take you with him." She started to speak, but K raised a finger, stopping her. "You need to find Jasper and make damn sure that Cameron doesn't. We must keep up the charade that Jasper is dead before someone catches up with him and makes it a reality."

The Rolls slowed to a crawl as its driver threaded his way through the scrum of cars, buses and taxis. Elspeth stared at the solitary flower seller marooned on the steps around the statue of Eros; right now, she'd give anything to swap places with her. K was still talking.

"I can't offer you much in the way of support once you're out of the country." She almost laughed; when had he ever given her support? He offered her a business card, a name and telephone number written on its reverse: Jude Faulkner. "Jude is our man in Istanbul. If you have to get out in a hurry, go to him, he should help you."

"Thank you." She took the card; it was the thinnest of lifelines.

"When is Cameron leaving?" asked K.

"This Friday."

The Rolls was easing its way into Coventry Street, barely moving at more than a walking pace.

"That doesn't give you much time to appeal to

20

Cameron's better nature. If you have to, take whatever train, plane, steamship or camel if it comes to it. Make sure you get there."

"Won't that make me look desperate?"

"Yes, but reprising your role as mad fiancé woman may just work as a cover." He glanced at his watch. "You'd better get started. Where can I drop you?"

"Here will be fine."

The Rolls came to a stop despite the taxi behind sounding its horn. So much for not attracting attention. As soon as she slammed the door shut, the Rolls cut into the traffic, carving a path through it. Elspeth glanced at the card in her hand.

"Thank you for nothing!"

That familiar bowling ball was sitting firmly in the pit of her stomach. It took all her will not to drop the card K had given her and start running. She took a deep breath and held it for a second before letting it go. If you start running now, when will you ever stop? An elbow caught her as someone in the crowd pushed past, their mumbled apology already lost in the traffic noise. Elspeth shoved the card into her coat pocket.

Ahead was a Lyons Corner House. She angled through the press of people on the pavement, heading for the temporary sanctuary of tea and starched white linen. How on earth was she going to play this? Did Cameron suspect her? If he did, then surely there was no way he would let her go with him. But, if he thought she was a plant, what better way to isolate her than take her to Istanbul? She pushed the door open. The bustle and clatter on the ground floor were barely less than the pavement outside. Elspeth took the lift to the restaurant.

She jumped as the attendant banged the lattice door shut, closing her in and taking away her control. The metaphor wasn't lost on her. K was manipulating her from the second she had stepped into the Rolls. Hell, he'd used her from the first moment they met three years ago. The subtle approach. The feigned interest in a freelance journalist trying to make a career. The not-so-gentle nudges on who to investigate and what stories to go after. The lift arrived, and the attendant had barely rattled back the door before Elspeth was stalking her way to the first empty table she could see.

The simmer of resentment was starting to boil. Elspeth flicked through the menu card, barely acknowledging what was written on it. Yes, K had manipulated her; directed her; told her what to do, but she had gone along with it. It'd be so easy to hang the blame on someone else. He made me do it. I had no choice. Oh, stop lying to yourself. You did these things because you wanted to, and now you're trapped.

A waitress was approaching the table. Elspeth scanned the menu. She wasn't hungry, but she needed a distraction. She snapped her order at the waitress; the girl all but jumped at her bark. The sting of regret at her words was near-instant. It's not that girl's fault. The waitress was already marching away, and it was too late to apologise. Elspeth's head sunk into her hands.

How did you get yourself into this mess? K's briefing from all that time ago was fresh in her mind: use your links from the paper; get close to a clique of high-society fascists; he'd help get her in. Report back to K the tittle-tattle and late-night gossip. Alcohol, parties and flirting had been her stock in trade, and it had paid off. It never failed to surprise her how many fat-headed fools wanted to boast about what should be kept secret.

It would be fine if that's all it was, just the bluster of self-deluding idiots. But sitting in the middle was a mole. A Communist mole. Someone with the will, and the skills, to nudge, steer and exploit a bunch of self-entitled shits: Lady Susan Linklater. She was more than vindictive; she was lethal.

Unmasking her had been hard. Jasper had dug the evidence out, but getting K to act had been a battle. He hadn't wanted to believe it, but Jasper had pursued it when K had tried to ignore it and when K could no longer turn a blind eye? He left Lady Susan in place where he could keep an eye on her and check what she and her OGPU[1] handlers were up to. What was the price for this window into the plots being woven by Moscow? Jasper's life was destroyed, but at least he still had one; it had cost Ruby hers.

The waitress returned with a pot of tea. As soon as she had gone, Elspeth poured some milk into her cup. Her hand shook, spilling milk onto the table cloth. She willed the tremor from her hand. There was no Sir Galahad on a white charger coming to her rescue, she'd got herself into this, and now she had to get herself out of it.

---

[1] OGPU, the secret service of the Soviet Union, the forerunner of the KGB.

3. A House Call

Thin spring sunshine washed a little colour into the tired façades of the houses in the street. Jasper loosened his scarf. The stiff march uphill from the ferry had pushed a little warmth into him, but it hadn't driven the chill from his bones. Creeping about on rooftops and lurking in alleyways during the small hours wasn't good for the constitution. His stomach rumbled. Neither was skipping breakfast.

He stopped outside a narrow building that seemed determined to cower between its neighbours. A couple of patches of peeling paintwork still clung to its wooden frame, hinting at past splendour. The first and second floors jutted out over the narrow street striving for a share of the sunlight. Faded Ottoman grandeur. Some would see it as charming; in this weather, it tended more towards draughty.

It was past ten, but the blinds were pulled down in the bay window on the first floor. Nobody home or was someone having a lie-in? Jasper shrugged; it didn't really matter, he had a key, and even if he didn't, he could still let himself in. As he trotted up the short flight of steps to the front door, a bearded face appeared at the ground-floor window. It was Tozan, the landlord of this shabby chateau. Jasper tipped his hat to him, and Tozan grinned back. Perhaps when he was finished, it might be worth dropping in on Tozan; with luck, he'd have some coffee that needed drinking.

The front door was unlocked, and the cramped corridor beyond led to the stairs. Jasper sniffed; no aroma of coffee or tea brewing. There again, he hadn't brought any baklava with him. His stomach rumbled once more in protest. The stairs groaned as he ran up them. A small face peered through bannisters from the second floor, saucer eyes fixing him with their stare. Jasper slowed his approach to the first-floor landing, his right hand sliding across and into his coat. A child's hand thrust between the uprights of the bannisters, its forefinger cocked and ready to fire.

"Bang! Bang!"

Jasper clapped a hand to his chest, staggering and swaying.

"You rat! You got me! Ugh!"

A triumphant squeal of laughter stormed down the stairs. Jasper grinned at the small lad, who continued miming gunshots at him. It was always better dodging pretend bullets than the real thing.

"Nikos!"

The mock assassin disappeared from view as a cascade of Greek, too fast for Jasper to follow, tumbled down the stairwell. No doubt, the forces of law and order had caught up with Nikos in the form of his mother or grandmother; there was always a price to pay for having fun. The verbal battle between Nikos and the fun-police spattered on until cut short by the slam of a door. Jasper walked softly to the second door on the first floor; he'd have to let Nikos take the rap. He knocked twice and let himself in.

The blinds had been opened. Dazzled by the unexpected deluge of daylight, Jasper raised a hand to shield his eyes.

"What kept you?"

"I got held up at finger point," replied Jasper.

Ruby limped over to the cast iron stove and shovelled a little coal into it.

"You shouldn't encourage that boy. He runs his mother

ragged." She straightened up, her eyes screwed shut, colour washing from her face. A sliver of ice slipped into Jasper's heart.

"Are you alright?"

He took a pace towards Ruby, but she waved him away, crumpling onto the unmade bed. Jasper remained still. The only sounds in the room were Ruby's breathing, accompanied by the occasional clink from the stove as the new coal started to catch fire. She breathed out loudly through her mouth, her eyes winching slowly open. Her pupils contracted swiftly, the pale blue of her eyes flooding her face with the only colour left in it.

"Hand me that hairbrush."

Jasper obeyed. Her dark hair, its sharp bangs framing her face, was immaculate. It always was, but there was no reason to point it out now. He handed her the brush. She snatched it away, starting to pull it through her hair.

"Perhaps we should get a doctor to have a look at you—"

"And what will he tell me that I don't already know? Tell me that!" A little colour had returned to her cheeks with the outburst. She dropped the hairbrush on the bed and pulled her robe around her.

"Sorry," she pulled a half-smile onto her face. "I know you're only trying to help." She shrugged; a wince pulled at the smile. The smile won. "I got shot. The bits left in my leg hurt like hell when it gets cold and damp. That's all there is to it, and there's nothing anyone can do."

The slither of ice twisted. Yes, she had been shot; several times. The bullet in her leg hurt her when it was damp, but the others hurt her all the time. If he hadn't run, then perhaps… If, perhaps, maybe. But he had run.

"So?" Ruby was staring at him. "What have you brought me?"

Jasper pulled the package from his coat pocket and tossed it to her. Ruby pulled the contents out, spreading them across her bed. She picked up the sheet with multiple stamps on it, peering at it closely. Jasper wandered over to the window and stared down into the street. A thump sounded from upstairs, followed by fast footsteps heading down. He counted the steps, timing them; it was a handy distraction from revisiting his regrets. Niko's mother was heading from the building, pulling her headscarf up against the cold.

"How many does Tozan have living upstairs now?" His gaze tracked the woman as she headed quickly away.

"Five." Ruby didn't look up from her inspection of the documents. "You were right. The French have changed them. We need Kerim to make some new stamps. Are these blank passports fake?"

"No. They're the real thing."

Ruby's eyes narrowed, her stare fixing him to the spot.

"How much, and who did you have to bribe to get them?"

"No-one." He slipped on his lopsided grin.

"That may work on the floozies in the clubs off the Grand Rue, but it doesn't cut the mustard with me!" The stare intensified, and his grin was starting to fade. "You burgled the French Consulate, didn't you?"

"Well, I… Burglary is such an ugly word—"

27

"Stop!" Ruby cut him off with her hand. "I told you it was too big a risk. We should be targeting something easier."

"But it's France and her colonies that our clients want to reach. The French have been tightening up on Russian refugees, and it's mostly Russians that need our help."

"And what happens when monsieur what's-his-face from the consulate realises half a dozen blank passports are missing from his filing cabinet? You don't think he's going to wonder about a recent visit from a Mr Max Bolton?"

"Don't worry, I had a good cover story."

"Don't tell me. Some twaddle about enquiring on behalf of a female friend. I bet you even delivered that line complete with faux embarrassment to make it sound like she was your lover."

Jasper's grin crumpled.

"How did you know?"

"I can read you like a book, Lewingdon. Lucky for you, though, I have a new customer who's very keen to get her hands on some good papers." Ruby picked up a blank passport and visa. "These should do the trick. And she has cash."

Jasper let his gaze fall to the floor.

"Well, who are we to refuse if she has cash?"

"Do I detect disapproval?"

How many times had they had this argument? Was it even an argument anymore? No, it was just two different points of view. But his view tended towards loathing their line of business. And that was the problem. What they were doing shouldn't be a business.

"They're refugees. They need our help, and we shouldn't… ."

His words evaporated, Ruby's stare dispelling them.

"Jasper, take a look at yourself in the mirror. We're refugees just as much as they are."

"That doesn't give us the right—"

"No, we have no rights; that's the point. But we still need to eat and pay for the roof, such that it is above our heads. If it wasn't us, then it'd—"

"It would be someone else," he finished her sentence for her, the words barely breathed towards the floor with its threadbare rug.

"And we'd be going hungry, or worse." Ruby got up and walked over to him, placing a hand on his arm. "At least this way, you know the papers they get will pass muster. You're not cheating anyone."

"We don't need to do this. I can access my old accounts and trust fund. We have plenty of money if I just make a few calls."

"The minute a so-called corpse called Jasper Lewingdon starts wiring to have money sent to Istanbul, thugs from both the OGPU and the IIB will be hot on your heels. I'm sure they'll be keen to enquire about your health. So you must keep your head down and your cover as Max Bolton intact."

Jasper looked away. Damn! He shouldn't have. He should have brazened it out and carried on like everything was fine.

"What?" The edge in Ruby's voice said that the headmistress wasn't likely to let him off. He pulled the envelope addressed to Max Bolton from his coat pocket and handed it to her. Ruby's eyes narrowed at him as she slid the paper cutting out; Jasper held his breath as she scanned it. How bad would this be? Slowly, deliberately, Ruby re-folded the cutting and then slid it back inside the envelope, her unblinking gaze never leaving him.

"A friend of yours?"

"I… I really have no idea. It was waiting for me in the Poste Restante." He took the envelope from her.

"Someone out there knows the connection between Max Bolton and Jasper Lewingdon. Let's hope it's your little darling Elspeth having a joke at your expense."

"You sound shrewish."

Ruby glared briefly at him.

"It's this leg. It always makes me bitchy when talking about… her."

Ruby's pause before uttering 'her' pulled a smirk onto his face; he couldn't help it. It was all he could do not to laugh out loud.

"You've never needed an excuse to be spiteful about Elspeth."

"And she didn't make any excuses for deceiving us at every turn."

Jasper shrugged. Ruby was right, but it didn't change the fact that he owed Elspeth.

"You're just bitter. She played us. You didn't spot it, and that still rankles."

Ruby pursed her lips, there was a flash of fire in her eyes, and then it was gone.

"You're right. She fooled me with that simpering, bobble-headed flapper routine instead of seeing her for the crafty, self-serving, devious little tramp she is!" Ruby sat back down on the bed. "Have you got any more poisonous adjectives I can use to describe her?"

"No, I think you were doing pretty well on your own."

"The fact remains that if it wasn't Elspeth that sent you that, then it's time we were moving on." She picked up a blank passport. "I suggest we save two of these for ourselves. Let's hope our new client is willing to part with plenty of cash, as we'll need it to get ourselves sorted."

"You think it's that serious?"

She nodded.

"We have a meeting arranged this afternoon. In the meantime, you can help me get dressed."

"Won't that sully your reputation in this household?"

Ruby snorted.

"Hardly; they think I'm a prostitute." She narrowed her eyes at him. "I don't know what you're smirking about. They're all convinced you're a pimp."

4. The business

Harrods was a mere corner shop grocer compared to the Grand Bazaar. Jasper unbuttoned his coat. They were only a few yards from the entrance, but the warmth from goodness knew how many people had pushed the temperature from winter into late spring. The high vaulted passage stretched off into the distance, with shops, stalls and booths lining its sides. A press of people near-swamped the space in between. A tea vendor, a large kettle strapped to his back, was making slow progress through the pack ice of shoppers. Shouts, calls, and cries to catch a shopper's attention clattered around the space. It was a veritable cathedral to commerce. Jasper felt a nudge in his side.

"Stop gawping, we're late," said Ruby.

"And whose fault is that?"

"Yours for not helping me to get dressed quicker."

"You changed your dress twice, your shoes three times and—"

Ruby dismissed his objections with a wave of her hand.

"It's important to make a good first impression." The long tan skirt and matching men's jacket certainly presented an air of business. Her eyes scanned him from head to foot. "Something you should take note of. Come on."

She pushed her way through the bustle ahead of them. Jasper followed in her wake; there wasn't enough room to walk next to her. He scanned the booths and side-alleys as they passed them. A lot of the bazaar was set out on a grid. It should be easy to navigate, but with the covered alleys and halls spread over seven acres, it was dead easy to get lost.

Dead easy; the words sucked the warmth from him. Dead easy to get lost, dead easy to miss someone on your tail, dead easy to get close... dead. Ruby was right; they needed money and a way out of Istanbul.

Despite the shove of shoppers, Ruby was rapidly carving a path forward; even the tea vendor had been left way behind. The shops selling silks and fabrics were starting to give way to rugs and carpets.

"Down here." Ruby darted left into a passage. The gap in the crowd she stepped through vanished as the crush closed up. Jasper hesitated as the sea of headscarves, hats and coats washed by. He pushed himself through the notion of a gap, the stream of people splitting around him. He stopped. Ruby had disappeared.

The spike of adrenalin was needle-sharp, his senses quickening along with his pulse. Act normal, walk normal, and don't start charging about. The side alley was not as busy as the central passage, but there were still plenty of people. Jasper pushed the panic down. Ahead, competing carpet sellers called to get his attention. Jasper let his gaze wash over them; their presence was an excellent excuse to look around him. He walked on, his pace kept to the steady amble of the dedicated window-shopper.

Still no sign of Ruby. He was at another crossroads. He turned right. More bustle, more bodies, and the static of sound in the arcade was numbing. Were any faces familiar, or were they all just perfect strangers? Dead easy to get lost, dead easy. Shut up and get on with it! Turn right, keep walking and keep looking. The main drag through the bazaar was just ahead. He slowed, slipping into the traffic, letting it carry him back to the passage where he'd last seen

Ruby.

The tea vendor pushed himself towards him, trying to catch his eye, and get a quick sale. A suddenly familiar face. A distraction to grab your attention? Jasper could feel his fists balling in his coat pockets. He smiled and shook his head at the tea vendor; a disappointed shrug was the only response. A fourth right, and now he'd been around the block. Still no sign of Ruby; had he really expected there to be? A sweet, strong tea would clear the dryness from his mouth. He all but jumped as a hand slipped through his arm.

"Been missing me?" asked Ruby.

"I'd feel happier if you'd let me trail you."

"But you're so much easier to follow, even when trying hard not to be followed."

Ruby stopped, bending to flick through a couple of rugs. She handed her clutch bag to Jasper. The carpet seller was already stepping forward, the grin of an easy sale stitched across his face. Sweet tea was almost certainly being prepared in anticipation of protracted negotiations.

"I thought we were running late?"

"We are." She let a rug flop back onto its pile. Then, with her hands on her hips, she scowled at another carpet. "I need some time to give the fool that was practically in your back pocket the chance to show himself again."

The old, unwelcome prickle ran up Jasper's spine. Dead easy to get close in a place like this.

"I do so enjoy being the bait."

"Sarcasm doesn't suit you." Ruby peered past his shoulder. A shout echoed above the babble of the bazaar.

Jasper turned, following Ruby's gaze. Another cry and heads turned as someone started to run. "Looks like it was a pickpocket, after all. Time to get moving."

Jasper shrugged an apology at the carpet seller; maybe another time, maybe never.

The throng had thickened; the sudden street theatre of a pickpocket on the run sticking shoppers' feet to the floor. Ruby shoved her way through, Jasper following close behind. The distraction was working to their advantage. Two turns later, the drama was way behind them, and the crowd had thinned to a trickle. A few bored carpet salesmen looked up, more out of habit than in expectation. This wasn't the fashionable corner for carpets. A brief glance behind, and they slipped through a dull doorway, the entrance half-obscured by a rug draped across it.

A pair of smoky lamps painted the room a pale yellow. The poorly trimmed wick on one light pulsed a stream of soot into space, the taste of paraffin just touching the tip of the tongue. Sat on a short stack of rugs was a big man. Long dark curls hung limply past his collar, merging in with a heavy beard streaked with white. He glanced up, the light from the oil lamps glittering in his eyes as he poured out three glasses of tea.

"Hello Viktor," said Ruby, "I wasn't expecting you. Where's our girl?"

"Sugar?" Viktor nodded towards the glasses of tea, and Ruby shook her head. "Of course not. You're sweet enough as it is." He chuckled. The sound had the hint of distant thunderstorms. "Please sit. The tea will get cold."

Ruby sat opposite Viktor, her clutch bag in her lap, her hands folded across it. Jasper stayed by the doorway. He glanced outside. It was still just the same bored carpet sellers with the odd shopper traipsing past; this wasn't a corner of the bazaar you went to unless you had to.

"So?" Ruby jabbed the question at Viktor. "Where is she?"

Viktor took a sip of tea, then carefully placed his glass on the beaten-brass table between them as if it might topple at any moment. Then, with his gaze still fixed on the glass, he ran a hand through the thick tangles of his beard. Ruby sat silent, her back ramrod straight, her stare fixed on Viktor. Jasper winced. The physical effort would be costing her, and this wasn't likely to end well.

"She's shy… no, that's not the right word." Viktor's heavy Russian accent thickened his words. "She's nervous, scared."

"Of what?" snapped Ruby.

Viktor shrugged, breaking eye contact.

"She's alone in a strange place. She doesn't know you and wants to get to France."

"How do I know she even exists?" Viktor's eyes snapped up at Ruby's words. "Is this just you trying to get your hands on some decent papers that you can sell on for a profit?"

"Ruby, how can you believe—"

"Believe that you'd double-cross us or sell us out to the Emniyet[2] for a handful of coins?"

Viktor grinned.

"For you, Ruby, it would have to be far more than a

---

[2] Emniyet: the Turkish secret police.

handful." He laughed. "We must make a living any way we can in these uncertain times. Once I was a clerk for a Duke. Now I help people who need help."

"You were a spy for the Okhrana, the Tsar's secret police."

Viktor shrugged.

"Before the revolution, so was half of Russia. Even the Bolshevik's beloved leader, Stalin, worked for them." He spat on the floor. "If you had doubts about me, you wouldn't be here now."

"I was expecting to see the girl you told me about. Does she have a name?"

"Yes. Anna. Anna Kravchenko. She's Ukrainian."

Viktor sipped his tea and then placed the glass back on the table. He stared at Ruby, and she stared back. How long would this go on for?

"Is that it? Nothing else?" Ruby had given in quickly; her leg must be hurting. "We're going to have to meet her. At the very least, take her photograph for the passport."

Viktor shook his head.

"She was adamant. She will only deal with me." He pulled a couple of small photographs from his coat pocket, tossing them onto the table. "Here, these will have to do."

Ruby picked the photographs up and glanced at them before handing them to Jasper.

"Will these be good enough?" she asked.

Jasper looked at the pair of pictures. They were prints from the same negative, one a little dog-eared but both good clear photographs. They'd be fine. There was nothing remarkable about the pictures themselves. But the face staring from them was anything but. The light-coloured hair, styled into a messy Eton crop, hardly hinted that this was a young woman. A hint of colour on her lips and cheeks suggested she wore makeup. It seemed in keeping with the loose blouse she wore. But it was her eyes that struck you. Her gaze was defiant, a challenge to the viewer. It seemed hard to believe that this woman could ever be nervous or scared.

"They'll do," replied Jasper. He took out his wallet and slipped the pictures inside it. "I'll take them over to Kerim this evening, and he can get started."

Viktor grinned, nodding gently at Jasper's words.

"Not so fast," said Ruby. Viktor's face froze, his eyes fixed on Ruby. She smiled back as if she had just been invited to tea at the Savoy. "There is the small issue of payment. All the more important as our client is little more than a name plucked out of the air and a couple of grubby photos taken by some shady backstreet snapper."

"I assure you Ruby—"

"You can assure me by paying upfront."

Ruby's smile notched up a fraction. Viktor's scowl started to match it in intensity.

"That's not possible! Where would I get that kind of cash?"

"Try the bulge on the left side of your coat."

Viktor glanced down, surprise flicked across his face. He reached inside his coat, his fingers searching out the seemingly strange lump. At the rustle and crackle of paper, Viktor looked at Ruby, a smile puckering at the corner of his mouth. With a flourish, he pulled a torn envelope from his pocket.

"And what do you do for an encore? Saw yourself in half?" asked Ruby.

The quip pulled a grimace from Viktor. He slid the envelope over to Ruby. She opened it and extracted a thin bundle of cash from it.

"US dollars, my favourite." She started counting the notes.

"There you are. Payment up front, just as you wanted."

Ruby smiled, or at least her mouth did.

"That's half of the payment up front, not quite what I wanted."

"You'll get the rest when you deliver the passport."

Jasper could see the tightening of Ruby's jaw, it was the barest of movements, but it seemed as sharp as a slap to him. The distant clatter of the bazaar started to push its way in against the stifling silence in the room. Viktor sat back, lifting a glass of tea to his lips, his eyes fixed on Ruby. She stared. An ice age appeared to pass before she put the money into her clutch bag.

"Agreed," said Ruby.

Jasper almost jumped as Viktor slapped his glass back on the table, his laugh a bellow like a bull. Ruby sat as still as a statue.

"Good! Good! I always like to do business with you. When will you have Anna's papers ready?"

"A week, maybe ten days."

A small shadow flitted across Viktor's face.

"No sooner?"

Ruby shrugged.

"The French have been changing things lately. It will take a bit of time to ensure we have the correct stamps and the right papers. Does it have to be a French passport? What about Spain or Portugal—"

"No!" Viktor hunched forward, his hands balling. Ruby hadn't shifted an inch. He forced a smile back onto his face, easing his big frame away from the small table. "Heh, heh. No, it must be France. I promised her. I wouldn't want to disappoint her. Not now."

"Is this girl in trouble? The Emniyet aren't out looking for her, are they?"

The old camouflage of confidence dropped back over Viktor's features. He slouched back, a grin spreading over his face.

"Would I be dealing with her if that were the case?"

"Of course not, Viktor. You'd have sold her to the highest bidder long ago."

The grin split into a laugh. Viktor hauled himself to his feet.

"I never know when you're making a joke or trying to provoke me. You know where to find me when you have to." He strode towards the door, stooping slightly in the cramped room. He patted a bear paw-sized hand on Jasper's shoulder. "I think you should make your peace with Cecile before her sister finds you."

The rug dropped across the door as Viktor left. Ruby

was still staring at the table with its collection of glasses.

"You didn't finish your tea," said Jasper.

Ruby turned to look at him, a wince crossed her face.

"And you have a new job."

Jasper raised an eyebrow a fraction.

"Placating a wannabe girlfriend before her sister catches up with me?" The lightness of his words didn't match the tension building in his back.

"No. Find Anna Kravchenko." Ruby stood up, pausing halfway through, her eyes screwed shut. Jasper forced himself to stay where he was. Finally, her eyes opened. "If she exists."

"You still think this is a scam by Viktor?"

Ruby pursed her lips.

"I don't know." The seconds drifted by as her frown deepened. "He wouldn't part with that much cash if he didn't stand to make a handsome profit. The trouble is…" She winced a smile. "It might be us that pays it."

"Do you want me to tail him?" Jasper started to lift the threadbare rug from the doorway.

"Not right now. You have something more pressing to do."

"What?"

"Buy me lunch."

5. A sister scorned

Tamara froze. It was him. The same shaven head, bare despite the cold. The slight stoop that always hinted he was embarrassed by his height; well, you never let that hold you back, did you? She took a step back into the alley. No point in being seen. Not yet. Not until it was far too late. How long has it been, Nathan? It must be twelve years since we cheered Lenin as he stepped off that train in St Petersburg. What different lives we're leading now.

Nathan Lavrov glanced round. Tamara fought the flutter in her stomach as his grey eyes scanned the street. He wouldn't have noticed her. Even if he had, would he have recognised her or even remembered her after all this time? The small group was moving off. No doubt, Trotsky hadn't liked what was in the store's window. Not good enough for you, Lev Davidovich[3]? Not quite your taste? You changed your name and murdered a nation claiming to save it. What's to your liking these days? We trusted you, believed in you, and you lied to us.

She pushed her fists deep into her coat pockets. Breathe, don't get angry. Keep control. She slipped out of the alley, joining the throng that near-choked the pavement in the Grand Rue.

Trotsky was the father of the Red Army, the great revolutionary thinker, and the instigator of the red terror. Now he was a refugee just like her. She almost laughed out loud. No, not like her. He was in exile in just about the only country that would take him, but the word was that the Soviet state wanted him alive. She was a non-person; they would snuff her out without even the effort of a show trial.

---

[3] Lev Davidovich Bronshtein: Trotsky's birth name.

Tamara hung back. A tram ground its way along the street, its driver furiously ringing the bell to get the crowd to part. Like an icebreaker in pack ice, slowly, it pushed its way through. Those separated from the spectacle of watching Trotsky go shopping ran around the back of the tram. Tamara followed, but Trotsky wasn't the draw for her.

Why are you here, Nathan? Are you the jailer or one of the dammed? She shook her head slowly. No, you aren't in exile; you were always too bright for that. Even if you didn't back the right horse at the start, you had no problem changing your mount halfway through the race. You lickspittle for Stalin! She checked her pace and forced her fists to uncurl, her fingertips brushing against the blade in her pocket. Would one stab do it, or should it be the frenzied, bloody attack beloved by headline writers worldwide?

The tram slid past. Trotsky had stopped, a ring of onlookers forming around him. Tamara walked towards the group, oblivious to the elbows and shoulders she jostled in the thickening crowd. Through gaps, she glimpsed the smile on his face as he started to speak. You never could resist the opportunity to lecture people, could you? Did you know that your jailer would recite your speeches to me as I lay in his arms? What does he sing to his lovers now, I wonder?

She scanned the crowd. Where was Nathan? Her heart quickened. A voice in the group heckled, and Trotsky laughed. More voices joined in, shouts and shoves following. Where the hell was he? Had she been spotted? Why hadn't she worn a scarf? Her straw-blond hair would stand out a mile. Trotsky's voice rose, and the heckling grew harsher. The ring of bodies no longer looked like an audience. Now it had the hint of the mob. The press behind her was pushing her closer to the scrum around Trotsky.

43

She had to get away.

Hard faces glared. A line of toughs pushed themselves between Trotsky and the crowd. Tamara elbowed her way to the right, but she was still being pressed closer. She could almost taste the tension, all it needed was one spark, and the violence would start. She'd seen it often enough, and God knew she had been that spark on too many occasions. A push in the small of her back made her stumble. She grabbed at an arm to stop her from falling. An angry curse as she was shrugged off. The hard pavement thumped against her knees. The press of people closed around. Pulse thumping, she clawed herself up, panic starting to take control.

Nathan Lavrov was in front of her. His back was to her as he forced a gap in the scrum that surrounded them, Trotsky close on his heels. Tamara felt for the knife. It was gone. It must have fallen when she did. She glanced down; the blade was by her foot. She lunged for the knife, but a boot kicked it beyond her reach. She looked up. That bastard Lavrov was getting away. She forced herself forward. A hand grabbed her arm.

"Anna! No!"

She drove her elbow backwards, feeling it thud home, exacting a gasp of pain. A thick arm wrapped itself around her, holding her fast. She raised her foot to drive her heel down her attacker's shin.

"Anna! You'll not get near him. Even if you stick your blade in Trotsky, it will be the rest of us that will suffer."

It was Viktor. She sagged as Nathan shepherded his charge away from danger and himself from her vengeance. The iron-like arm loosened, and she turned to look at the mountain that was Viktor. His sad brown eyes, framed by a mane of dark hair and a full beard, said more in one look than Trotsky had ever said in a thousand speeches. Now was the time to play the part of Anna Kravchenko once more.

"You don't understand, Viktor. He was just there, and God gave me one chance, and I lost it."

"No girl, you don't understand. If you'd touched one hair on Trotsky's head, every poor Russian refugee in this city would pay the price. Those Bolshevik bastards would blame the Turks for not keeping us under control. The Turks understand this, and they would exact a heavy price if you'd succeeded. So take a good look."

Tamara looked up the street. Trotsky was being herded towards the Tokatlian hotel where he was staying. Between him and the crowd, which was already dispersing, was a line of three men. They were clearly Turks with nothing Russian about them. The message was clear: the Emniyet, the Turkish secret police, would not allow anything to happen to Trotsky unless they wanted it to.

"I'm sorry, Viktor, I couldn't help myself. I just saw him and—"

The words died in her mouth. Nathan was staring at her, his eyes widening in recognition. One of the men with Trotsky called to him, but his gaze held her rigid. He took a pace towards her. She shrugged off Viktor's hand and ran. The crowd had dwindled, yet she still had to jink and dart to make it to a side street. Once there, she sprinted as hard as she could.

She knew what deal Nathan had cut with the Englishman in Baku. Nathan knew that, and now he would want her dead. She had to escape Istanbul before he could find her.

* * *

Ekrem looked up, squinting slightly. A length of ash
clung to the end of the cigarette clamped between his lips.
Jasper nodded to him as he headed past the desk towards
the back stairs of the club. Ekrem shrugged and returned to
his newspaper. The ash gave up its fight against gravity. It
fell, spattering across the newspaper. Jasper jogged down
the stairs, its creaks and groans barely covering Ekrem's
muttered curses as he shook ash from his newspaper.

At La Mouette, the basement stood in for backstage.
The place might be a flea pit, but it was a cut above the
majority of the corner clubs, third-rate restaurants, and two-
bit bars that infested the backstreets from the Galata bridge
all the way to Taksim Square. Welcome to Beyoğlu. One
thing La Mouette did have was changing rooms for its acts,
assuming the manager, Oktan, thought you were worthy.
Jasper smiled. His brother, Ekrem, was allowed a desk at
the top of the stairs; your act had better be worth more than
family, or you were changing in the toilet.

A single wall lamp struggled to illuminate the
basement passage; mostly, it added depth to the darkness.
The fabled dressing rooms were to his left, with the toilet at
the end of the corridor. Its door barely stifled the hint of
sewage and the hiss from its cistern. Jasper shuddered. This
place always gave him the creeps; even a grave-hunting
ghoul would have second thoughts before taking up
residence here. Above, in the club, a band started up; no
doubt an audition for Oktan, perfect.

Jasper grasped the door handle of the nearest door. He
waited until a cornet's wail cut through the stillness of the

46

basement and opened the door a couple of inches. A light was on.

"Cecile?" No answer, but he'd barely whispered her name. Several heartbeats passed. Perhaps he should come back another time. Don't be a fool. Deep breath; fortune favours the brave and all that. Jasper put his head round the door. "Cecile?"

A glass skimmed his hair, smashing against the wall. Jasper ducked back, yanking the door shut.

"You shit! You utter piece of shit! How could you?" Salome's wail would have cut grass.

Shit! Shit! Shit! She must have swapped dressing rooms with Cecile. Salome's scream vied with the cornet, and another glass shattered against the door. Can't just stand here, Ekrem will come and investigate, and then he'll summon Oktan. Get stabbed by Salome, or be battered by Ekrem and Oktan? Not much of a choice. Jasper flung the door open and charged in.

"No! Wait!" Salome had an ashtray in her hand, ready to hurl. "Let me explain."

He cowered, one arm up to ward off the expected missile.

"Can you?"

Say something. Say something quick, and say something smart.

"No."

Jasper squeezed his eyes shut, tensing, waiting for the inevitable. He winced at a clunk from across the room. No impact, no sudden pain. He counted to three and opened an eye. Salome stood in front of an untidy dressing table, her

47

arms crossed. Her dark eyes were pebbles against her pale skin, and a riot of raven curls hung to her shoulders. A splash of red lipstick reminded him what ran in her veins and what could be spilt from his. The ashtray was still within grabbing range. Jasper unbent. Salome's arms tightened, but she hadn't reached for the ashtray.

"What is it that I've done? What is it I have to explain?" They seemed like reasonable questions. The flare in Salome's eyes said they weren't.

"You miserable little toad!" Her hand reached for the ashtray. Jasper ducked.

"No! Wait! I really have no idea what you're talking about!"

Salome had the weapon above her head, ready to hurl. Jasper kept his eyes on her, tensing, ready to dive aside. Salome's eyes narrowed.

"That little tart you're keeping in Balat."

"What on earth?" He started to straighten up, and Salome brandished the ashtray.

"Don't lie to me! You make eyes at my sister, lead her on, and the whole time you have some little whore in a house that you call on. I hear she isn't even that pretty!"

Suspicion set solid; she was talking about Ruby. Jasper stood up and faced Salome. He'd always taken care when he visited Ruby, made sure he hadn't been followed. Not careful enough. Someone was watching, but who? First, the press cutting, and now this. It looked like his old life was keen to catch up with him, him and Ruby. His gaze had dropped to the stained carpet; no answers were to be found there. He looked back at Salome. The ashtray was still in her hand, but the tightness had leeched from her face.

48

"Who told you about Ruby?"

He wanted to shout, but he kept his voice even. Salome's grip on the ashtray tightened.

"You admit it? This Ruby, she's your little tart?"

The edge in her voice had dulled, and the ashtray was starting to look heavy. There should be triumph in her eyes, not doubt.

"She's not a tart. She's a refugee, just like you and me."

Salome's snort of laughter lacked fire; she was having to work at being angry.

"What do you know about being a refugee?" It was a good question, one he should have expected. Revolution and civil war hadn't chased him out of his homeland. But he clung to this refuge just as much as Salome and her sister did. He shrugged. No point in getting into an argument about who was the more desperate. "If she's not your tart, then who is this Ruby to you?"

"I owe her my life. I nearly cost her hers."

The ashtray clunked as Salome half-tossed and half-dropped it onto the dressing table. A bottle of nail polish toppled onto the floor. Her shoulders sagged as she watched the bottle roll across the floor. Jasper picked it up.

"Scarlet Heart. I thought you preferred Brazen Blush."

"It's Cecile's. I borrowed it." She stared at him. Making her mind up, or getting ready for another assault? "You swear that this Ruby is…that she's… ."

Salome was struggling to find an adjective. He could help her, but was there a word to describe what Ruby was to him? Boss, partner, spy: none of these was going to help. Salome muttered something in Russian and then swore; she was stoking the anger again. Her glare nailed him to the spot.

"Are you fucking her?" she demanded, her hands locked to her hips. Salome was nothing if not direct. It was something he'd always liked about her.

"No! She's married."

"Ha! When has that ever made a difference?"

Jasper sighed. He was just confirming Salome's suspicions.

"We work together. She has contacts in this town, contacts we need to help us get papers organised for real refugees."

A wrinkle of amusement crossed Salome's lips, but it didn't touch her eyes.

"Rich refugees." The rise of her eyebrow turned the flat statement into a question. "Not destitute dancers like Cecile and me?"

The jibe bit. Jasper could feel the tightness in his jaw. The thin smile on Salome's lips said she could see it too.

"We've all got to eat. I haven't the talents to persuade Oktan to hire me, let alone spare one of his dressing rooms."

It was a feeble justification. Salome's smile, more of a sneer than a smile, agreed with him.

"I've seen you play: piano, drums, and even a trumpet when you've been drinking. I could get you work here if you wanted." She was studying him, waiting for him to come up with some half-baked justification, some smart-arse quip. Now was the time to keep his mouth shut. She sighed. "No. You like to play at things. Look at me the playboy, look at me the hero, look at me the… what would you like to be?" She cocked her head to underline the question.

Right now, somewhere else.

"We're keeping our heads down, waiting until it's safe to go somewhere else." Or too dangerous to stay where we are.

"What about Cecile? What are you going to do about her?"

"I like Cecile, I'm fond of her, but… ."

Salome rolled her eyes.

"But. A small word that says so much." She dragged a chair free of the cluttered dressing table and sat down. She extracted a hairbrush from the detritus on the table and pulled it through her hair. "You know she's dreaming up fantasies about the two of you? She's convinced she'll be Mrs Max Bolton, and you'll be whisking her away to a life of luxury in England."

"Salome, I've never promised Cecile—"

She held up her hand, cutting him off.

"I know." She sniggered. "Anyway, with that suit, you wouldn't get past the front door of the Ritz. Only my sister would dream that you were anything other than a small-time crook."

Salome's slander stung; the suit was Saville Row and had been through the front door of the Ritz on several occasions. At least it was Max Bolton that was being

51

labelled as a petty villain, which had to count for something.

"Would you have been happier if I was some second or third son of a minor lord, slumming it in the clubs and brothels of Beyoğlu?"

She was working hard to hide the pout, but it was there. Salome's gaze dropped to the floor before she spoke.

"No. There are plenty of shits like that, and I can spot them a mile away." She shrugged. "It would have been worse if you were everything she dreamt of; you'd take her away, and where would that leave me?"

Salome's stare was defiant, daring him to judge her.

"I couldn't break up a good double act," said Jasper.

A small smile took the edge off Salome's face, but this time, her eyes added to it.

"You and Ruby?"

Jasper nodded.

"Me and Ruby."

She sighed, the anger now spent.

"Why were you looking for Cecile?" asked Salome. "Was it to tell her that you were leaving?"

Jasper shook his head. Time to ask the question, and possibly time for another eruption from Salome?

"I wanted her to put in a good word with you, so I could ask for a favour."

Salome laughed. The sound was as sharp as a paper cut.

"You're either very brave or very stupid. Which is it?"

"Possibly both."

He slipped on his lop-sided grin. Salome's face remained as flat as an iron and just about as soft.

"So what is this favour you want so badly?"

"I'm looking for someone—"

"A girl?" Salome's interruption was like a slap, but she hadn't made a move for the ashtray. He nodded. "What a surprise," she muttered.

Jasper swallowed or tried to; his mouth was suddenly paper dry.

"This girl is... she's."

"Oh, for God's sake, get on with it! I'm not going to throw anything at you! We're past that stage for now"

He winced a smile at her.

"She's called Anna Kravchenko. Viktor Volkov wants us to get some papers for her, papers to get her into France."

"Viktor Volkov is paying you to do this?" Jasper nodded. A frown formed on Salome's face. "If that man told me it was Monday, I'd assume it was Tuesday."

"I don't trust him either, so I want to find this girl before I hand anything over to him."

"You know what he was back in Russia?"

"I've heard stories, rumours, nothing more."

"Watch out for him. He still thinks he's playing the Great Game and doesn't care who he drags into it. So what

53

makes you think I can help you?"

"You know anyone who is anyone, amongst the Russian exiles and quite a few beyond. So I thought there'd be a chance you'd recognise her."

He handed Salome the picture of Anna Kravchenko.

"Pretty girl. If she can sing or dance, I'd give her a job with Cecile and me," shaking her head, she handed the picture back, "but I've never seen her."

A dead-end; it looked like he would have to tail Viktor after all. If the rumours were true, that wouldn't be easy and might turn out to be unhealthy, verging on fatal.

"She might be a new arrival," said Salome, "Russia is still bleeding exiles and escapees. Of course, you could ask around at the soup kitchens the church runs, but if she's Viktor Volkov's creature, he won't have left her to fend for herself." She shook her head. "Forget the soup kitchens. Do you know Kimon Panakis?"

Tension twanged in Jasper's shoulders.

"Short chap runs a stall by the Galata Bridge hawking cigarettes and shoelaces to passers-by?"

He had to force the grin to stay in place. Salome paused mid-brush, and the frown was now a full-on scowl. Putting the brush down, she shook her head slowly.

"What does my sister see in you?"

She murmured the words, but they were meant to be heard. Jasper let the grin fade. He knew very well who Kimon Panakis was; there were few drifting around the underbelly of this city that didn't know of him. He was a pimp, pornographer, and trafficker in anyone or anything he could make a profit from; his reputation was a stain on the

Bosphorus.

"What of him?"

"Volkov does business with him. He uses him to get people in and out of Odessa, or so it's rumoured."

Everything was rumours about Panakis, right up to the moment someone stuck a knife in your ribs to remind you not to ask questions.

"Viktor used Panakis to bring her here?"

Salome shrugged.

"I don't know, but Panakis has a place near the rail tracks where they head out of Haydarpasa station. I'm told it's where he keeps new girls before he finds work for them." Her face was looking flinty. "You could try looking for her there."

Tailing Viktor was looking more appealing by the second.

"Who told you about Ruby? Was it Viktor?"

She shook her head slowly.

"No, it wasn't Viktor," her eyes lost focus, her voice trailing off.

"Salome?"

Her gaze swung back to him.

"It was an Englishman."

"You're sure?"

Salome nodded.

"He was here at the club two nights ago." A dozen cold

showers couldn't have made him more alert. "At first, I thought he was trying to chat me up, even bought the real champagne instead of the cat's piss that Oktan sells."

An invisible hand was tightening around Jasper's innards. Two nights ago, he'd been in this very club watching Cecile and Salome dance before heading off to burgle the French Consulate. And now it looked like his stalker had also been along for the show. Ruby was right that this wasn't a coincidence. Sod finding Anna Kravchenko, they had to get out of Istanbul.

"What did this chap look like?" asked Jasper. He'd snapped the words at her. Faking disinterest now was unlikely to cover the unease he was feeling. A wrinkle of interest was creeping up Salome's face.

"You owe him money?"

He pressed his smile into service. It was false, but it might divert Salome.

"Something like that. So what did he look like?"

Salome shrugged. For God's sake, please don't start playing games, not now.

"I can't remember—"

"Salome!"

She stared, her eyes widening, but the cynical smile didn't appear.

"It was dark. I'd been on my feet all night, and to be honest, one lothario looks much the same as any other." She shrugged a smile on. "I was watching the champagne. By the time I realised he was talking about you, he'd gone. Just like you."

One more spook sliding through the shadows of the backstreets of Beyoğlu, it figured. Salome was studying him.

"This is more than money, isn't it?" she asked. Jasper nodded; there wasn't any point in denying the obvious. Salome's face hardened. "May the saints protect you, but if any of this comes back on Cecile, I will kill you."

Jasper winced a smile at her.

"I know you will."

6. Dearly departed

The ferry was taking forever to cross the choppy waters of the Golden Horn. Strangling the railings on the side of the boat wasn't making it move any faster. Jasper leapt ashore before the boatman had barely thrown a loop around the bollard at the jetty. Head down, his hands shoved into his coat pockets, he stalked through the narrow streets that snaked uphill. It was all he could do not to run. The weather had improved, sunshine gracing the city for the first time in weeks. A trickle of sweat was working itself down his back. Despite the physical effort, nothing would dispel the sense of apprehension that had built like a thunderstorm.

Jasper slowed down. Ruby's lodgings were just around the next corner. He swallowed; it was probably nothing, and coincidences happened all the time. A group of girls were taking the opportunity of the sudden sunshine to play outside. A skipping rope whirred in time with the slap of feet on the pavement. Jasper detoured around them. Sunlight and laughter, how could anything be wrong on a day like this? From the corner, he could see Nikos sitting on the steps outside the lodgings. No doubt he'd been exiled from beneath his mother's feet now that the weather had changed. He was too young to play with the bigger boys and too aware of being male to play with the girls. He was scowling at the ground.

As Jasper approached, Nikos looked up, a smile springing onto his face. A few feet from the house, Nikos brought up his finger, ready to fire. Jasper shook his head.

"Sorry, Nikos, I haven't got time today."

Nikos's hand dropped. His lower lip bulged as his brows knitted themselves together. Then, as Jasper's shoe reached the first step, Nikos suddenly beamed at him.

"Have you got toffees?"

His hand shot out as the smile notched up a couple more levels. Jasper couldn't help but grin. Five years old and already on the make.

"No toffees. They're bad for your teeth."

The stunning smile collapsed in an instant to be replaced by a prodigious pout, and Nikos went back to scowling at the street. Jasper stifled the urge to laugh as he headed for the front door. He'd have to bring him some toffees next time.

"The other man gave me toffees."

Jasper's hand froze on the front door's handle.

"What man?" Nikos shrugged and continued to scowl at the street. "Nikos?" Nikos half-turned to look at Jasper, his lips clamped shut. "I promise I'll bring toffees with me next time."

"The man."

The man. What man? When was he here? What did he look like? Jasper wanted to shout the questions, but this was a five-year-old boy in a sulk. And all he had was the promise of fictional toffees to get him talking.

"When was this? Today?"

Nikos pursed his lips; was this in thought, or was he stretching out the sulk?

"Today."

Terror was tightening its grip, but he had to control it. So act natural, and don't scare the boy.

59

"Have you seen him before?"

"No." Hardly surprising, but the boy's grin said he had more to say. "He has a hat just like yours."

Jasper could feel his face freeze. His hat had come from Jermyn Street in London; it wasn't unique but clearly English in style and rare on the streets of Istanbul. A third time couldn't be a coincidence; the Englishman was haunting him. He shoved the door open and went inside.

"You bring me toffees tomorrow!" Nikos's wail pursued Jasper as he headed for the stairs. He'd bring toffees tomorrow, assuming there was a tomorrow. He paused halfway up the staircase. Voices drifted down to him, muted from behind a closed door. It wasn't English, but it could be Greek. Probably Nikos' mother and grandmother. Jasper kept to the side of the stairs, softening his tread as he approached the landing.

Ruby's door was shut. Jasper pressed his ear to it. Nothing. No voices, no movements. It was as quiet as the grave. He tried the handle, but the door wasn't locked. He let it swing open, revealing the room.

The light from the window picked out every detail: the cast-off clothes on the back of the chair; shoes scattered across the floor; a discarded syringe; Ruby staring sightlessly at the ceiling from the unmade bed. Jasper watched himself walk into the room and carefully close the door. The key was still in the lock. He turned it. He watched himself lift Ruby's wrist checking for a pulse; he knew there wouldn't be one. Her skin was cool, almost cold, but not quite. A smear of dried blood marked the crook of her arm where the needle had punctured her skin.

An inquest would see this for what it was: just another overdose. One too many injections of morphine to control the pain. A pain that never left her. A pain that she had lived with since the day he'd abandoned her in Albania. He thought she'd died that day on the mountainside. Perhaps it would have been better if she had. Better for who? Better to die in a noble act of self-sacrifice than from an accidental overdose? He let go of her hand.

But this was murder.

Ruby only ever injected herself in the thigh; that way, she could always hide the bruising. Her arms were sacred. No track marks or blemishes were ever allowed to be seen there. Someone had ended their partnership.

Jasper let his gaze track around the room. The details started to tell a different tale than the one that Ruby's killer intended. The shoes carelessly kicked to one side, the dress in a heap by the bed. She was untidy, but those shoes and that dress were her favourites; she'd never treat them like that. Ruby was leaving him a message; she had been forced. The solitary chair was angled towards the bed. It's back bore an impression, her blouse pressed and creased into it. Had he sat there while she had pushed the syringe into her arm? Sat there and watched as her life left her?

Jasper's hands curled into fists, his nails digging deep into his palms. Don't, not now! You need to be rational. You need a plan, and you need to get away! He squeezed his eyes shut, breathing deeply. She was dead, and he couldn't bring her back. Not this time. And you're still alive, but you won't be if you don't act now!

His eyes flashed open, fixing on the dressing table. He pulled the table from the wall and dug his fingers behind the skirting board. With a yank, it pulled away, revealing the small space behind it. Jasper felt inside; nothing. His pulse started to quicken. Had the killer taken it? He pushed his hand further in, his fingers fixing on a package. Jasper

61

pulled it out and opened it. Inside were the blank passports and papers he'd taken from the French Consulate and a thin bundle of US dollars.

He slipped the dollars into his pocket. How many passports should he take? What about the visas? Did he really need them? For God's sake! You haven't got time for this, move!

A loose floorboard on the landing sang. Jasper glanced out of the window. Nikos was still sitting hunched on the front steps of the house. Another creek, much quieter but closer than the first. It looked like he had company. Jasper dropped the papers on the dressing table and grabbed the chair. He pushed it against the door jamming its back under the handle. Well, now he'd just trapped himself inside the room.

"I'm buying myself time." He muttered the words to the room; maybe the room would believe them, but he certainly didn't. If he had a gun… if he didn't have such a hang-up about killing people… if.

The handle on the door started to turn. Jasper stared at it, almost hypnotised by its motion. There was a slight click as the handle reached the limit of its travel. The chair creaked as whoever was on the other side tried to open the door. A two-second pause and then a shove. The chair's legs dug in. The door banged, but its lock held.

Move! Now!

Jasper grabbed the passports and then tried to pull open the sash window. It shifted a couple of inches and then jammed. He tugged at the window; it shuddered but refused to open further. The doorknob rattled, and then someone slammed against the door. The chair's legs quivered but didn't give in. It wouldn't survive much longer. He looked around for a weapon. No matter how expensive, an abandoned stiletto wouldn't give him an edge against a gun.

The door shuddered once more. The chair was losing its fight. The next hit, and it'd be open. Jasper covered his head and leapt through the window. The impact, surrounded by the sound of shattering glass, instantly turned to weightlessness. Jasper tried to twist and soften his landing. The pavement beat the breath from him. Stunned, he rolled onto his side, trying to suck in some air. Nikos was staring at him. Across the road, he could hear the scream of girls.

Struggling to his knees, Jasper gasped in a lungful of air. Pain shot through his legs; he had no feeling in one arm, but he was alive. Then, from above, he heard a crash; the chair had just lost its fight. Jasper staggered upright. His hat was still in his hand; how had that happened? Niko's shocked stare snapped from him to the window he'd just crashed through.

Run!

He stumbled forward, his ribs stabbing into his side. The corner was a few feet away, but he was making headway. The girls with the skipping rope stared at him. Jasper gasped as he staggered on. He tensed; any second, a bullet would find him. The girls scattered as he pitched forward against the wall.

Move, you idiot! Move! It was no good. It was all his legs could do to hold him up. Jasper clung to the battered brickwork of the wall. Then, gritting his teeth, he half-turned. His ribs ploughed pain through his side. Might as well get a look at Ruby's murderer before he dispatched him as well.

The empty window stared back at him. Had he just imagined the whole thing? A hint of a silhouette moved in the room and then stopped. Was the killer lining him up for the coup de grace? Jasper's hat slipped from his numbed fingers. Enjoying the view? Having fun? Like what you see? The mangled blind flapped against the shattered window frame, its crack like a pistol shot. Jasper flinched.

Move! You're no use to anyone dead, least of all yourself!

Ruby's voice was as clear as if she was standing next to him. Jasper turned and staggered away. She was right. He had to escape, find somewhere to hide, and figure out a plan.

7. Arrival

The shriek of the guard's whistle echoed through the station. The train's whistle joined in, followed an instant later by a whoosh of steam as the locomotive eased past the line of carriages sat in Sirkeci Station. Smoke and soot pulsed into the morning sky to join the damp, grey clouds above. The platform's canopy captured every sound from the bustle of bodies beneath it.

Elspeth glanced down the platform. She could see a porter pushing a trolley with what looked like her trunk and a matching pair of suitcases balanced on it. He was heading for the exit; probably a good idea to follow him. Three days on a train across Europe was enough for anyone, even if it was in the much-touted luxury of the Orient Express. She intercepted the porter as he entered the ticket hall of the station.

"Taxi? Taxi to the Pera Palace?" The porter frowned. Elspeth repeated the question. What was Turkish for a taxi? Did she know any words in Turkish? It could be her accent; perhaps she should try French. She gave English one more try.

"Pera Palace?"

The porter smiled and nodded.

"Yes, yes. Pera Palace. This way."

The porter carved his way through the throng, barking at idlers to get out of his way, clipping the careless with the trolley when they didn't move fast enough. Elspeth followed in his wake, avoiding eye contact with the casualties left behind. The trunk and cases were hauled aboard a waiting taxi, instructions bellowed at the driver, a tip discreetly passed, and she was heading from the station.

The last few days had a single objective: get to Istanbul. Now what? Find Jasper and warn him. Warn him of what exactly? Did she know anything with any degree of certainty? It was all suspicion and guesswork, but she'd built a whole career on that. The taxi lurched to a halt as a tram rattled onto the Galata Bridge ahead of them. Elspeth could feel the vibrations of the tram through the thin padding of the taxi's seat; it added to the lumpy shudder from the engine. It was like she was sitting on a nervous horse, ready to bolt; perhaps she should bolt too. The taxi stuttered forward onto the bridge.

It hadn't taken much wheedling to get Cameron to give in and let her accompany him to Istanbul. Two berths booked on the Orient Express, the promise that this would be a fine adventure. A chance to think about their lives together. But business had got in the way. Cameron had to go ahead; he'd meet her at the hotel. No, no need for her to miss out on the fun of the Orient Express. Enjoy the journey, take in the sights, and don't rush. It's just some business that needs sorting. Suspicion and guesswork; your mind can write some pretty good stories when you have three days on a train to fill.

The taxi was across the bridge and starting a chaotic climb through streets that seemed more like alleys. Despite the damp, these same alleys were shared by shoppers, idlers, and the occasional handcart loaded to the gunwales. The place felt alive. It felt more like a snapshot of life in London than a glimpse of the Orient. What had she expected? Minarets and veils? Men huddled around hookahs? A waft of strong coffee crept into the cab. At least that fitted with the clichés flitting through her head.

The cab clawed its way out of a side street. The driver braked as a tram grumbled across the road in front of them. Elspeth stared. Wasn't that the tram that had beaten them onto the bridge? Maybe the driver had wanted to show her the scenic route through the backstreets of Beyoğlu. She shook the notion away. Now wasn't the time to get suspicious; there would be plenty of time for that over the next few days or weeks, assuming she had that long.

The driver slewed the cab across the road and halted outside the Pera Palace Hotel. A doorman was already reaching to open the passenger door. Elspeth pressed some lira into the driver's palm; judging by the smile, she'd overdone the tip. She got out of the cab. Her luggage had been unloaded and was preceding her into the hotel's lobby. She held a breath, counting slow seconds as they passed. It was time to play her part, pin that mask back in place and dive in.

* * *

The last bellhop had left the room. Elspeth pushed the door shut, the click of the lock signifying solitude for now. She turned and leaned against the door. The slight vibration of the lift was noticeable even if the sound of it wasn't. Her eyes dropped to the collection of cases and the trunk. A proper lady would have a lady's maid to unpack and organise her wardrobe for her. If only she were a proper lady. It could all wait. For the last three days, she'd lived out of one case. Why had she brought so much? Because you're playing a part, and this is all just set-dressing, that's why.

Elspeth sighed. Better unpack some of the set-dressing, at least get her evening dresses hung up. She wandered across to the window, ignoring the trunk. The French doors opened onto a small balcony. The view from here was across the waters of the Golden Horn, the ancient Ottoman city draped across the hills opposite. Minarets and domes, palaces and parks; if she'd wanted the clichéd tourist image of the city, she couldn't have asked for better. She pushed the French doors open. A flurry of wind fluttered the drapes. The spray of flowers on the writing desk threatened to topple, and the card propped next to them skittered onto the floor. Elspeth pushed the windows shut and then went to retrieve the card.

The card and the flowers were from Cameron; she should have guessed. Sorry, I can't be there…business is taking longer than expected…see you for dinner. Bland declarations of regret, just the kind of thing Cameron's secretary would have written on his behalf. A half-formed suspicion flitted through her mind. Elspeth picked up the telephone and dialled the reception.

"Oh, hello, this is Elspeth Stirling. Could you put me through to David Mill's room?"

She waited. Muffled sounds of a conversation drifted through the earpiece, followed by a clunk as the receptionist fumbled for something. Tens of seconds passed before the receptionist came back.

"I'm sorry, miss, but we do not appear to have a David Mills staying here. Have I got the name correct?"

"Yes, it's definitely David Mills. He should be travelling with my fiancé, Cameron Lowe."

There was more muffled discussion, a little more urgent at the mention of Cameron's name.

"I'm terribly sorry, miss, but I'm quite certain that Mr Mills is not staying with us. Would you like me to call around some of the other hotels in case he has booked in somewhere else?"

"No, no, thank you. I'm sure he'll turn up."

Elspeth hung up. Cameron was here on business but didn't have his secretary with him. There was a first time for anything, but Cameron never did business without David on hand to prepare, collect, and manage the paperwork; he was fastidious in that regard. Perhaps David was just in another hotel. She reached for the telephone and changed her mind. No, if Cameron was here for any commercial reason, then David would be at his immediate beck and call, with an adjacent room in the same hotel. There was little point in highlighting her interest in what Cameron was up to by trying to track down his secretary.

If Cameron wasn't here purely to close a deal, what was the real reason he was here? K had been more interested in what Cameron was up to than he had let on to her. An excellent place to start looking would be in Cameron's hotel room. To do that, she needed a burglar, and the best burglar she knew was somewhere in Istanbul. Elspeth opened her travelling case and emptied the clothes onto the bed; she could sort the mess later, but right now, she had to get out and track down Jasper.

* * *

The tram ground to a halt. Elspeth half-rose from her seat, only for a sudden shoulder to dump her back into it. She checked the urge to shove back, but this was public transport worldwide. The locals knew the score: don't make eye contact; get half a shoulder forward; don't give a break to the stranger; you've got the right of way. It was the same

69

in London as in Paris, and it would also appear in Istanbul. A few bodies shuffled forward. Elspeth pushed her way into the jam and fought her way off the tram. Half a step onto the pavement, the driver sounded the bell. One step later and the tram lurched off. She glared at the departing tram; that driver could get a job anytime on the North Acton line. She stalked a few paces onto the pavement and checked her map.

She was in Sirkeci, not far from where she'd arrived, not much more than an hour ago. The concierge had obliged her with a city map. He'd marked all the places of interest that a young English woman could want to see: the bazaar, the spice market, the Grand Post Office for sending postcards. He'd pressed her to take a guide, but she'd made her excuses and headed off. What could possibly go wrong? Lots, and having a hanger-on trying to show her trinkets and baubles to buy wasn't going to change that.

Two short streets and she was at Grand Post Office. Where else would you be going if you wanted to send a few postcards? The unwelcome voice in her head reminded her of the offer from the concierge to post them and another polite excuse hidden behind a smile delivered to deflect him. Don't get tangled in your feeble cover story. Stop explaining yourself; just get on with what you're here to do!

A dozen conversations echoed around the hall of the post office. Letters being franked, and the clatter of the doors punctuated the buzz. Elspeth headed to a stand of desks and pulled out the postcards she'd brought from the hotel. Who to send them to? A card to Michael back at the office, teasing him about all the chores she was expecting him to do in her absence and highlighting all the supposed fun she was having out here. The other? Perhaps a short line to K asking what on earth she was doing here. Elspeth

70

shoved the second card back in her bag and scribbled a couple of bland lines to Michael on the first.

She glanced up. The post office was busy, but there were still several empty counters manned by bored clerks. Perfect; less chance of someone at your shoulder eavesdropping on your business. She walked to the nearest counter, and the young man behind it looked up. Elspeth let a smile slip onto her face.

"Hello, could I send this to London, please?"

She pushed the postcard across the counter, holding the man's gaze. He started as their fingers touched.

"I'm sorry, miss."

When he looked back up, Elspeth notched up her smile.

"That's quite alright."

There was a little colour creeping beyond the young man's stiff white collar and tie; this might be easier than she had expected. A couple of stamps were quickly fixed to the card, and with a flourish, it was franked.

"That will be thirty-five piastres, miss."

Elspeth pulled a small purse from her bag, opened it, and then scattered half a dozen coins across the counter. She tried but failed to corral the coins, her efforts mostly impeding the clerk behind the counter.

"I'm so sorry. I can't believe I'm so clumsy!"

"It's quite alright, miss. This happens all the time." The clerk quickly collected the coins and handed the change back to her. "Is there anything else I can help you with?"

"Well, yes, there is, but I don't want to put you out."

71

"That's quite alright, miss. This is my job."

He was beaming a smile back at her. Elspeth took a white envelope from her bag and slid it over the counter.

"Can I leave this to be picked up?"

The clerk picked it up and read the name on the envelope.

"Of course, miss. Just leave it with me—"

"Could you just check if any other letters or packages are waiting for Mr Bolton to pick them up?"

The clerk hesitated. His facial gymnastics betrayed the conflict inside him.

"I'm sorry, miss. That would be against the post office rules."

Elspeth let her smile crumple. A tear would be too much, at least just now.

"I wouldn't want you to do anything that would get you into trouble. It's just that I haven't heard from my brother in over two months, and the family have been sending letters and packages for him to pick up from here. So I just thought that if I could check, I'd have some idea if he was still in the city. But if you can't …"

How far could she play this? The young clerk glanced behind him.

"Just wait here, miss. I'll be right back."

He took the envelope and headed through a door behind the counters. With any luck, he was off to break the post office rules and not ask permission from a higher authority. Elspeth's stomach tightened. What if he brought someone with him? Someone that was unlikely to be so easily swayed by her limited charms? Especially if that someone wanted proof of her identity. Elspeth looked at the exit; it was pretty close. Bluff it out or leave right now?

"Miss?"

Elspeth jumped. Play it up, act the idiot, let them make assumptions and use them.

"Gosh! You startled me. I was miles away."

Thank God, the clerk was on his own. He leant forward.

"There was just the one letter addressed to your brother. It was sent from London three days ago."

"Oh, thank you! That is such good news. He must still be in the city."

The clerk beamed at her; she could practically feel his smile as she sauntered from the post office. If only her spirits matched it. That letter from London must have been the one she posted before setting off for Istanbul. It didn't mean Jasper was here. K had practically exiled him. Would he have regularly checked for anything sent under his cover name of Max Bolton? It was the only link Jasper had to his old life. Surely he would have. Surely…of course, he would…you just keep telling yourself that because you haven't got any plan other than to hope he gets the message and contacts you at the Pera Palace.

"Elspeth!"

Elspeth froze. She turned slowly. What the hell was that woman doing here? You know damn well; she's here for the same reason as you.

"Elspeth darling. Such luck finding you here."

Lady Susan Linklater was striding towards her. Her face held a smile, but that didn't mean any friendly intent. She carved her way past the people on the pavement, her unruly red hair breaking free from her cloche hat. In the dark grey tweeds she wore, she seemed like a destroyer running down its target. Elspeth forced a smile onto her face.

"Susan, what a lovely surprise. I didn't know you were in Istanbul." If I had, I'd have run a thousand miles in the opposite direction!

"Cameron told me you were arriving today. I was hoping to catch up with you."

Oh, I bet you were. Elspeth's smile was starting to ache.

"I've only just arrived, but no sign of Cameron, though. Instead, he's fobbed me off with flowers and a promise of dinner tonight."

Lady Susan slipped her arm through Elspeth's, gently steering her along the pavement.

"Oh dear," Lady Susan stopped, a hint of concern touching her eyes. "I'm so sorry, but I sort of invited myself along tonight. I hope you don't mind. I didn't think—"

"That's quite alright," replied Elspeth. Keeping the smile from turning into a glare took every bit of her self-control. "You're an old friend, practically family." She patted Lady Susan's hand, which held her captive. "In the meantime, you can show me the bazaar and fill me in on what clubs we will visit tonight."

8. Tamara

Viktor scowled through the narrow window, glaring at everything but looking at nothing. His beard bristled as his hands clamped around the top of the chair. Its creaks and groans went unheeded.

"I still need to get papers for you. Good papers. But that bastard has run off with my money!"

His hands continued to worry the chair, pulling more protests from it. Tamara didn't disagree, but time was getting tight.

"Why do I need a French passport and papers? I could travel on a Nansen passport for now. It'd get me out of here."

Nathan Lavrov knew she was here. She had to get out of Istanbul and quickly. She couldn't tell Viktor that. Perhaps if she worked on him and pushed not needing a French passport. Persuaded him it was more important to get her out of this place than wait for some fancy French documents. Viktor stopped pulling the chair apart and swung his scowl to her instead; it was almost physical in its intensity. So much for changing his mind. That look said his mind was fixed.

"With refugee papers, that's all you'll be. Stuck in some transit camp and left to rot! You need to be in Paris. You need to be there to carry on the fight against the Bolsheviks. Without proper documents, you won't get in."

He shrugged and sagged down onto the chair. The Russian bear was looking tired. No, he looked exhausted. A twang of sympathy flared for him and then just as quickly died.

"What did you see at Tozan's house?" she asked.

"Not much. There were police about, and I didn't want to hang around."

"You're sure that your contact is dead?"

Viktor nodded, his gaze stapled to the floor.

"Yes. I got the story from that bum, Tozan. Looks like there was a fight. That bastard killed Ruby and ran off with my money!"

"Are the police looking for him?"

Another shrug from Viktor.

"I don't know. Why would they? One dead foreigner, another on the run, and nobody making a fuss." Viktor chuckled. "Except Tozan. He wants someone to pay for his window."

"What happened to his window?"

"After killing Ruby, that bastard jumped through it and ran off. He didn't bother to open it first."

Tamara stared at Viktor. He was still studying the floor. Why would someone leap through a window after committing a murder? Why had he killed his partner in the first place? Viktor thought it was over money, but Tamara had shadowed them after their meeting with Viktor. Whatever this was, it wasn't about money.

"Are you sure he killed Ruby?"

She hadn't meant to speak. The question had all but asked itself, betraying her doubts about Viktor's story. He looked up, the scowl etched deep on his forehead.

"Of course I'm sure. Who else could it have been?"

How about whoever it was he leapt through a window to get away from? At least she managed to keep those words private. No point in antagonising Viktor as she still needed him. She half-smiled and shrugged.

"You're right. There's no one else."

Viktor's scowl subsided to a frown. His wrong-headed self-assurance was surprising, given how many years he'd spent as a spy. Maybe that was why he was in this hovel overlooking the train tracks leading out of Istanbul. That failure to look behind the convenient may not have cost him his life, but it had cost the lives of plenty of others. Did you ever catch a real Bolshevik, or was it too easy to torture an easy mark to cover your self-doubt? Can you even spot a real Bolshevik even when she is standing right in front of you, you shit?

"So what is your plan now, Viktor Fedorovich?" asked Tamara.

Viktor grinned; it wasn't a pleasant sight. Such a smile meant mischief for somebody, and Tamara could guess who.

"I've spoken to Kimon Panakis. We've struck a deal. His people are keeping an eye out around the city, especially the port and stations." Viktor chuckled. The sound was reminiscent of the rumble of trains. "Mr Max Bolton will not leave this city until I get my money back. Back with considerable interest."

Tamara fixed her smile in place.

"What does Kimon get in return?"

"Oh, the usual," said Viktor. He stood up and shoved the chair under the rough wooden table against the wall.

77

"The usual?"

Viktor stared at himself in the small oval mirror hung from a nail over the table. He pulled his fingers through his mane of hair and then straightened his tie. He glanced at Tamara over his shoulder.

"Organise a couple more trips from Odessa. Still plenty of people trying to escape those Bolshevik bastards. It shouldn't take too much effort to fill a couple of ships." He grinned. "And, of course, with a cut of the passage fees, I'll be able to support the cause!"

He picked his hat up and left. Tamara stared at the ill-fitting door to the room. The squeal of a train crawling along the cutting behind the house drowned the clump of Viktor's footsteps. Despite the coolness of the room, she could feel heat climbing her neck.

Two more ship-loads of counter-revolutionaries free to spread their lies. Two more ship-loads of enemies ready to try and destroy the Soviet Socialist Republic. Enemies… Tamara closed her eyes, and the heat cooled. Two more ship-loads of the desperate; she'd seen them, shared their journey, felt their fears. Nathan had always said that doubt was the first step on the road to being a traitor to the cause.

Tamara shook her head. She wasn't a traitor. She had a mission, but to complete it, she had to get out of Istanbul before Nathan Lavrov found her. To do that, she had to get decent documents that would put her identity beyond question. That meant tracking down a man that had leapt through a closed window.

* * *

78

From the corner of the street, Tamara studied the house. One half of the first-floor window was boarded up; there was no doubt that this was the right house. Apart from her, the street was empty: no one else taking an interest in a run-down boarding house, no one loafing on a street corner on a chilly March afternoon. She crossed quickly to the house. As she got halfway up the short flight of steps to the front door, a bearded face appeared at the ground-floor window; had he been watching her hover near the corner? Tamara smiled and went into the house.

The cramped corridor of the entrance hallway dog-legged around the foot of the stairs. A waft of boiled cabbage competed with the aroma of damp that clung to the place. A squeak from the first-floor landing suggested that she was being watched. Then, as Tamara closed the front door behind her, she heard another door open. She turned, and the bearded man from the front window was standing in the hallway.

"What do you want?" he asked. He pulled his long coat around him, keeping his distance from her. Tamara smiled at him, shrugging her hair free from her scarf. This must be Tozan; he didn't return the smile.

"I was told you had a room."

His eyes scanned her. Tamara fought the urge to scowl. No doubt Tozan was making a mental calculation to decide what ridiculous price he could demand for the room.

"Can I see the room?" she asked. Tozan twitched, her question distracting him from the complex task of thinking of a number and then doubling it. "It's this way, isn't it?"

Tamara was already halfway up the stairs before Tozan reacted. She could feel a smile curling at the corner of her mouth as he spluttered and then shuffled after her. His protests echoed as she strode up the stairs. The smile spread into a grin; that little parasite on the poor didn't frighten her. He was practically shouting as she reached the door and turned its handle.

The handle pulled itself from her grasp. A small dark-haired woman stood in front of her, barring the way. She fired a salvo of questions at her. Tamara could barely catch one word in five, but the meaning was clear. Tozan caught up with her, placing his hand on her elbow.

"Miss, please…I was trying to tell you. The room, it is already taken."

Tamara stepped back, and the door banged shut. She turned and glared at Tozan; he flinched away. Who was she angry at? This pathetic peasant? No, it's your own arrogance. You came and saw what you expected to, and you didn't wait and think. Call yourself a professional? You almost deserve that bullet that will find you if you don't get this right. Her shoulders slumped, contrition crawling onto her face.

"I'm so sorry. I was desperate, and one of the girls at the refuge said that she had heard of a room… I'm sorry, I'll go. Please forgive me…" If she worked at it, she knew she could force a few tears to add to the performance. She brushed past Tozan, pressing her face into her hand, a sob ready to be deployed if necessary.

Barely two days had passed since Ruby's death, but Tozan had already moved someone else in. There was no chance of getting a good look at the room and its contents. What had happened to the dead woman's belongings? She glanced back at the house as she trudged away. A figure stepped back from the unbroken part of the window. What now? She couldn't risk hanging about. She had to keep to her cover as the refugee, not so far from the truth.

80

A couple of girls ran around the corner laughing, almost colliding with her but skimming either side. Tamara's hand dropped to check her pocket. Always think the worst. It was second nature; that's what life had taught her. A boy slouched round the corner. He stopped and scowled after the girls; this extracted even more laughter from them as they scampered away. The boy, head down, his lips pushed into a pout, scuffed his way past Tamara heading for the steps in front of Tozan's slum. No doubt he'd been the butt of some joke or petty meanness at the hands of the two girls. It was an early lesson in life.

Tamara studied him. He must be about five, maybe six. Older? Perhaps, if his family had had some hard years. Everyone around here was having some hard years. But he was clean and had shoes. The hat he had clasped in his hands was way too big; it was clearly a man's hat. It was a hat she'd seen before, and that time it had been on the head of the man she needed to find. Tamara fixed a smile on her face and walked over to the boy.

"Hello, are you alright?" The boy stared up at her. "Were those girls being horrible to you?"

The boy nodded.

"They won't play detectives with me."

Tamara squeezed some sympathy into her eyes.

"That's a shame. They don't know what fun they're missing out on." The boy shrugged and turned his face once more to the ground. Tamara pulled a small bar of chocolate from her pocket and snapped a piece off, handing it to the boy. "All good detectives need some chocolate."

The boy's eyes widened, and he snatched the gift away, and the hat dropped from his grasp and rolled to Tamara's feet. She picked it up. The inside had been partly stuffed with paper to make it fit on the head of a small boy. Tamara ran her fingers around the inside of the sweatband; nothing. She handed the pale grey fedora back to the boy.

"That's a nice hat. Is it your father's?"

"No, it's my friend's hat. I'm looking after it for him."

Judging by the grime it had acquired and the battered brim, it wasn't getting that much care.

"Is he coming back soon?"

The boy shrugged.

"I don't know," a frown flitted across his face, quickly swept away by a smile. "He'd give me toffees!"

Tamara hesitated a second before pulling the remains of the chocolate bar from her pocket. This child was already lost to the capitalist world, but she needed to keep him talking. She handed the last of the chocolate over.

"Why did he leave his hat with you?"

"It fell off." The boy shoved the remaining chocolate into his mouth. "When he jumped out of that window."

He pointed at the boarded-up window.

"Goodness me! Why on earth would he do that?"

A smear of chocolate was now ringing the boy's mouth like some loathsome lip-liner. Tamara fought the urge to wipe the child's face clean, but not wanting to get too close to a sticky child was deterrence enough.

"He was running away from the other man."

Tamara mugged surprise.

"Was he playing detectives?"

A slight frown creased the boy's forehead, and he carried on chewing for several seconds.

"No." The boy looked up at Tamara, his brow still carrying the frown but something else as well. "My mother said not to talk about the other man."

"Your mother is a sensible woman," said Tamara. His mother probably knew a lot more about this other man and Ruby's death. "Did she say why she didn't want you to talk about him?"

The boy shook his head.

"I didn't like him. He kept asking me where Max had gone, where he could find him."

"But you didn't tell him."

"No. Not even when he shouted and my mother threatened to beat me."

"You're a good friend to Max. Do you think he will come back for his hat?"

He stared at his feet and shook his head slowly.

"No. He'll have stowed away on a steamer heading to Egypt."

"How can you be so sure?"

"He would tell me about all the different ships and where they went. He could watch them from his room. It looked out over the docks—"

A window above rattled open.

"Nikos!"

The boy flinched. Tamara looked up, and the dark-haired woman she'd encountered earlier glared at her. Nikos jumped up.

"I have to go."

He ran inside as his mother slammed the window down, all the time scowling at Tamara. It was time to go but maybe not too far. Tamara walked along the street until she was out of view of Nikos' mother. Pulling her scarf further around her face, she waited. Time was crawling past, it certainly wasn't in any hurry to move, and neither was Nikos' mother. Tamara glanced at her watch. Over twenty minutes had passed; five minutes more, and she would give up. She was probably reading too much into the situation.

A door banged further up the street. Tamara glanced around the corner she was concealed behind. Nikos' mother emerged, heading across the street and down the hill. She was wearing a long tan skirt with a matching man's jacket set off with a fetching cloche hat and a decent pair of shoes. That explained why Nikos' mother had taken so long to come out; she was changing to meet someone she wanted to impress. It also explained what had happened to Ruby's belongings; they were the same clothes Ruby had been wearing when she met Viktor in the bazaar.

Tamara hung back, the streets weren't busy, and she didn't want to get caught out if Nikos' mother looked around. There again, Nikos' mother was in a hurry to get somewhere. This should be an easy trail, but she'd had a good look at her face. Why the hell was she taking this risk? What did she hope to gain? Find out who else was looking for the same man that she needed to find, that's what! With luck, she'd be able to trail them…but then you get there second, and he'll be dead. The argument continued to circle all the way to the jetty, where Nikos'

mother boarded a small ferry across the Golden Horn.
Tamara swore. Now what?

9. Keep your friends close

Elspeth winced as the wail of a cornet cut through the conversation, such as it was. Cameron's lips were still moving, but she couldn't make out what he was saying. She leant forward.

"I said that this is a lovely little dive you've dragged us to." Cameron's eyes twinkled, his grin matching them. Elspeth smiled back.

"That's why you should bring me on more of your business trips. Just look at the places I take you to."

To be honest, she'd been in worse, but this place had something. Peeling paint, sticky carpet, mismatched furniture, it had plenty of things. But it also had an atmosphere. Michael would have pronounced it as having 'the vibe', and he'd be right. A good band, decent dancers, plus a hint of chaos in the proceedings; Jasper would love this place. Elspeth reached for her glass; it helped to cover the flutter in her stomach as she swept the thought away. Cameron was staring at her.

"How did you find it?" he asked. "Some international underground organisation that swaps tips on the best clubs and bars?"

Elspeth sipped her drink, shuddering at the bite of the alcohol.

"If there is such a brotherhood, or in my case, a sisterhood, I'd ask them to hand back my membership fee." She put the glass back on the table as if it contained nitroglycerine. Perhaps it did. "I'm afraid it's Susan you have to thank for this."

"Oh." Cameron mugged surprise; it was a compelling

act. Why had that bitch nudged them towards this place? It wasn't like her to do anything without an ulterior motive, and it certainly wasn't to advertise the charms of a backstreet basement club like this. How much did Cameron know, and how much poison had Susan dripped into his ear?

"How's your mission going to find a Turkish partner?"

Cameron shrugged.

"Slowly, but I'm making progress."

"Why not let David do the donkey work? Isn't that what a secretary is there for?"

"If only he was here." Cameron slouched back into his chair.

"Where is he?"

"Tending to his sick mother, would you believe?" Elspeth squeezed concern onto her face; it was struggling to displace the disbelief she was feeling. "That's why I had to rush out here and pick up the pieces."

Of course you did. It's not like you don't pay David enough to employ a nurse, is it?

"The poor chap. I do hope his mother is all right."

"Death's door, I'm afraid, last rites and all that. Sorry to put a dampener on tonight."

Elspeth reached across the table and patted Cameron's hand.

"Not at all. I'm sure that she'll pull through."

The strain of holding onto the smile was taking a toll. It seemed unlikely that David Mill's mother would pull

87

through unless the last rites were from a witch doctor; she'd been buried in 1926. Why was Cameron getting caught out with such a crap cover story? What was so important to bring him on his own to Istanbul and in such a rush?

That flutter in her stomach was starting to stretch its wings. What if Cameron didn't give a damn about continuing a crap cover story? Maybe he had already achieved his aim of getting her away from London. Who was it who said to stay away from a spook in a hurry? Well, he didn't have to hurry anymore. The band kicked in with a surge of saxophone. Two dancers strutted onto the floor, one dark, the other with fair curls. Cameron's attention swung to them.

K had said that if it all started to fall apart, she should contact his man in Istanbul, and he'd do his best to get her out. Elspeth glanced at Cameron. His gaze was fixed firmly on the cleavage of the dark-haired dancer. Perhaps while Cameron was ogling, she should slip away and phone her only ally in this city, Jude Faulkner. No, not her only ally, just the only person she had a half-believable contact for.

The dark-haired dancer was starting to return some of Cameron's interest. A quick smile here, a glance there, subtle but effective. She really made an art of flirting. Elspeth studied the covert communication. As the fiancé, she should feel put out by Cameron's shameless display. Rich idiot tempted by the charms of a gold-digging dancer. As a column header, it needed work, but it had the right feel. Such a line would put the reader on the side of the slighted fiancé, who would be reported fleeing from the club in tears… No, stormed out in fury after hurling her drink in the face of the now ex-fiancé. Such a tale would explain the quick packing and a ticket on any train out of Istanbul. As a cover story, it had an appeal, and it fitted with K's suggestion she re-visit the role of the mad fiancé

88

woman.

The band struck their final note, and the dancers took their bow. The club's clientele clearly enjoyed the performance, judging by the avalanche of applause. Cameron was clapping so hard his palms must be stinging. The dark-haired dancer blew him a kiss as she sashayed from the dancefloor. Cameron was grinning so hard the top of his head might just fall off. This tall tale was telling itself now. Elspeth's hand tightened around her glass. Now or never. Cameron turned, and his eyes widened.

"I'm sorry. I got a little carried away." He was wearing his schoolboy smile, the naughty boy caught out in class. His eyes flicked up. "Oh look, here's Susan!"

Elspeth half-turned, following Cameron's cue. Damn! She shouldn't have. The moment was gone. Half a heartbeat earlier and the furious fiancé routine was believable. Now? Cameron wasn't stupid. Try it now, and he'd sense she was acting, and then he'd wonder why. Her fingers shrank from the glass.

Lady Susan was just a couple of tables away, heading towards them. Her pale green satin dress complimented her flame-red hair to perfection, emphasising her eyes which were fixed on Elspeth. A smile was inching onto her face. It didn't say hello, but hinted at 'caught you'. Cameron stood, pulling a chair free from the table for her.

"Susan, where have you been? I'd almost given up on you," said Cameron.

Lady Susan let her gaze slide to Cameron.

"Oh, that would never do," she replied, her hand dropping to the back of the spare chair, momentarily holding Cameron's hand captive. "I was running a little late, but Jude chivvied me along, so here we are."

Lady Susan glanced at the man who had followed her to the table.

"This is our man in Istanbul, Jude Faulkner." A frown flitted across her face as she studied him. "I'm not really sure what you do in the British Consulate." She turned her gaze once more to Elspeth. "But he's been so helpful with my stay here."

Her smile was as dazzling as a thousand icebergs, and its temperature matched the ice in Elspeth's veins.

"Can I get you a drink?" asked Cameron.

The band had shifted into something with a soft melody, and several couples were already seeking out the dancefloor in response.

"Oh, leave that to Jude; he knows what I like. You can take me for a turn around the floor. You don't mind, do you, Elspeth?"

"Of course not. Cameron always complains that I move with the grace of a wounded gazelle."

"That's not true," said Cameron, his grin inching up in intensity. "It's a wounded buffalo, not a gazelle."

The effort of holding the smile and laughing at the pitiful pun was almost enough to raise a sweat. Buffalo or gazelle, it didn't really matter. Both were big-game creatures to be chased down and killed; the simile didn't feel that far from the truth. She watched Cameron lead Lady Susan to the dancefloor and almost jumped as the chair beside her moved.

"Sorry," said Jude, "I didn't mean to make you start."

Elspeth looked at the man now sitting next to her. He didn't have the swarthy matinee-idol good looks that Lady Susan usually went for. Brown hair brushed back with a hint of hair oil, grey-green eyes, and high cheekbones. It was a face that could easily be lost in a crowd if it wanted to be. Did K know he was sharing his man in Istanbul with a known Soviet agent?

"Not at all." Elspeth waived to get a waiter's attention. "Might as well order some drinks. So what has Lady Susan been getting you to do for her?"

"Good grief, what hasn't she had me do? She seems to have confused the services of the British Consulate with those of Thomas Cook. Today she has a bee in her bonnet about Leon Trotsky having a suite of rooms in the same hotel as her."

"She's expecting you to find her an alternative hotel?" It was ironic that a Soviet agent was objecting to the presence of a communist icon, even if he was an out of favour one. No doubt Lady Susan would be shortly arriving at the Pera Palace, probably in a room next to hers. A smirk shuttled across Jude's face.

"If only her demands were that simple."

"Lady Susan, demanding? Surely not."

"She seems to be under the impression I can get the Turkish authorities to expel Leon Trotsky from his hotel, if not the country."

"How difficult can that be for someone with your skills and influence?" Elspeth mugged a grin at him and got a thin smile in return.

"I'm a minor official in the British Consulate. I have barely enough influence to get a train ticket out of

Istanbul."

Elspeth studied the face of the young man staring at her. Was that a threat or an offer? Jude's face wasn't offering any further clues.

"I'm sure you're much more than a minor official."

Jude's smile hardened, his eyes growing cooler. A waiter arrived at their table. A congenial curtain dropped across Jude's features as he sat back.

"I'm practically parched. What would you like?"

"Surprise me!"

She gave Jude her best diamond smile; it was a performance to match the one he was delivering. Elspeth glanced at the dancefloor. It was full but not packed. Being half a head taller than most men, it was easy to track Cameron, and the occasional flash of red hair pressed against his shoulder helped. It didn't look like they would return to the table anytime soon. The waiter had gone, and Jude was looking at her.

"What errands are you running for Lady Susan tomorrow?" she asked.

The smirk had found its way back onto his face.

"Trying to get one of the architects of the Bolshevik revolution expelled is bound to take up my time and make me difficult to contact. I think I can safely hide for a couple of days, don't you think?"

The waiter returned. He placed a bottle of champagne in an ice bucket on the table. Then, before retreating, he polished four glasses and put them on the table with a small flourish.

"What's all this for?" asked Elspeth.

"You said to surprise you."

Jude started to fill her glass. If the label on the bottle were to be believed, then this was an expensive surprise.

"Is this to be charged to sundry expenses in the British Consulate?"

A grin spread across Jude's face as he filled his glass, his attention focused on the rising froth of bubbles. A hand reached past Elspeth and plucked her drink from the table. She turned and stared as the dark-haired dancer took a sip from it. Jude's face had frozen, and the champagne followed over the top of his glass.

"I wouldn't waste that. It's not the cat's piss we usually sell here," said the dancer.

Jude took a napkin and methodically mopped up the spill.

"Hello, Salome," he said, "I thought your dance was terrific. Would you care to join us?"

The sunshine in his voice suggested he was pleased to see her, and the surprised smile he wore came complete with wrinkles around the eyes. Elspeth snuck a look at Salome; it was hardly surprising that Jude was pleased to see her; most of the men in the room were. Salome finished the glass.

"Don't drag me, and especially Cecile, into your little schemes! I told your friend that you're looking for him, and what you said about the woman in Balat!"

Salome smacked the empty glass onto the table and stalked away. Jude's attention snapped to Elspeth.

"I have to go; please make my apologies for me." He started to get up.

"But—"

"No. Listen. Call me tomorrow on the number K gave you. I need your help."

Elspeth watched Jude all but run from the club. She glanced at the dancefloor. Lady Susan was also watching him leave, a smile crawling onto her face.

10.   Disinformation and deceit

The scent of disinfectant seemed to cling to the very fabric of the building. The white-tiled walls of the corridor shone in the glare of the lamps set high along the wall. Elspeth shivered. Was that the cold of the corridor or a response to her own notions about the surroundings? The morgue. Probably a bit of both. She looked towards the double doors at the end of the corridor. Speedy steps were approaching. The near-opaque glass panels of the doors made it impossible to determine who it was. The left-hand door clattered open as a white-coated figure, head-down and clasping a clipboard, marched through, barely slowing his pace. The man glanced at her, a question starting to form on his face, but he strode past.

Elspeth settled back on her chair. She sighed, the sound seemingly magnified in the still of the space. Her watch claimed she'd been here for thirty-five minutes, but it felt like five hundred. So where the hell was Jude? She'd phoned the number K had given her, but there had been no reply. No, not exactly. The phone had rung for a while before someone picked up, and the connection had cut off. Further attempts just got an engaged tone.

Calling the British Consulate had been almost as frustrating. Jude who? No, I'm sorry, madam... I'm sure we don't have anyone by that name... you're calling on behalf of? One moment while I check... Several muffled and whispered conversations and implied threats later, she'd been allowed to leave a contact telephone number. A telegram had arrived about half an hour afterwards asking to meet at the morgue. It was signed J. There had been a flare of hope that J was Jasper, but she'd snuffed that out as soon as it started. Be realistic.

A murmur of voices, accompanied by a slow tread,

seeped past the double doors. The sudden squeeze in her stomach stamped out the anger she was stoking at Jude Faulkner. She'd been summoned to a morgue, and it wasn't for afternoon tea. Whose corpse was she about to be asked to identify? The doors swung open, and Jude walked in, head down and listening to the white-coated man with him. Elspeth stood up. Right now, another five hundred minutes of waiting would be welcome. Jude looked up.

"Elspeth, thank goodness my telegram reached you. I'm hoping you can help the doctor and me."

Jude's smile looked sincere, but none of this explained his dramatic exit from the club or the urgent appeal for her help. He fell into step beside her as they followed the doctor along the corridor and deeper into the building. The smell of antiseptic grew stronger, as did her apprehension.

"What's going on?" Elspeth focused on the doctor's back. It helped to keep her voice level.

"A little delicate, I'm afraid. A body…" he grimaced. "But I guess you've already worked that out from where we are."

"Who is it?"

They stopped at a large door. The doctor fished out a bunch of keys, fumbling to find the right one before unlocking the door. As he pushed it open, a rush of cool air streamed out. The doctor went in, but Jude paused. The screw in her stomach turned some more. It looked like someone had got to Jasper before she had.

"I don't know. She didn't have any identification on her. The landlord of the doss house she was found in said she was English, which makes it my problem to find out."

Elspeth dug her nails into her palm. She. It wasn't

96

Jasper.

"I don't understand. Why might I know her?"

"The police interviewed the other people in the house, and they said she had a male friend, an Englishman named Max." He was studying her face. Elspeth pushed her nails deeper, fighting to keep a straight face. How much did Jude know?

"What did K tell you?" she asked.

"That you're trying to find a man called Max Bolton."

"And this woman is linked to him?"

"I hope not, as the police think he was the woman's pimp."

The doctor beckoned them into the mortuary. Elspeth followed behind Jude. What the hell had Jasper got himself into? Was it just a coincidence that some poor girl was mixed up with another Englishman named Max in Istanbul? Not inconceivable. The girl was probably some out-of-work actress or dancer who had headed out here searching for work. Times get tough, and some sleaze moves in. It wouldn't be the first time. She squeezed her hand. Stop making up stories! You don't know anything. At least, not yet.

In the centre of the room was a trolley. A body lay on it covered with a white sheet. Whoever she was, she couldn't be much more than five feet tall. The doctor was stood at the head, his gaze fixed on Elspeth. She took a breath as the doctor glanced at Jude. Jude nodded. The doctor folded the sheet away from the corpse's face.

The corpse. Without a name, she was just that. A body. A thing. But she wasn't. In life, her skin had been pale, but now she was grey. Her hair was still smart, its sharp bangs framing her face. The mouth was no longer ready to snap out a spiteful, smart-arse comment, but it was her. That woman. Ruby. Elspeth's nails were once more puncturing her palms. Jasper said she had died in Albania. So how come she was now lying in an Istanbul morgue? Not quite as fresh as a daisy but remarkably well-preserved for someone who was supposed to have been killed over two years ago. Jude was staring at her.

"Do you recognise her?"

Of course she recognised her. She'd never forget that smug, lying, two-faced bitch. The question was whether Jude recognised her, and if he didn't know who she was, what she had been, it was better he stay that way.

"No, I'm sorry, I've never seen her before in my life."

A frown flitted across Jude's brow. Disappointment or disbelief? Jude looked at the doctor and shook his head. The doctor shrugged and covered Ruby's face with the sheet as Jude headed for the door. Elspeth followed him.

"How did she die?"

"A drug overdose. Maybe a mistake or a way out? Who knows?"

Overdose, suicide? Neither of those tallied with the woman she'd known. That wasn't true either; she'd never known Ruby. She was pretty sure that even Jasper didn't really know her. You only ever got to see the face that she presented to you. But if Ruby was in a morgue, what did that mean for Jasper? Face down in the Bosphorus, or still on the run?

"Do you think this Max could have killed her?" she asked.

Jude stopped and looked at her.

"What makes you think that?"

He knew more than he'd told her, and she'd have to tease it out of him.

"A woman in a morgue. Your sudden exit from the club last night." She searched his face for any sign she was on the right path, but Jude's poker face blanked her. "Is this the woman in Balat?"

There was the slightest flicker in his eye, then a nod.

"What happened?" she asked.

"Much as I told you…"

"But?"

"A man was seen running from the doss house after jumping through a first-floor window. He didn't bother to open it first."

"Escaping the scene of the crime?"

They headed back along the corridor, Jude more engaged with studying the floor than answering the question.

"Escaping, yes. But what or whom, I don't know. The chap you're looking for, is he likely to be a pimp or capable of murder?"

How long had Jude entertained the thought that Ruby's death wasn't straightforward? She couldn't see Jasper being a pimp, not in a thousand years. Capable of killing Ruby? That was equally absurd, but why the charade that she'd died in Albania? Should she blacken Jasper's name and push Jude further from the truth? She shook her head.

"No, I can't see him being involved with any of that."

Jude held her gaze for a fraction longer than was comfortable.

"That's a shame, as we might have been able to use the local police to find him. The Emniyet have shown an interest in the man who jumped out of the window." He shrugged. "Can't be helped. I was hoping I could get a name for the dead woman, at least to let her family know."

"Sorry, I couldn't help." Elspeth slipped a sympathetic smile onto her face.

Her family. Good luck with that. Her husband is a leading communist spy; they'd set up a network together in Trieste. Jasper cut a deal with him in Berlin to blackmail Lady Susan's brother. Lady Susan's brother is murdered shortly after Jasper leaves London, and now Ruby turns up dead two years after she was meant to have died. Coincidence? With luck, it was, but lately, she'd been right out of luck.

"If you need any help tracking down your chap, just ask." Jude slipped a smile on. "I need an excuse to dodge Lady Susan."

"Don't worry, I will."

She was replying to his back as Jude strode off down the corridor. Now what? Same as before, find Jasper. At least now she knew someone who had seen him in the last few days; the dancer in the club, Salome. In the meantime, she had to hope that Jasper would keep his head down and out of trouble.

* * *

The bellow of the steamer's horn echoed from the buildings lining the dockside. Gulls screamed in response. The line holding her bow slipped clear of the bollard on the quay. It was rapidly hauled inboard as the ship's engine nudged her briefly astern. The rope of the stern spring tightened with a twang, the ship's bow swinging away from the quayside and pointing out into the Bosphorus. Another bellow from the steamer's horn and the water beneath her stern boiled as the ship's screw started to push her forward on her voyage.

Jasper was impressed. The captain handled two thousand tonnes of steamship as if it were a London cab swinging out into the traffic on Shaftesbury Avenue during rush hour. A safe pair of hands that could be relied on to get you to your destination. The thought sunk like a stone hurled into the sea. If he had any sense, he'd be on that ship right now and heading to Beirut. So why are you still here? Why indeed.

A couple of faces peered down from the ship's side, an arm waving goodbye. A small group of people pressed up against the railings separating the quayside from the road; they waved back. At least someone was on their way. A port official closed the gate to the dockside. There were no more departures today. He started packing up the tools of his trade, dropping his stamps and ink into a tin. He folded away his chair and propped it inside the sentry hut by the gate. Finally, he closed the ledger, where he recorded the names of the passengers that had departed on the steamer.

A pair of men, one sharp and wiry, the other tall and tree-like, ambled up to the official. Jasper tensed. Suddenly this alley he was lurking in felt far too close for comfort. He slipped back a little, his eyes fixed on the trio by the

101

gate. The official paused and stared at the pair, his brow knotting. Finally, the shorter man said something, the words lost in the bustle of the dockside. The official shook his head and reached for the ledger. The taller beat him to it, handing the book to the shorter man. The frown on the official's face deepened. The shorter man flicked through the pages, the official shaking his head in response to more questions. Finally, the shorter man tossed the ledger to the official before turning and sauntering away. His tree-like companion leant close to say something to the official before following. From the look on the man's face, he hadn't wished him good health.

A truck shuddered its way past, blocking the view. When it had gone, there was just the official. Jasper scanned the area. There was no sign of the pair that had been hounding the man, just a mixture of stevedores, workmen, and the occasional overcoat wearing a wide-brimmed hat. Little and large had slipped away. It was time to do the same.

Head down, Jasper headed away along the road. Away; that was the key word. Away from where you had to go. Away from whoever it was, that was hunting you. He turned his collar up against the salt-laden breeze. He'd have pulled his hat down if he still had it. Who was that pair? Police? The quality of their coats and shoes said no. Whoever they were, they were the reason he hadn't tried to board the Cresta today. Last night in the bar, her first mate had warned him that someone had been asking about passenger lists. He'd laughed it off at the time, but that niggle had clung on, and today's adventure confirmed it; he was being hunted.

The breeze was stiffening, and the start of a shower just added to the fun. Jasper pulled himself further into the illusory shelter of his coat. His room was only a couple of streets away, but with that pair out there and God knows who else, he'd have to take his time. If only he knew who was after him, he could work out a plan B. The rain was stepping up its assault. A man in a suit, a newspaper clutched to his head, sprinted past. Jasper sidestepped into the alley on his left. He upped his pace; time to put a bit of distance between himself and the docks.

So who were the likely suspects on his tail? IIB? OGPU? Emniyet? It had to be someone who knew he was using the cover name of Max Bolton. Did that narrow it down? Not really. There wasn't any reason for the Emniyet to be looking for him unless those stolen passports were coming back to haunt him, but that didn't explain the press cutting. He slowed, crossing the street and using it as an excuse to glance behind; nothing.

There were undoubtedly people in both the IIB and OGPU who had a burning desire to catch up with him, chiefly in the shape of Lady Susan Linklater. His foot caught the edge of an uneven step, forcing a stumble. He stifled an oath and kept on up the steep alley, his hands shoved deep into his coat pockets. Is that what this was about? Is that why Ruby was murdered? A settling of scores. But who was keeping count? Lady Susan Linklater. His hands balled into fists, each footfall punching the pavement. Surely not. Her OGPU handlers would never let her indulge in such private vendettas.

The alley dog-legged to the left, tumbling out into a shop-lined street. The weather had beaten all but the most determined or desperate shoppers away. Jasper trudged on, cutting across the road, slipping between a cart and a bus. When had Lady Susan ever let anyone tell her what she could or couldn't do? Never, but her Soviet spymasters weren't just anyone; they expected, no, they demanded obedience. But this felt personal. Why else bother with this

103

haunting? If someone in the OGPU wanted him dead and knew where he was, he'd be dead already. Instead, they'd murdered Ruby.

* * *

Elspeth checked her watch. She was a good fifteen minutes late, just as she had planned. Salome and her sister, Cecile, were sat at a table at one end of the tea lounge of the Pera Palace hotel. The soothing melody played by the hotel's pianist drifted up to Elspeth's vantage point. The hotel's first-floor corridor ran around the central court; it provided the perfect place to discreetly observe anyone sitting in the lounge on the ground floor taking tea. Elspeth studied the pair. Despite the genteel Ottoman surroundings, it certainly wasn't all tea and charm for Salome and her sister.

Salome's scowl was as sharp as steel, not that it was having any effect. Cecile was staring down the length of the lounge, arms crossed, head turned away, and her lips pressed into a pout. She was pretty; with her blonde hair pressed into a tight Marcel wave and the bright red lipstick, she'd be exactly Jasper's type. Ha! Kick that thought away; it's irrelevant! You're here to find out what Salome knows if anything. Don't start delving into daydreams. But Cecile is his type; suspicion is so hard to stifle once it's got its claws into you.

Salome leant forward, speaking. Cecile's head snapped around; her reply caused a couple of faces to turn, but the pianist didn't miss a note. She grabbed her purse from the table and marched towards the exit. Time to make an entrance. Elspeth hurried to the staircase, taking the first

104

flight at a jog and then slowing to a saunter as she descended the last flight into the foyer. The staccato clack of Cecile's heels was like machine gun fire as she stalked past. Elspeth hastened into the tea lounge. She scanned the faces there before finally fixing on Salome. Her apologies were already forming on her face as she bustled over to Salome's table.

"Oh gosh, I'm so sorry. My editor kept me on the phone, but I couldn't get away. He kept banging on about getting an article from Istanbul. What's hot and what's not, who to watch for, you know what it can be like."

It was easy to let the words tumble with barely a full stop between them; don't overdo the play-acting, as your mark isn't stupid! Salome was smiling.

"It is not a problem, I haven't been here that long, and the surroundings are ..." she glanced around, "charming. Is that what the English would say?"

Elspeth smiled in return and sat down. Salome's act was near-perfect; if she hadn't just seen her sister storm off, she wouldn't have been any the wiser that anything was amiss. Elspeth rummaged through her bag and pulled out her pad and pencil.

"Wasn't that your sister I passed on the way in?" asked Elspeth, her pencil paused above her pad; it was worth seeing how in control Salome really was.

"Yes." Salome shrugged. "She has boyfriend trouble."

Salome let her gaze wander across the room and settle briefly on something beyond Elspeth's shoulder before she brought it back to her. It was a deft deflection, but suspicion was digging in.

"Oh dear, poor thing," said Elspeth. "I was worried it

105

was my tardiness. I hope this boyfriend thing isn't serious enough to stop the pair of you from performing?"

"No. We know what puts food on the table and keeps a roof over our heads." It was a pragmatic if bleak, summary. "I don't think this boyfriend will be around much longer." Salome's smile shone. "You said you wanted to interview me for your column in a London paper. What would you like to know?"

Elspeth smiled back. It wasn't a complete lie. She had a column in a London paper, and yes, it would be interesting to include some snippets from the local celebrities and denizens that made up the nightlife of Istanbul. But that soon-to-be-gone boyfriend was too interesting to let go of. Tease out the tale or dive straight in? Elspeth rummaged in her bag.

"Is that your sister's boyfriend?"

She tossed a passport-sized photograph of Jasper onto the table. Now for the fireworks. Salome glanced at the picture and then glared at Elspeth. It was hard work keeping her face blank as her innards squirmed. Right now, there were things lying in the gutter that wouldn't have got a look like the one Salome was giving her. But she hadn't stormed off like her sister; that had to mean something. Salome sighed and flicked the photograph back across the table.

"Everybody wants to find Max."

Elspeth nodded, taking the photo and putting it back in her bag.

"Do you know where he is?"

Salome shrugged.

"How should I know? He's gone. Good riddance, why should I care?" she leant forward. "Why should I talk to you?"

"Tell me about the woman in Balat."

Salome's face was hardening.

"Why don't you go and ask his little tart yourself!"

She snatched her bag and stood up.

"I visited her this morning," said Elspeth. "She didn't have much to say. She was in the morgue. Know anything about how she got there?"

A couple of heads turned to look at Salome; no doubt afternoon tea at the Pera Palace was sparkier than usual. Salome sat down, taking a few moments to smooth her skirt. Elspeth smiled at the gawpers. They looked away; watching a domestic drama is only fun when you don't get caught.

"Are you threatening me?"

"No. I'm curious about Max. His partner turns up dead, and you say he's soon to be an ex as well."

"I didn't mean—"

"What did you mean?"

Salome's glare could have cooked kippers.

"I didn't kill her!"

"I never said you did." Elspeth beamed at her. "Shall I order some tea, or would you like something stronger?" Silent seconds ticked by. "No? Well, I certainly will."

Elspeth glanced up searching for any signs of a waiter.

"You said she was his partner; that's what he called her. What happened?" asked Salome. Her words were quiet, barely above the level of the piano. Elspeth looked at her. The fire had left her eyes replaced by something else. Concern? If so, then who for?

"It looked like she took her life. An overdose of morphine."

A waiter was making a beeline to their table. The buggers were never there when you want one and just when you don't … Salome was studying her as the waiter arrived. Elspeth looked up.

"Can we have a couple of mint juleps, please?"

The waiter smiled, nodded then headed away. Elspeth looked back at Salome; a little confidence had clambered back into those eyes. That was an interruption she could have done without. The pressure was to speak, to fill the awkward space. No, wait it out. She eased back in her chair.

"You don't believe she killed herself," said Salome. "Why?"

"Max was seen running from the house." Salome's eyes narrowed. "After he jumped through a shut window."

Salome snorted.

"He didn't kill her. He wouldn't have."

"How can you be so sure?"

"He came to see me. Asking about some girl they were getting papers for."

Papers. A girl. What scam had Ruby gotten them into?

"Who was the girl?"

"Some Ukrainian refugee, Anna Kravchenko, if you believe the name."

"And you don't?"

Salome shrugged.

"She's Viktor Fedorovich Volkov's creature. Who knows what her real name is," she chuckled. "Maybe even Viktor doesn't know or care. As long as Max and his… partner come up with a passport carrying her picture and that name, then nobody cares."

Names and a scam that linked them. All this was great if she had someone reliable to take it to. Someone to trust. The trouble was the only person she knew in this town was Jude Faulkner. The very same Jude Faulkner who'd also been looking for Jasper even if he didn't know it. But if you can't trust Jude, what about Jasper? He'd said Ruby died over two years ago. Then it turns out she's in Istanbul running some racket with refugees and Jasper as her loyal lieutenant. Salome's eyes narrowed.

"Why are you keen to catch up with Max?"

"Why do you think?"

With any luck, Salome would offer up a half-decent reason she could adopt as a cover story. That question had caught her off guard; she should have expected it. Where was that bloody waiter with their drinks? A wrinkle of amusement appeared at the corner of Salome's mouth.

"Another rival for his affections? Just like your friend with the red hair." Salome's eyes dropped to Elspeth's engagement ring. "But I must be wrong."

The effort to push a smile onto her face was phenomenal. Salome's gibe confirmed what she had feared;

Lady Susan was in Istanbul to find Jasper. How much did that cow know?

"Purely professional, I assure you."

"You must be very keen to interview him, but I'm guessing it's not for his musical skills."

That was one way to put it. So what the hell was Jasper up to, and why all the charade about Ruby's death? Who was he really working for? Elspeth's stomach squirmed. If Lady Susan had found Jasper, her cover was well and truly blown. Sod finding him, she should get out of Istanbul now, but where to?

"I need to get to him before someone else does. Someone that would do him harm. I think he'll come to you."

Salome shook her head.

"No. He's used up all his favours from me, and he knows it."

"Who else might he go to if he's on the run?"

Was she likely to get an answer to that one? The look on Salome's face said no. The waiter arrived with their drinks, a small hiatus in a deluge of disappointment. She would need a few more glasses before the day was out.

"Thank you," said Elspeth as she signed the waiter's pad. Salome was sipping her drink, her dark eyes fixed on Elspeth. She placed her glass down.

"There is someone he might go to, Kerim Yazaroğlu. He's a small-time crook with expensive tastes, a bit like Max." Salome smirked. She picked up her glass and finished it. "Now, what are you going to write about me for your paper?"

11.   Frying pans and fires

The courtyard behind the butchers was silent. The lamp
above the shop's backdoor could barely lift the shadows in
the yard, but shadows were good as you could hide in them.
There again, so could anyone waiting for you to show your
face. Jasper shivered. The drizzle had eased and now
shimmered in the lamplight. Several hours had sloughed
past since Little and Large had leant on the customs man at
the docks, so where were they now? They'd be in that dark
doorway across the yard from the butcher's shop if they had
an idea of where his room was. Wouldn't they have got
bored by now? There was an easy way to find out. A cat
sauntered across the yard, making for the doorway. It
paused by the door and then carried on past. Had it seen
something? What did that hesitation mean? God knows. Go
and ask the cat!

A light flickered on, drenching the doorway in light.
That's why you wouldn't hide there, but it meant someone
was coming down the stairs from one of the apartments
above, Little and Large? Jasper squeezed himself deeper
into the shadows. The sound of steps echoed from the
doorway. It was just one person. A figure emerged, hunched
against the cold and damp, pausing to light a cigarette.
Jasper breathed out. It was Emile. No doubt he was off to
wait tables and then onto a club to play the clarinet; lucky
him. But that meant the stairs were clear up to the top of the
building, lucky me.

Jasper jogged across the yard. No point in hanging
about. Get in, get your gear together, and get out. There was
no time to waste. He stopped at the foot of the stairwell and
listened. Okay, there was always time to be cautious. His
room was four flights up, three landings holding a possible
ambush. Emile's body language hadn't hinted that anything

was up, but you never knew. He breathed in, holding it for several heartbeats. They flew past in a second at the express-train rate his heart was going. You have no choice. You just have to go.

He headed up. The stairs felt solid, but he kept to the sides. How often do you notice your stairs' noise when you use them? Almost never until your life might depend on it. At the first landing, he peered up the stairwell. At the top was darkness. He waited. No movements, no sounds. Everyone was out. Just the thump of his pulse to keep him company. Keep moving!

Second floor, third. Now he was outside Emile's door. The light for the next flight, and his own room, was out. Hardly surprising, he'd removed the bulb himself. Was that a smart move? Ask yourself that one when you're on a train out of Istanbul. Barely breathing, he headed up the final flight. No sudden assault, no shouts of alarm. He'd made it. He pulled his cigarette lighter out and coaxed it into life. In the flame's fluttering light, Jasper could see a scrap of a cigarette packet wedged between the door jamb and the door itself. He breathed out. It was still there, so no one had been inside.

His key turned the lock smoothly. It was one of the few things about this place that worked as it should. The door swung open. The scrap of cigarette packet dropped onto the floor. Don't want to leave any clues behind. Jasper stooped to pick it up. His fingers froze around the fragment; he wasn't alone.

"Come in."

The voice came from his room, the accent hinted at Turkish, but you can never be sure in Istanbul. How close were they? Jasper looked up. The muzzle of a revolver was staring at him with interest. Too close. He let the scrap fall from his fingers and slowly straightened up. The light in his room flicked on. Little was standing in front of him about three feet away. Too far to rush him and too close to flee and not get shot.

"I hope you haven't been waiting long. I had a few errands to run," said Jasper. The smart-arse words were betrayed by the tremble in his voice. The smile on Little's face said he'd noticed it.

"You're a funny man. That's good, and Kimon Panakis likes funny men. Maybe he will pay me a bit extra for you. Come in and close the door."

Jasper stepped inside, nudging the door with his elbow. It swung shut smoothly, the click of the lock smugly informing him he was trapped. Little backed out of the short entrance corridor. The bedsit had gone from sanctuary to snare in a matter of seconds.

"Where's your partner?"

Little retreated into the corner of the room, motioning Jasper to sit in the armchair wedged between the bed and the wall. The soft springs of the chair creaked as he sat. Little slouched against the washstand, but the revolver in his hand didn't look quite so at ease. The muted wail of a steamer's whistle echoed from across the Bosphorus. A blob of bile tried to fight its way into Jasper's mouth; he swallowed it back down. Little grinned at Jasper.

"My friend will be along soon. He also had to run some errands."

The steamer's whistle sounded again. Little glanced out of the window; there was a good view over the docks from here. His attention snapped back to Jasper.

"Don't move!" the words were underlined with a thrust

114

of the revolver. Jasper remained stationary; he hadn't moved in the first place. Little was on edge.

"How much am I worth?" asked Jasper.

Little stared at him, the smile from the seconds before replaced with sourness.

"What do you mean?"

"How much is Panakis paying you?"

"What do you care?"

"I can pay you more." It was a gamble, but what had he to lose?

Little smirked. Jasper studied him as Little's eyes took in the shabby sheets, the damp patch on the ceiling and the blemishes of mould in the corners of the room. There was something rat-like about Little's face. He laughed.

"How can you afford more than what he's offering?"

Offering. Not paying, just offering. It was a small thing to hold onto, but it allowed hope, however fleeting.

"Do you know why Panakis wants me?" The corner of Little's eye twitched. Did he know? Did he care? The silence said no to the first question and maybe to the second. Jasper pushed a half-smile onto his face. "Panakis isn't someone to throw his money about. If he wants me, I must have something worth more than what he's offering you."

Little's rat-like face twitched a bit more. Would he take the bait?

"What did you steal from him?"

"Enough to share and still be a rich man."

Little eased himself away from the wall, the revolver still steady.

"Where is it? Is it here?" He gestured with the revolver; it was the first time it hadn't been aimed directly at Jasper.

"No. It's safe."

"Where?"

The sneer didn't add to Little's limited charms as he brandished the revolver, but at least he was getting engaged in the tale.

"I'll take you there. We need to go before your partner gets back." Little's eyes narrowed. "Splitting the gold three ways means less for you. Less to enjoy. Less to make sure Panakis can never find you."

Little grinned; it wasn't a pleasing sight.

"Or, me and my partner beat you until you tell us where it is. We go and get it, split it and both be rich."

"Won't Panakis come looking for you, and then you end up in a room somewhere with someone pointing a gun at you?"

Little sniggered.

"He doesn't know we have you. Your secret is safe with us."

It looked like Little and Large were freelancers. If he could deal with Little before his partner got back, he could get out of the city and have a decent chance of staying alive. If. If he could get past a man with a gun. If other likely lads didn't spot him first. If.

"How did you know where to find me?"

"The first mate on the Cresta. Sold you for a few dollars. I thought it was too expensive." Little's grin was back in full force. "My partner thought it was cheap. I think he was right."

Jasper mugged a smile at Little. With any luck, the first mate of the Cresta would pick up a lethal dose of Gonorrhoea in Beirut. More importantly, how to avoid a fatal beating in your own bedsit? Little glanced out of the window. Something held his attention for a few seconds before his gaze snapped back, the revolver translating his tension into threat.

"Where's your partner got to? You've sprung your little trap, and now he's taking his time. Something up?"

Jasper forced a thin smile onto his face. The effort felt Herculean, but it had nothing to do with the trickle of ice running down his back. The rat-like twitch was back on Little's face.

"Shut up!"

"Perhaps he's wondering if he should share that finder's fee that Panakis is offering." Jasper notched the smile up a level. "Loyalty can be such an over-rated commodity, especially when it's all one way."

Little was on his feet now, the twitch almost making his eye flutter.

"I said, shut up!" The words were practically sieved through the grimace contorting Little's features.

"Lucky your man doesn't know about the gold. Do you think he'll share with you?"

Little snarled, taking a pace forward. The revolver was raised ready to strike. Jasper tensed. Now or never.

Someone rapped on the door. Little stopped, the sneer seeping back onto his face. The ice pit in Jasper's guts was overflowing. It was too late; he'd missed his chance. Little backed away, the revolver held low and aimed squarely at Jasper's chest once more.

"Don't go anywhere. I need to answer the door." Little's grin had triumph written all over it.

Jasper looked at the window. He was four floors up; there was no way he'd survive the jump. There was no way he was going to survive these two comedians or whatever Panakis had planned for him either. He stood up. Little's partner banged on the door again.

"All right, all right!"

He could hear Little fumbling with the latch. Jasper scrambled over the bed to the window. The wooden frame was old and barely had any paint on it. Jasper pushed at it. The thing had been shut all winter and must have swollen with all the damp. The knocking sounded again. Jasper heaved, and the window started to open.

"What—" Little's words cut off.

The bedsit's door slammed open, followed by a metallic clatter. Jasper turned. Little staggered into the room, his hand clasped to his throat, blood coursing through his fingers. Little's eyes were fixed on Jasper as he crumpled onto the floor and stopped moving. In the doorway stood a slim woman with short, straw-blonde hair. Jasper stared at her. In her left hand was the revolver. In her right, she held a thin blade. It was Anna Kravchenko.

The window was partially open. With a push, he could be halfway out before Anna got to him. She was as still as a statue, but her eyes pinned him in place. Jasper's eyes

dropped to the knife in her hand; a single bead of blood
crept down the blade balling at its tip.

"Are you going to jump, or shall I give you a leg up?"

Jasper blinked. Anna's monotone delivery hinted at
sarcasm, but nothing was in her eyes to back it up. At least
she wasn't pointing the revolver at him. Anna stooped and
wiped her blade on Little's corpse; she kept her eyes fixed
on Jasper.

"You have something I need. Once I have it, you can
go where you like or jump out the window if that pleases
you."

So it was sarcasm, but still scary. Jasper stepped back
from the window, turning to face Anna.

"Something you need or Viktor wants? Has he sent you
to get his money back when he couldn't get it from Ruby?"

Jasper's pulse was starting to rattle. Salome had
warned him about Viktor. It was a pity that the warning
hadn't been sooner.

"Yes, Viktor wants his money—"

"And you murdered her for him."

Jasper took a pace towards Anna. Even before his back
was away from the wall, the blade was up and ready.

"Stop." Her voice was quiet but had a hint of steel; the
blade merely underlined the threat. "I didn't kill your
friend. Viktor thinks you did and have run off with his
money. It's Viktor that put these creatures on your trail."
She nodded towards Little.

Anna slipped the revolver into her coat pocket, but the
blade never wavered.

119

"I know you didn't kill your friend. Why would you jump out of her window unless someone was after you?" said Anna. Jasper eased back against the wall. His pulse still hammered, but it was time to listen. "Viktor doesn't know I'm here. I need those papers. The passport that you were getting for me. Please, give that to me, and we can both leave."

It was phrased as an appeal, but the threat was clear.

"I don't have it."

Anna's pale blue eyes made flint look soft. She hadn't moved, but the blade seemed closer and just that bit sharper.

"Maybe Viktor was right."

"No!" the denial snapped out, driven by more than a hint of desperation. "I don't have the passport or the papers. Kerim is still working on them."

"And where is Kerim?"

A flutter in the guts; hope or fear? That depends on how this ends.

"I... I can take you to him."

The stutter was real and not faked for effect. Take her to Kerim, and then what? Would Kerim have the finished passport with all the correct stamps? Perhaps, assuming he'd been burning the midnight oil and not trawling the bars and clubs along the Grande Rue flush with the money he'd had as a down payment. Even if he hadn't finished the documents, he'd want the rest of his money. But Viktor had that. Would Kerim hand over the passport? Jasper's eyes dipped to the blade in Anna's hand, then focused on her flinty face. Payment in cash would be the least of Kerim's problems.

"We'd better move before Little's friend comes back," said Jasper.

"I've dealt with him."

The flat calmness in Anna's voice suggested she'd just booked tickets to the theatre. Of course you've dealt with him. Who else have you dealt with on your travels? Her photograph said this was a woman who wasn't afraid of anything, and meeting her in the flesh hadn't changed his view.

"But you are correct," said Anna. "We should go before someone finds the body."

"Hang on."

Jasper moved towards the head of the narrow bed. He looked at Anna. She hadn't moved, but the knife wasn't any more threatening than it was two seconds ago. She shrugged. Jasper pulled the bed away from the wall and felt behind it. It was a lousy hiding place, but at least it was one. He pulled out the two blue passports he'd stashed there and a tragically thin roll of dollars. Anna's eyes narrowed.

"My passports," said Jasper waving them apologetically and slipping the cash from view.

"Why do you have two passports?"

"Sometimes I find it's better to be someone else. Would you like to check them?"

Anna's blank-faced stare held him, his arm half outstretched, proffering the dog-eared documents.

"No. We must go."

* * *

The drizzle made the dark seem all that more dense. The lack of a hat wasn't helping, but taking one from Little's corpse just hadn't felt right. Better to stay wet and stick to a semblance of a moral code. But decorum didn't keep you dry. Jasper hunched inside his coat as he trudged on uphill. Why the hell was everything in this bloody city uphill? The scuff of a shoe behind him was the reminder that Anna was just a couple of paces behind. Close enough for a stab if he made a run for it? But she still had Little's pistol; running wasn't an option.

"How far is it to your friend Kerim's house?"

Jasper could feel himself start at her voice, almost the words of a wraith.

"Not far now." They were in the maze of narrow streets clinging to the slopes below the Galata Tower. Tall apartment blocks and buildings squeezed the senses forming chasms of what were little more than alleys. Lights in windows studded the facades drawing the shadows in the streets just that bit deeper. Jasper slowed as they neared a corner, and Anna drew alongside.

"What is it?" she asked.

"Probably nothing. Kerim's apartment is in the block at the end of the next street. It might be wise to head straight past. Take the chance to see if anyone is hanging about that shouldn't be."

"You don't trust him?"

"About as far as I trust all the small-time crooks in this city."

122

It was hard to make out her features in the gloom, but there might just be the hint of a smile on her face.

"Alright, we'll do this your way. But if you're going to run off, then do it now and save me the time and effort of chasing after you."

Jasper turned right into Kerim's street. Anna was alongside him, matching him step for step. To anyone watching, they would look like any other couple. Kerim's block was about seventy yards ahead, where the road took a sharp left. Jasper glanced behind. The street wasn't empty; a figure was heading away downhill. A smattering of singing floated down from above, followed by the strains of a violin. The effect would be soothing any other time, but tonight it just added to the tension.

As they got closer, Jasper saw a figure huddled in a doorway to their right. At least it might be a figure, more of a bundle or a sack of rags. Anna's hand slipped into the crook of his left arm. The bundle shifted, and a boot stuck out from beneath a blanket or coat. Ahead a trio of men turned the corner, one talking loudly. Jasper half-checked his pace. The pressure from Anna's hand increased, propelling him forward. The other two men burst into laughter as they split on either side of Jasper and Anna but barely looked up. Ten yards, five yards, they were almost at Kerim's block.

"What floor is your friend's apartment on?" asked Anna. The comedian and his two friends had stopped further down the street. Jasper fought the urge to turn and look. Anna's fingers dug into his arm. "What floor?"

"The fourth. Apartment seven."

The comedian had started another tale, judging by the chuckles from the other two. Anna's hand dropped from his arm. Jasper stared at her.

"Go," she said, "I can do the rest."

Jasper glanced down the street. The comedian and his friends stood a few yards past the sleeper in the doorway. A match flared, etching their features into being before the shadows made them outlines once more.

"No, I'll come with you." Anna was studying him, searching his face for whatever angle she must think he was trying. "It will go better if I explain to him. I know him, and I got him into this."

Jasper glanced once more down the street. The comedian and friends were heading off down the hill. When he looked at Anna, she nodded and headed for Kerim's. She pushed at the tall door, but it didn't budge. Then, her brow furrowing, she reached for the panel of buzzers for the apartments.

"Hang on," said Jasper.

"You have his front door key?"

"Not exactly." Jasper pulled the lock picks from his coat pocket. This wasn't the first time he'd had to let himself into Kerim's building. The familiar lock gave in without an argument; it wouldn't have been much quicker if he did have Kerim's keys. Jasper pushed the door open and then followed Anna inside. An elegant staircase swept up the wide stairwell, complimented by a fine brass bannister and a stylish carpet. Anna glanced at him.

"Your friend is doing better than you." She set off up the stairs, and Jasper headed after her. Yes, Kerim had done alright for himself; how much longer would that last?

At the rate Anna climbed the stairs, it didn't take long

to reach the fourth floor. There were two apartments, their front doors opposite each other sharing the landing. Anna went straight to Kerim's at number seven. Jasper lagged behind; maybe he should have left Anna to do this; after all, he liked Kerim. Anna looked at him.

"Now that you are here, do you want to do the introductions?"

The line was delivered with all the flatness of a straight man in a comedy double act. What did that make him? Reluctant at best, a traitor at worst. He glanced out the window to his left at the street they'd just walked up. It was too dark to make out anything, but he'd be conspicuous for any jokers out there watching. He pressed the buzzer in the centre of the gloss-black door. A distant drone sounded from beyond the door. Now for a wait. Time to rehearse a line. A chance to plan. The lock rattled, and the door opened. Kerim's round face appeared, his smile frozen in surprise.

"Hello, Kerim, sorry to barge in like this, but... ." Jasper was already walking in, all but forcing Kerim to take several paces backwards. The door clicked shut behind them.

"Wh... what are you doing here?" Kerim had stopped, finally able to hold his ground. His eyes flicked between Jasper and Anna.

"I'm sorry, I would have called you, but things have become somewhat pressing of late. Anna here needs that passport that you've been working on. Thought we'd drop by and get it."

"But, look, these things take time—"

"Why don't we go into your lounge, far more

comfortable than your hallway?"

Jasper put his hand on Kerim's shoulder. Kerim's eyes flicked once more towards Anna before he gave way and led them into his lounge.

"Yes, of course. I forget my manners. Would you like something to drink?"

Jasper's eyes scanned Kerim's lounge; you could fit his bedsit into it twice over. Two tall windows looked over the street with the cream drapes pulled open. A pair of sofas, a chaise longue and several chairs appeared to have been casually scattered across the room. Still, Jasper knew they had been placed with the same precision and care that Kerim put into his work. He had expensive tastes, and his rates reflected them. Kerim Yazaroğlu was a fine forger and could charge accordingly. He headed over to the concoction of glass, chrome and mirrors against the far wall that was his drinks cabinet.

"What would you like?" asked Kerim, his reflection looking at Jasper.

"The usual, whisky with a little soda."

Bottles chinked as Kerim opened the cabinet. Jasper smiled. Kerim was ridiculously proud of his drinks cabinet, having imported it from Paris. It was impossible to do business with him until he'd had a chance to show it off or talk about the latest picture adorning his walls. Any business usually had to wait until the first, or occasionally the third, cocktail had been sampled. Anna perched on the chaise longue, and Jasper stayed by the window, searching the street outside for signs of a threat.

"Has anyone been asking about me in the last few days?" asked Jasper. The last syllable died in his throat.

126

Rather than a tumbler with a fine malt, Kerim's hand held a small automatic pistol.

"I'm sorry, but I must insist you put your hands up."

Judging by the ragged look on Kerim's face, the apology was genuine. Slowly, Jasper raised his hands to shoulder height.

"I'm guessing from the gun in your hand that the answer to my question was yes," said Jasper.

"They said you murdered Ruby."

There was a tremor in Kerim's voice. It was nothing compared to the hawser-like tension twisting every fibre in Jasper's body. He could feel his hands curling into fists as they dropped down at his sides. His pulse should have been hammering, but it wasn't, just a steady thump as he started towards Kerim.

"And you believed them?"

That steady thump was now a pounding in his head.

"Stop! I'll shoot!" Kerim thrust the automatic forward to back up his threat.

"It isn't me you should be pointing it at."

Kerim glanced left. Anna had the revolver trained on him. The tremor in his voice had made its way to his hand. Jasper stepped forward and took the pistol from him. The safety was still on; Kerim was a lousy choice for a killer.

"Who've you sold me to?"

Kerim took a pace backwards and came up against his precious drinks cabinet. The jolt made the bottle of malt whisky topple onto its side, its cap rolling onto the floor, its contents slopping across the top of the cabinet.

"I... I didn't have a choice. They said I had to help, they said—"

Jasper shoved Kerim against the drinks cabinet scattering the bottles and glasses across its surface.

"Who are they?"

"I... I don't know!"

"Who are they?" Jasper grabbed him by the lapels of his blazer, yelling the question into Kerim's face. Kerim turned his head away, his eyes screwed shut and no doubt fearing a fist or worse.

"I don't know!"

Jasper could feel Kerim shaking; he was terrified, but who was he more scared of? He'd believed that Jasper had killed Ruby; why wouldn't he? Jasper was just another piece of trash that had washed up in Istanbul, looking to find an edge. Of course Kerim would believe he'd murdered Ruby. It wasn't like he was being given an option by whoever had killed her. Jasper breathed out as his hands uncurled from Kerim's jacket. Kerim sagged against the cabinet and looked up at him.

"There were three of them. The one doing the talking was Russian."

Jasper took a step back, his gaze drifting around the room, pausing on the picture above the fireplace and the shining standard lamps holding court in opposite corners of the room. The clink of bottle and glass pulled his attention back to Kerim. He had rescued the whisky and was pouring himself a large measure.

"How much is he paying you?" asked Jasper.

Kerim placed the bottle back on the cabinet. The

128

tremor had left his hand.

"Nothing. He threatened me. He said that if I didn't tell them where you were, he'd inform the Emniyet about our passport scheme." Kerim took a sip from his glass, his eyes never leaving Jasper.

"And what did you tell him?"

"What could I tell him?" Kerim's voice rose in pitch.

"That I'd be along for that passport you've been working on. Perhaps for a reward, you'd let him know when I was turning up to collect it?" Jasper glanced at the painting; it was new.

"No!" The tumbler clunked down on the cabinet. "I swear I haven't—"

The slow metallic click of Anna's revolver being cocked cut Kerim's words short.

"Please give me my passport," said Anna.

The temperature in the room seemed to fall.

"I… I don't have it…"

"Kerim, don't mess us about," said Jasper. "She's killed two people tonight that I know of, don't make it a hat trick!"

Anna stood up, her face like flint.

"I'm not lying! He took it! He asked to see what I was working on. I showed him the documents I was making for you, and when he saw her one, he said he'd take it for safekeeping!"

Anna moved towards Kerim; her revolver levelled with the centre of his forehead. Kerim backed against the cabinet, his back arching as he tried to get further away. Jasper slipped his hand into his pocket, his fingers curling around the butt of Kerim's automatic.

"Describe him!" demanded Anna. A hint of colour touched her cheeks; it was the closest to an emotion that Jasper had seen from her. Kerim's eyes were fixed on the muzzle of the revolver.

"He was tall, thin. Shaved head, his face hard! I don't know. What do you want me to say?"

"Nothing," replied Anna. Kerim twitched as she de-cocked the revolver; its click seemed as loud as a slap. Kerim sagged against the cabinet, his hand searching for the whisky tumbler. Jasper breathed out. Anna looked at him, her gaze dropping to his pocket with the automatic in it.

"Come on," she said, "it's time to go."

The buzzer to the flat sounded. Kerim started, the contents of his glass splashing across the carpet. Anna's revolver was back up at his eye level.

"Expecting company?" asked Jasper.

"It's not my doing!" Kerim's eyes were fixed on the revolver.

The buzzer sounded again, only this time longer, more urgent.

"What's not your doing, Kerim?"

The buzzer sounded a third time. Kerim's gaze flicked from the muzzle of Anna's revolver to the lounge door. Jasper stepped over to the windows. There were three figures clustered around the front door to the building. One looked like he was trying to get a key to turn. Another was by the panel of buzzers, glancing up.

"No point in looking for your newfound friends to come to the rescue. I bolted the front door from the inside before we came up. Wanted to make sure we weren't disturbed."

"Is there another way out of here?" asked Anna.

"Maybe."

"What about him?"

It was an obvious question. If only it was a question and not a suggestion. Kerim was staring at him, the colour flooding from his face. The second they left, Kerim would be racing down the stairs to let his new friends in. That wouldn't leave them enough time. Sorry, Kerim, there really was no option. Jasper pulled the automatic from his pocket.

"No! Please! I wouldn't … please! Let me live!"

"Shut up, Kerim! Don't want to upset the neighbours, do we?"

He grabbed Kerim by the shoulder and spun him round. Then, pushing the automatic into Kerim's back, he shoved him through the lounge door and into the short passage that led into the rest of the apartment.

"Go left!" Jasper underlined the order with a nudge from the automatic. Kerim stumbled forward into the kitchen at the back of his apartment.

"Please! I beg you. You can have what money I have. I'll give you anything."

It might seem like a tempting offer, but Kerim ran his life on credit. Keeping pace with the latest European fashions was expensive, and his safe held little more than cobwebs. Jasper opened the pantry.

"Get in!"

Kerim stared at him.

"I said get in!"

Jasper shoved him into the cupboard. There was plenty of space; Kerim always ate out, usually at someone else's expense. Jasper forced a chair under the door handle, giving it a kick to keep it in place. Anna was leaning against the kitchen wall with her arms folded. She raised an eyebrow.

"What?" asked Jasper.

"My way would have been quicker."

A distant crash grabbed their attention. Jasper pulled open the small sash window at the back of the kitchen.

"We'll have to go down the drainpipe and into the yard. There's an alley from there we can use."

He clambered out of the window using the drainpipe to pull himself up. Below, the yard was mostly in darkness. A few floors down, a light flicked into life, but it added little detail other than how far down the yard was. Hanging onto the drainpipe, Jasper hopped across to the adjacent window sill. Anna's head appeared from Kerim's kitchen. Jasper held a finger to his lips and then beckoned her out.

The sill he stood on was narrow, but it was enough. He pulled his picks from his pocket and set to work on the woodwork around the window latch. Again, more banging sounded, but this time it was closer.

"Come on!" Anna hissed at him.

Almost there, almost. A thud followed by a crash; that

must have been Kerim's front door. The sash slid open. Jasper slipped inside. He turned to help Anna, but she had already jumped across. He pulled her into the darkened kitchen. They slid the window shut and waited.

The occasional thump of a door seeped through the darkness, but no shouts, no screams. Someone was working their way through Kerim's apartment. The last thump was closer; the kitchen. The clatter of a chair being kicked away, muffled voices; one shrill and the other measured. They'd found Kerim. Jasper closed his eyes. If there was a time to pray, this was it.

The drone of voices filtered through the adjoining wall. For the second, or possibly a third time, that day, Kerim was being interrogated. The pitch of his voice was rising; they weren't buying what he was telling them. That familiar sliver of angst was back in the pit of Jasper's stomach. He opened his eyes; in the gloom, he saw Anna staring at him. Maybe her way would have been better. The tone of the voice next door changed. It was shorter and sharper, giving orders. The sound of running. Silence from next door. Had it worked? Please, God, let it have worked, and let them think they'd escaped down the drainpipe.

"Smart idea." Anna's voice was barely above a whisper, but it still made him jump. "How long do you plan on us sitting here in the dark?"

Ten minutes? Half an hour? How about the rest of his life? He shuddered. If the ploy hadn't worked, the rest of his life might not make it to ten minutes, let alone half an hour.

"I don't know. The owner uses this place to bring his girlfriends when his wife is in town, which thankfully she isn't." Jasper stood up. A tremble was making itself felt now the immediate danger had passed. The hum of a voice pawed at the fringe of his hearing. No, the threat hadn't gone, not yet. He headed into the dark apartment.

"Where are you going?" asked Anna.

The tremble was waning, tiredness taking its place.

"I'm going to lie down or change my clothes, probably both. If you're lucky, there'll be something in one of the wardrobes that'll fit you."

"Why should I change my clothes?"

Even in a whisper, there was a challenge in her voice.

"Kerim's Russian friends have a pretty good idea of what we look like and what we're wearing. So when the police turn up and start asking questions, we need to look like the kind of people that fit with this place when we walk out past them, and not like a pair of rain-drenched refugees."

Anna's silence stretched the seconds.

"Okay. Where?"

"Second door on the left, there's a dressing room."

"You've been in here before?"

"Yes. I thought it might be worth burgling if things ever got tight." Why the need to justify? Could things be any tighter than now? Anna chuckled.

"You are not the total fool I took you for."

12.   Follow your sources

Elspeth swore; it was another dead end. She turned and retraced her steps. The ten-minute stroll from the Pera Palace to the Galata Tower had been almost pleasant. The light breeze and sunshine made this near-ideal weather if you were sightseeing, but she wasn't. The concierge's map was fine for finding the landmarks, but it wasn't up to navigating the scrum of streets that colonised the slopes around the tower. She trudged back up the hill. At least she could see the top of Galata Tower, which meant she had something to head for. It was better than wandering aimlessly through this maze of alleys and side streets. Despite the sunshine, it was still cold, even with all this exercise.

Elspeth paused at a crossroads. There was the red brick minaret of a small mosque to her right. She stared. The minaret was quite pretty, but the police car parked opposite it and half-blocking the way through wasn't. A couple of bored-looking police officers stood at the back of the car, shoulders hunched inside their coats, shuffling their feet, trying to generate warmth. Elspeth pulled her map from her pocket and checked it. The few clues on it confirmed the sinking feeling in her stomach; Kerim Yazaroğlu's apartment was on the other side of the policemen.

Nothing for it but to head down there and find out what was happening. Her heels clacked lightly on the cobbled surface. It looked like there was someone in the car. That was probably why the two men stood outside rather than keeping warm inside. One officer looked up, a slight frown appearing on his face. Elspeth put a smile on hers. The policeman nudged his colleague, who looked at Elspeth and straightened up. Elspeth let her gaze drift away from the pair fixing on a spot beyond them, her pace not slowing.

A muffled voice from the car dragged the attention of the taller of the two officers away from Elspeth. A swift elbow in his colleague's side swung his attention to whoever was sitting in the back of the police car. Elspeth sailed past the pair; their slouches had been replaced by ramrod backs. Elspeth suppressed a smile. No doubt their change in demeanour was in response to the string of invective coming from the car. She stopped a few yards past the police car. Another crossroads. The narrow alley to her left ran uphill towards the Galata Tower. The street to her right ran downhill, probably ending somewhere near the Galata Bridge. Ahead must be Kerim Yazaroğlu's apartment. She checked the address that Salome had given her. Yes, there it was: a tall building just before the bend with several balconies above the entrance.

She'd had plenty of time to come up with a decent cover story, but inspiration hadn't taken hold in the last few hours. So what should be her opening gambit? Hello, I'm a friend of Max's. Can you tell me where he is before a vengeful witch puts a bullet in him? At least it was direct and to the point, if not the wisest course of action. It didn't matter anyway if she couldn't get into the apartment block, but… Her hand clenched. The apartment block's door was opening, and a smartly-dressed woman was coming out. Elspeth stepped forward. Thank you to whatever God is smiling on me today; luck was on her side this morning.

The woman stopped and turned to say something to someone behind her. Elspeth upped her pace, her heel catching on a cobble, the sound unnaturally loud. The woman turned to look at her. Keep going, push a smile onto your face, and don't be desperate; you're going to ask her a favour. A man emerged from the building wearing a dark fedora and a smart suit. He said something to the woman and then turned. Elspeth stopped. It was Jasper, and he was looking directly at her.

"Elspeth!"

Jasper's mouth hadn't moved. The voice came from her left. Her feet froze to the spot, and the world slowed as she turned towards the voice.

"Cameron darling! What on earth are you doing here?" said Elspeth.

Striding down the alleyway from the direction of the Galata Tower was Cameron Lowe wearing a matinee idol grin to match the swagger of his step. With him was another man. Tall, slim, almost angular, with a bare-shaven head despite the cool weather. His long coat gave him the air of a vampire. The man's face was a neutral mask, but his eyes were locked on Elspeth.

"I might ask you the same thing."

The laughter in Cameron's voice seemed genuine; somehow, she had to play along despite the twist in her stomach. Jasper must have recognised her, and he couldn't have failed to hear Cameron's voice. She glanced right. Jasper and the woman were heading away but not fast enough. Elspeth started towards Cameron; he was still grinning, but the vampire was studying her. Had he noticed her glance and wondered what was of interest around the corner?

"I went sight-seeing." She waved the map at him. "I'm not very good at it!"

Cameron laughed. The vampire stared at her.

"Where are you off to?" asked Elspeth. Business or pleasure; maybe it's both. And who is your new friend? She shone her smile at them.

"Just off to meet a potential investor in a new venture. All dull stuff, really." He shrugged, but the schoolboy enthusiasm clung to him. Elspeth eyed the vampire.

"You must be Cameron's Turkish business partner that he's been so coy about introducing me to."

The vampire smirked.

"This is Nathan," said Cameron. "We're still working out the fine details of our arrangements, but hopefully, everything will be settled any day soon."

Everything will be settled any day soon. Despite the sunny smile, the words chilled her to her core. Behind her, a car door slammed. Nathan and Cameron looked to their right. Elspeth turned and followed their gaze. A tall thin man in a pale grey uniform was heading towards them. The sun glinted from the shine on his boots and the Sam Browne belt he wore. From the white of his moustache and wrinkles around his eyes, Elspeth guessed he must have been in his sixties. This must have been the man in the back of the police car. The two police officers were practically standing at attention but hadn't left the car's side. Cameron and Nathan were still looking at the man as he reached them. The smile he wore and the wrinkles around his eyes gave him the look of a friendly uncle. But the large holster on his hip did not.

"Mr Lowe, Mr Lavrov, what a surprise to meet you here." He looked at Elspeth. "And you must be Miss Stirling. What a shame that Mr Lowe hasn't introduced me to you before now." He looked back at Cameron.

Cameron's matinee idol grin was starting to look a little shabby at the edges. Nathan Lavrov's expression wasn't exuding happiness either.

"Darling," said Cameron, "this is Colonel Göçek of the ahh… Turkish police."

Colonel Göçek bowed from the waist, the grandfatherly smile fixed on his face.

"It is a pleasure to meet you in person, Miss Stirling. I am a fan of your newspaper column. It's always most amusing to find out about the goings-on in London. You have most remarkable detective skills."

Elspeth simpered at him; it was better than running at full pelt down the street.

"I'm afraid there is little sleuthing involved. It's mostly just gossip offered up by the aggrieved or the jealous."

Colonel Göçek chuckled.

"Much like police work, then." He glanced at the map still clutched in her hand. "You were perhaps a little lost? May I offer my assistance?"

He was already reaching to take the map from her hand. Her heart froze. She could hardly say no. Had she marked the map with Kerim Yazaroğlu's address? Her mind was blank. Colonel Göçek rubbed his chin as he studied the map before handing it back to her.

"I think what you are looking for is up that street," he pointed up the alleyway that Cameron had come from. "Head past the tower and then the first right."

"Thank you, Colonel." She pressed her best smile into service; it sometimes worked on older men. "What brings you to this part of town?"

The wrinkles on the Colonel's face deepened into a frown.

"A little unpleasantness over there," he nodded in the direction of Kerim Yazaroğlu's apartment. "A murder, I'm afraid." He pressed his smile back into service. "Hopefully, we will meet again under happier circumstances, Miss Stirling. Good luck with your souvenir hunting."

* * *

The man sitting behind the desk shook his head slowly as he replaced the telephone's handset in its cradle.

"I'm sorry, but there is no answer. Perhaps if you—"

"Try it again!" Elspeth practically spat the words at him.

"But, miss. I've tried the number twice already—"

"Just do it!"

She loomed over him, her fingers digging into his desk. Where the hell was Jude? Why does he never answer the bloody telephone? The clerk was redialling the number. The bottomless pit in her stomach was filling. The man was right; if Jude or anyone hadn't answered the phone before, what on earth makes you think they will now? Desperation, that's what.

It should have been a twenty-minute walk to reach the British Consulate. It would have been if she hadn't spent an additional forty minutes trying to shake off whoever was following her. Had she actually seen anyone? Had she managed to trap them into revealing their presence? Confirmed her fears and made the doubts concrete? No. Just hints, shadows, and sounds. She'd been dancing with spectres, and her subconscious had filled in the rest. Her hands uncurled from the clerk's desk, and his eyes rested briefly on her as he listened to a distant ringtone for the third time.

Why not just grab your passport, buy a train ticket and get the hell out of this city? What's stopping you? Nothing. Nothing apart from the conviction that someone out there is on your tail. Had they been there since she'd arrived in Istanbul? She hadn't picked up on anything before now. The feeling had only been there since she had all but fled from Cameron and his new best friend, Nathan Lavrov.

The clerk's face crumpled into what was bound to be another apology. It wasn't the man's fault. No point in launching another attack on him. He had the handset away from his ear and already heading for its cradle. What now? Head for the station and trap yourself on a train?

"Hello, hello?" The clerk half-jumped at the sound of the disembodied voice coming from the handset. He pulled it back to his ear.

"Hello, sir. This is Grahams at the front desk reception. I have a young lady here who is quite insistent that she talk to you… ."

Grahams blinked and then stared at the handset as if it were new and unfamiliar.

"I'm sorry, miss. He hung up. Are you sure that was the correct number? Would you like me to try again?"

Well, that was her answer. You're on your own now, so make the best of it. She gave Grahams a brief smile.

"That's alright. You've been terribly helpful. I'm sorry for my appalling manners."

She turned and headed across the consulate's foyer

towards the revolving doors. Wasn't the consulate meant to represent safety and security? The black and white chequered flooring gave the impression of a giant chess board. How appropriate; she was a pawn in this game, and it looked like she'd just been sacrificed.

"Miss Stirling! Elspeth!" It was Jude.

She stopped. Jude was rushing down the staircase into the Foyer. He nodded to Grahams, who smiled before returning to the paperwork on his desk.

"I'm so sorry. I had no idea you were trying to get in touch with me."

The apologies were painted across his face; did they sit any deeper than his skin? Did it really matter? At least his was an outwardly friendly face.

"That's alright; I thought you were avoiding me. Do you get many distraught women turning up here demanding to see you?"

Jude's eyes flicked towards Grahams, who kept his head engrossed in the ledger on his desk.

"How about we go somewhere a bit more private?"

She followed Jude through a door skulking beneath the sweep of the main staircase. A thin corridor headed deep into the building. The lights studding the ceiling struggled to lift the gloom of institute-grey painted walls. The muted clatter of a typewriter was the only sound that accompanied their footsteps. Several plain wooden doors marked the corridor's length; the place had the feel of a cellblock. Jude stopped. Elspeth half expected him to pull out a bunch of keys on a chain.

Jude opened a door stepping to one side to let her in.

The bars inside the window did little to dispel the sense of a cell. An austere desk cut the room in two. The desk lamp raised on a couple of telephone directories shone a puddle of light across the blotter on the desk's surface. A black telephone sat silently on the end of the desk. Was this the same telephone that had been ignored so many times? If it was, then why had Jude come running from upstairs?

"Sit down. Make yourself comfortable." The second sentence sounded like an afterthought.

Jude headed for the other side of the desk. He slipped his jacket off and hung it on the stand lurking in the shadows of the corner of the room. He didn't offer to take Elspeth's coat. Elspeth stared at him as he sat down and started flicking through a sheaf of papers on the desk. Maybe he wasn't expecting this to take long. Elspeth pulled a chair clear of the desk and sat down. Jude was still examining the papers.

"I found Max Bolton," she said.

Jude stared at her for a second and then pushed the papers to one side.

"Where is he?"

"I don't know." A frown creased Jude's brow. "I can tell you where he was about an hour ago, and that's about it."

The frown deepened as the seconds sped by.

"How about we stop messing about?" He forced the words out. The frown had become a scowl.

"Yes, let's!" Elspeth mugged a stiff smile at him. If that's how he wanted to play this crappy little charade, so be it. "How about you drop the mock police cell interrogation and start giving me the support you're supposed to."

"Hah! That's good." He shook his head slowly. "How about you stop lying to me?"

Elspeth folded her arms and shrugged.

"I don't know—"

"The woman in Balat! Remember? The girl in the morgue that you said you'd never seen before."

"What about her?"

"She was part of some racket getting papers and false passports for refugees. Refugees, criminals, anyone willing to pay and to hell with the reason." He was searching her face, leaning forward into the pool of light from the lamp. How long before he tried the B-movie routine and shone it in her face? "Your chap is in it up to his arm pits. Don't tell me you don't know her." He sat back, smoothing his tie. "Does the name Ruby ring any bells?"

So he did know more than he'd let on. There again, so did she. But, right now, she needed his help, and it didn't seem like he was that keen on hers.

"Yes, I lied." Jude's eyes widened a fraction. Wasn't expecting her to give in so easily? Perhaps she could buy a little more. "Her name is Ruby Stevens, and the last time I saw her was in Albania two years ago. Where did you get her name from?"

"What was she doing in Albania? What's this got to do with your man, Max?"

"If K has briefed you, then you already know. We were all working together. And for the record, my man Max is officially a dead man called Jasper Lewingdon."

The scowl slipped from Jude's face. I've shared some of mine; now, are you going to share some of yours? There again, this could all turn into a perpetual staring contest. Jude's scowl was creeping back. Staring contest it was then. But who's going to win? Now her eyes had adjusted, Elspeth could make out the few features of the room a bit better. A near-empty bookcase took up one wall facing off against the obligatory portrait of the King on the other. Sunlight cast shadows of nearby trees across the barred window. The glass was opaque, presumably to prevent prying eyes from taking in the spectacle of standoffs such as this. Jude cleared his throat. Elspeth let her gaze drift back to his face. Had she won?

"A contact gave me her name."

Elspeth stared at him. A contact. Thank you for nothing. An agent, an acquaintance from a bar, a girlfriend?

"What kind of contact?" she asked. Jude's mouth tightened. Was that real or just her imagination? "Ruby wasn't just anybody. She was a professional, one of K's best." It irked her to admit it, but it was true. "If someone knew her real name, they probably did business with her. If that's the case, it links them to my man."

Did she really have to spell this out? Desperation was morphing into irritation. Why waste more time here when she could already be on a train out of here? Jude was looking uncomfortable. Push him, or just let the silence do the dirty work? Finally, he spoke.

"Since the end of the civil war in Russia, Istanbul has become a clearing house for refugees fleeing the delights of Communism and looking to start again. There are those still keen to help people to get out and head to the West or where ever. These same people also help us get our people into southern Russia. My contact is one of these—"

145

"Viktor Volkov?"

He swept the reaction away behind the neutral mask he usually wore, but the surprise on Jude's face had been evident. Throwing that name in had been a gamble, but it had been worth it.

"Where did you get that from?"

Elspeth fought hard to keep her face straight. The way he'd snapped that question back at her confirmed she was right. Thank you, Salome.

"I have contacts too."

It was hard not to let a little smugness creep into her voice. Now was the time to be professional and milk this for everything she could get out of it. Jude's mouth looked tighter than before. It wasn't a good sign, and it didn't look like he would open up further about his dealings with Viktor Volkov. She shouldn't have let that triumphant smirk flash across her face. But she was human, after all. There was no point in prolonging this.

"I need your help to get out of Istanbul." She noted the rise in Jude's eyebrow in response to her words.

"Why? What's happened?"

Simple question. But what had happened? Did she have any evidence?

"My cover is blown. The sooner I get away, the less chance your favourite task mistress, Lady Susan Linklater, will get her opportunity to take revenge on me."

"Revenge? For what?"

"Lady Susan believes that Jasper murdered her brother. To the world, Jasper Lewingdon drowned in the Thames,

146

but as we know, an hour ago, he was alive and well in a backstreet in Galata. Lady Susan is here trying to find him, no doubt aided by my soon-to-be ex-fiancé and his new best friend, Nathan Lavrov."

"Nathan Lavrov!" Surprise splashed across Jude's features, and he wasn't making any effort to hide it. "Are you sure?"

Elspeth could feel her stomach stiffen; such sudden interest couldn't signal anything good.

"Why? Who is he?"

"Officially, he's an attaché in the Russian consulate. He doesn't appear to have any obvious job there but turns up at events and spends his time making friends."

"Much like you?"

Jude shrugged a smile at her.

"He arrived around the time that Trotsky was exiled here."

"And Lavrov turning up at the same time makes him important?"

"It's obvious he's a spook." He was pinning her with his smile, urging her to buy into his belief. Elspeth crossed her arms, leaning back in her chair. Jude hunched forward. "The rumour is that Lavrov's star is on the rise."

"The rumour?" Was that it? A rumour, backstairs gossip, diplomatic small talk? She couldn't stifle the scepticism in her voice. Jude carried on.

"Look, if you're right and he's mixed up with Cameron Lowe, this might be something we can use against him." Unfortunately, Jude's enthusiasm was tinged with overconfidence. It was a bad combination, and the pit of her stomach confirmed it.

"Lavrov is mixed up with Cameron," said Elspeth confirming Jude's suggestion. She suppressed the shudder at the memory of seeing the pair walking towards her and Cameron's words that soon everything would be settled. "And now you tell me he's a Soviet spook. That's all the more reason for me to get out of Istanbul."

"You're missing the bigger picture—"

"No! You're missing my need to get out of Istanbul before you have to identify my body in that morgue!"

"Just think about it…" He paused. Expecting her to slap him down again? Let's see where he wants to go with this. She shrugged at him. He went on. "We have a Soviet diplomat cosying up with someone that pretty much represents everything their regime despises. Judging by the editorial in his papers, Cameron's a borderline fascist. So why on earth would Lavrov be doing that? Aren't you even the least bit curious to find out?"

Curious? Yes, that was one way to describe how she felt. Terrified as to what it signified for her would be a better one. But if this was all about her, why involve some Soviet spook out here in Istanbul? If Cameron wanted her out of the way, surely there were less cumbersome ways of achieving that. A suspicion was starting to make itself felt. There was something inevitable about where this was all going.

"Whatever Cameron and Lavrov are up to, it involves Jasper and the racket he's caught up in." She could see the question forming on Jude's face in response to her words. "The last place I saw Jasper was where I ran into Cameron and Lavrov."

A scrap of smugness skimmed across Jude's face.

"And you want to leave just as things are getting exciting?"

"Recent experience tells me that exciting can quickly turn into terrifying." Often with a supporting cast of torture and corpses. But what on earth is Cameron up to? Was this the real reason that K had sent her out here? "Who is Colonel Göçek?"

Jude broke eye contact a moment, a frown settling across his features.

"Where did you meet him?"

"I think he was waiting for Cameron and Lavrov, and you haven't answered my question."

"In short, bad news. He's the head of the Emniyet in Istanbul."

"Other than being the head of the secret police, why is he such bad news? He looks like someone's favourite grandfather."

The frown deepened as Jude tapped his index finger on the table top. Finally, he spoke.

"He's been showing an interest in your man, and was very keen to put a name to the woman in Balat."

"Hardly surprising the police are taking an interest."

"Except he's taking a personal interest. He even dropped by to talk to the Consul in person. He asked how we were getting on with our enquiries. In particular, he asked if we had been able to contact any of her relatives."

"But he didn't mention anything about Cameron or Lavrov?"

149

"No, but if he's involved with them, that makes things more awkward."

"You're not getting cold feet, are you?"

Jude sighed, and a wrinkle of a grimace inched onto his face.

"Göçek is a crafty old fox. He was sending a message. He's watching us, and if we step out of line, he will make it the Consul's problem. Which, of course, means it will be my problem, or at least it will be me that gets sent home in disgrace for diplomatic expediency."

"At least you'd get to go home. Ruby ended up in the morgue." And Jasper is still on the run somewhere in this city. Shouldn't she leave before she joined Ruby? But there was a story here, and she could feel it in her bones. "We need to talk to Viktor Volkov. Where can we find him?"

13.   Ghosts

Tamara slouched in the shadows. They'd followed the woman to the British Consulate. Thirty precious minutes wasted, and for what? She looked at her companion. Is that what he was? She'd hunted him down, aiming to get hold of the papers she could use to get across any border with no questions asked. And now? Not only did Nathan Lavrov know she was in Istanbul, but he had the very documents she'd risked herself trying to get hold of. Was there an upside to this? She was alive.

"We should move," said Tamara.

Max didn't look like he was in any hurry to leave his vantage point on Graveyard street; quite an appropriate name. He looked at her.

"Where to?"

It was a fair question.

"Anywhere but here. If we don't move, someone will start wondering what we're up to."

Max shrugged.

"I was hoping to see where she went when she leaves the consulate."

After leaving Kerim's apartment, they had hardly exchanged a word; they'd been too busy keeping on the trail of the woman. No, he'd been busy trailing the woman. She'd been too busy making sure that no one had been following them as they'd pursued the woman through endless alleys and back streets.

"So what's so important about this woman that we chase her across half of the town?"

151

"She shouldn't be here. The fact that she is, means… I don't know what, but I need to know."

The woman had recognised Max; that much was certain. The man that had called out to her had called her Elspeth; pity she hadn't seen his face. The woman's name didn't mean anything to her, but the man's voice? That voice was one from her past.

"You're right. We'd better get moving." Max stared at her. "Are you alright? You look like you've seen a ghost."

* * *

Baku, September 1918.

The distant crackle of rifle fire had been almost constant throughout the day. However, the firing was more sporadic now that the sun had set. Ottoman forces were at the city's edge, and it wouldn't be long before they broke through. The house seemed to be holding its breath. Tamara stepped softly, making her way down the stairs in the darkness. Voices were coming from the kitchen. It sounded as if Nathan had a visitor.

"We're pulling out tomorrow night. Make sure you're at the quayside at seven o'clock and give the guard this. He'll be expecting you."

The voice sounded English, but not quite, a hint of American? Maybe Canadian. Tamara took a couple more paces closer. The door to the kitchen was ajar. Nathan was planning something, but he hadn't shared any details. With luck, she could get a look at this mystery man.

"What about you? How will you get out?" asked

Nathan.

The man chuckled.

"Don't you worry about me."

Nathan laughed. A bottle and glasses clinked.

"It's not you that I'm worried about. It's our mutual friend sitting in prison waiting for rescue."

"I've got it all covered. As soon as the Turks start their attack, we'll bust the jail open and get our friend down to the docks and away to safety. Well, for now, anyway."

Glasses clinked, followed by a chuckle.

"I don't understand why you want me to get this guy out of jail when you could leave him for the Turks to finish off. It's a waste of good dynamite and bullets."

"He'd become another martyr to the revolution. I need him alive long enough to kill his reputation. After that, some central committee or other will deal with the mundane business of killing his body," replied Nathan.

"Tough business being a revolutionary." The glug of liquor being poured was followed by another clink of glasses. "I feel a bit of a heel doing this to him. He was always straight with me when I was trying to get a deal to supply us with oil and keep it out of the Turk's hands. You sure this is necessary?"

"Yes. He's wedded to Trotsky's faction, so he needs to be… moved out of the way."

"I thought Trotsky's star was flying high. If anyone is going to replace Lenin, it'll be him. I thought he was your man. So why bet against him?"

"I'm ambitious, and Stepan is Trotsky's favourite."

The pair laughed. "With Stepan out of the way and with my man's backing, I'll be in a position to run things here."

"Assuming you can boot the Turks out when the Brits have gone."

The crump of a shell shook the house. Tamara gasped. She clasped her hand to her mouth, but the sound was out.

"Tamara? Is that you?" called Nathan.

She strode into the kitchen. The oil lamp painted the tableau for her. Nathan was half out of his chair, a crease of concern puckering his face. A bottle of vodka sat in the middle of the small table, along with a pair of shot glasses. A big man with dark hair brushed back and a thick moustache was sprawled in the other chair. In contrast to Nathan, his face held a huge grin, his eyes joining in as he looked at her. Tamara fixed the bottle with a glare.

"Where is my glass?" she demanded.

The man draped in the chair let out a bellow of a laugh. Nathan stood up.

"I'll get you one," he said.

Tamara studied the man, her hands fixed to her hips. She had to keep control of this, don't let Nathan steer the situation and wonder how much she had heard.

"No one told me that we had a visitor, or I would have found something for us to eat," she said, the edge of a rebuke in her voice.

The man unhooked a canvas satchel from his chair and pulled a small loaf and a block of cheese from it.

"I brought my own. I know what a hopeless host Nathan can be!"

Nathan put an extra glass on the table and filled all three.

"How do you know Nathan?" asked Tamara.

The man started to open his mouth, but Nathan cut in.

"This is Cameron Lowe. He's found us a safe passage out of Baku."

* * *

"Anna!" Max's voice jolted her from the past. "Are you sure you're okay?"

His face wore an inkling of unease. She fixed a smile in place.

"Of course. We must move. Now."

Tamara headed down the alley, away from Graveyard Street, away from the British Consulate, and with luck, away from Nathan Lavrov. She was still striding, her eyes fixed ahead, as Max caught up.

"What's going on?" he asked.

"We need to move, that's all."

She slowed her pace. Max glanced behind. A few loafers were hanging about, waiting for the trade to pick up. A few faces looked their way. Of course they would. Right now, she looked like the kind of woman with money to waste in tourist traps selling trinkets and baubles. She needed to shed these clothes, assume an identity that blended into the background, and return to being Anna. But being this woman had worked earlier, and that was Max's idea. It all depended on the environment; if she was to make it to Paris, this might be the persona she needed. She slowed to an amble glancing at the well-stocked windows of the boutiques lining the street.

Max was joining in the charade of window shopping. The act was good; either he was a natural or well-practised. But where had he been practising? She'd assumed he was yet another piece of flotsam scratching a living among the margins of Istanbul's migrants. That looked like an act as well. She re-ran the memory of the scene outside Kerim's apartment. It wasn't just the woman Max had recognised; he'd reacted when she'd said Cameron's name.

"Are we looking for something special?"

Tamara stopped and studied his face. Who are you really, Mr Max Bolton?

"Who is Cameron?" she asked.

The surprise looked real, and maybe it was. But the reaction was masking something else. He'd done it well; if she hadn't been looking for it, she'd be none the wiser. But what was he covering up?

"He's…"

Tamara almost smirked; this would be a lie, and he'd telegraphed it with his hesitation. Maybe he wasn't that good after all. Max half-chuckled, maybe at a memory half dredged up or perhaps at the size of the lie he was going sell.

"He's Elspeth's fiancé."

Tamara blinked. That wasn't what she'd expected. It seemed too odd, too specific to be false. Surely it couldn't be real? Max had walked ahead a couple of paces. He turned, waiting for her to catch up. He was grinning, but there was a brittleness to it. The humour seeped from his face.

"And he's probably the most dangerous man I've ever met."

Tamara stared at him. That had the ring of truth, but a good liar always hid behind the truth.

"You know him?"

"I know of him." Max looked down at the pavement before continuing. "I've met him, but I don't know him."

"But the woman, Elspeth, you know her?"

"Yes."

Well, that much was obvious. But what was Elspeth to Max? And why did this mean a man from a past she thought buried was here? They stepped onto the Grande Rue, stopping to let a tram grumble past before heading to the far side.

"What makes him so dangerous?"

They drifted along the bustling pavement. Where were they heading? That would depend on what Max knew about Cameron Lowe. The street was busy but not teeming with people. Enough to help cover an escape but not so many that you would miss who was following you. Max stopped and peered at a display in a shop window, and Tamara echoed his apparent interest.

"He's rich, influential, and has a private spy ring at his disposal."

Max's voice was barely audible above the background babble of the street.

"And he's here to find you?"

Max nodded and then carried on along the street.

"What makes you so important to him?"

Max let out another half-laugh; it seemed tinged with bitterness.

"I'm not important to Cameron Lowe, but he has a close friend that would dearly love to see me squirm. No, he has a friend that is no doubt watching me squirm and loving every second of it," he looked over his shoulder, scanning the street, "right up to the point I stop breathing."

"They killed your partner?"

He looked at her for several seconds.

"If it wasn't you and Viktor, then I can't think of any other candidates."

Did he still have suspicions about her? He'd be a fool not to, and recent events suggested he wasn't the clown he made himself out to be. Could she rely on him?

"The woman warned you outside Kerim's." Max's eyes narrowed at her words. "Why did she do that? Was she—?"

"No." Max started walking, and she fell into step with him. Let the silence build. The pressure would be on him to fill it. "No, there was never anything between us. Events brought us together, but now? Who knows?"

"She thought there was enough there to warn you. Does she know what Cameron is?"

"Without a doubt."

He'd upped his pace, his hands shoved into his coat

pockets. No doubt those hands would be balled into fists.

"Why would she marry such a man?"

"I don't know." Tamara smiled to herself; that was the lie he was covering. "Maybe it's his bank balance, there again, he owns several newspapers, and she's an ambitious journalist. Desire can blind you to many things."

He was trying hard to blacken her character. It felt like misdirection, but the edge in his voice hinted at more. He glanced at her.

"What about the Russian at Kerim's?" His voice was level. How long had he been nursing that question? It was an obvious tactic to change the subject.

"What about him?" she replied.

"Who is he? Why is he so interested in you? And why was he looking for me at Kerim's?"

How much should she tell him? He'd already shared, and what he'd said about Cameron fitted with the man she'd known in Baku. Unfortunately, this man who claimed to be Max Bolton isn't what he presented to the world; an out-and-out lie wouldn't be good enough.

"Nathan Lavrov. We were lovers. He left me to die in Baku; if he catches me here, he will kill me. I don't know why he is looking for you, but you are in more danger than you realise."

He didn't look surprised. If anything, he looked bored. Everything she'd said was true, even if it wasn't everything.

"It must have been one hell of a lover's tiff if he's still out to kill you."

They ambled further along the Grand Rue, presenting the fiction that they were just another well-to-do couple looking for a little late-morning distraction. His words hadn't offered any comfort, and his silence was little consolation, but that wasn't what she needed.

"What were you doing in Baku?" Max asked.

His curiosity had got the better of him. Good, it was something that she could use.

"Nathan was part of the Cheka. You know what that is?"

"Yes. The Bolshevik's bully boys and murderers tasked with keeping the revolution on track."

He stared down at the pavement, his hands still pushed into his coat pockets. His words didn't mark him out as a fellow traveller. There would be no point in appealing to his politics.

"When the Bolshevik's enemies invited the British into Baku to save them from the Turks, most of Nathan's comrades were arrested, but he managed to escape."

"Leaving you behind?"

An easy assumption to make, the story of an abandoned woman would flow easily from it. And it felt like a snare for the unwary. This man is not a fool.

"If only he had."

Max stopped. Now she had his full attention and not just the part expecting a pitiful tale of betrayal, although that would be weaved into what she had. She stared at him, almost counting the seconds before she spoke.

"I need your help. Not just to get out of this city but

out of Turkey and far beyond." His face didn't quite say what's in it for me, but it didn't need to. "I know your man, Cameron Lowe. He was in Baku."

"That doesn't surprise me."

His bearing was all bluff. His words were a verbal shrug, a challenge for her to offer more.

"He was making a deal with Nathan Lavrov. I know what it was and how it all played out. Help me get away, and I will tell you everything."

"What makes you think I can give you what you want?"

"Cameron Lowe and Nathan Lavrov are searching for you. Viktor Volkov has put a bounty on your head. Yet, despite all this, you're still alive."

"I've just been lucky so far."

"No, you've been expecting this day. You've planned a way out, and I want you to take me too."

How deep did his Sir Galahad streak run?

"You're deluding yourself. Do you think I'd still be here if I did have a way out?"

Max shook his head and started to walk. It looked like the Galahad streak wasn't deep enough.

"Cameron killed your partner. What I know about Cameron Lowe and Nathan Lavrov makes me worth killing. In the right hands, it's enough to get Nathan hanged or worse. What do you think you could do to Cameron Lowe with it? Don't you want to avenge your partner?"

Max stopped and turned. Tamara held her breath.

"Okay. You're going to need a passport. I think I know where we can get one, but first, we're going to have to make a deal with someone."

14.   Burning down the house

Jude switched the ignition off, and the car shuddered into silence. The breeze from the Bosphorus sent a shiver through the trees lining the track leading from the coast road. Elspeth looked at Jude. His gaze was fixed ahead, and he still had his hands on the steering wheel.

"We're not driving up to Volkov's front door?" she asked.

The question was a gibe to get a response from him. The thirty-minute drive from Istanbul had been in almost total silence. The tightness in Jude's jaw didn't suggest that the silence was about to end anytime soon. Maybe she should walk back into the small town at the start of the track. The place felt like it had money. There was a fine café there; she could order some lunch and then get a taxi to take her back into Istanbul before boarding a train out of here.

"I thought it would be better if we didn't announce ourselves. I don't want to give him the option to be out when we call."

Jude's words almost made her jump. He was still staring ahead, his hands glued to the steering wheel.

"It looks like you're having second thoughts about this. What's changed?"

"Nothing's changed, but…" Jude's hands slipped from the wheel, and he slumped slightly into his seat. "Göçek's involvement in all this worries me."

"Why? It doesn't seem unexpected that the head of the secret police is going to take an interest."

"The Emniyet tolerate what Volkov and others do, but

I'm wondering whether they're sending out a message that they won't tolerate it anymore."

"You think they're behind Ruby's death?"

"Maybe, I wouldn't put it beyond them. Behind Göçek's grandfatherly exterior is a cold-blooded killer with no love for the British."

"That sounds like you have a history with him."

Jude shook his head.

"Just his reputation." Jude opened the car door and started clambering out. "Come on, Volkov's place is beyond the crest. He likes his privacy."

Elspeth frowned and fumbled with her door catch. Jude was already striding up the track before she could get out of the car. She half-ran to catch up with him. No doubt that sudden leap into action was to distract her from digging further into Göçek's background or, more likely, his. Near the crest, Jude slowed, approaching half-crouched as if he expected a sniper. Elspeth hung back. Surely all this Boy Scout stuff was a little over the top? She glanced down. The grass at the edge of the track had been pressed flat by a tyre. The crushed grass stalks were still green. Something had passed by recently but was it heading to or from Volkov's?

"Come on, it looks clear."

Elspeth looked up at Jude's words. He was already heading over the crest. Had he seen the tyre tracks? Elspeth caught up with him. The route meandered down a gentle gradient. The outline of a large Ottoman villa could be made out through the trees that screened it from the track. It was an idyllic hideaway if you were a movie star or a holidaying socialite. It didn't feel like the kind of place to find a people smuggler running rackets in the black market, but what had she expected?

"We'll head around the back and see if we can get in," said Jude.

"What about the staff? A place that size is bound to have some servants."

"We should be alright. Volkov only uses a few rooms, and much of the house is closed up. I think he has a cook and cleaner come up from the village, but that's about it."

Jude headed off the track and through the trees. What the hell was up with him? One minute he could barely prise himself from the car, and now he was practically scampering through the woods with no idea of what was waiting for them. Elspeth picked her way after him. The undergrowth was sparse, as if someone had spent time keeping the grounds under control. So much for just an occasional domestic visit from the nearby village. This place needed and probably had full-time staff. Jude had stopped a few yards ahead and crouched down. Elspeth crept up to his side.

"Volkov has visitors."

The back of the house was about fifty yards from the trees and shrubs they were hiding in, separated by an abandoned tennis court. Shutters covered the windows of the upper storey, supporting Jude's view that the house was in hibernation rather than inhabited. The ground sloped away to the right of the house, where there was a garage and a gravel driveway. Two cars sat on the driveway: a glistening bright red Hispano-Suiza two-seater and a dusty black model-A Ford saloon parked at an angle across the drive.

"The Hispano-Suiza is Volkov's," whispered Jude.

"And the Ford?"

"No idea. Let's go and find out."

"Hang on." Jude was already rising from a crouch. "We've no idea who's in there with Volkov. We need to take things carefully."

Jude grinned.

"Don't worry, I will. You stay here if you want, but I want to find out what Volkov is up to."

He turned and headed for the back of the house, adopting his Boy Scout half-crouch again. It looked like the lethal cocktail of over-confidence and ignorance had pushed aside Jude's earlier reticence. He skirted around the edge of the tennis court and stopped at its corner. The court's low wall and chain-link fencing gave him a crumb of cover but not much. At least from there, he should be able to see through the French doors that opened onto the sunken paved area behind the villa.

Elspeth counted the seconds as they passed, ignoring the onset of pins and needles in her leg. What the hell could he see? What was he up to? She couldn't just sit here hiding behind a bloody bush; she'd also have to go down there. She started to get up and then froze. Jude was moving again. He half-ran, half-scampered across the back of the house. What had spooked him? The right side of the house had an extension or wing that jutted out. Jude headed for it and into the dead ground. Now what? She couldn't see him and had no idea what he was doing.

A man appeared at the French doors; was this Viktor Volkov? Whoever it was, it must be who Jude had run from. The man stood for a few moments, a frown forming. His head turned as if responding to a question from someone in the room before returning to his vigil. Where the hell was Jude?

A twig snapped behind her. Elspeth turned. Nothing but trees; no assailant, no threat. Shit! She shouldn't have moved. Elspeth looked back at the house. The man at the French doors was still there, but now he was staring in her direction. Had he seen the movement? She willed herself to be still. What could he see? If she ran now, then Jude was as good as caught. A camel hair coat and dark blue felt hat were hardly the greatest camouflage, but at least she wasn't wearing anything too bright. If she kept still, she might be taken for a shadow. Time ticked by. The man spoke to someone behind him, and another figure appeared at the doors. Elspeth felt her chest tighten; it was Lavrov.

The man spoke again to Lavrov. He shrugged and then also stared in her direction. The man started to open the French doors. Her heart was hammering. If she was going to run, it had to be now. One-half of the French doors banged open. A crash sounded to Elspeth's right. A deer broke cover and hurtled away to another patch of trees. Lavrov and the other man stepped out onto the sunken patio. She could hear Lavrov laughing as he clapped the other man on the shoulders. A few more crashes sounded as two more deer headed after the first. Still chuckling, Lavrov headed back inside the villa, but the other man stayed where he was scanning the treeline. Finally, after what seemed like a thousand years, he went into the building pulling the door shut behind him.

Elspeth breathed out. Her pulse was still pinging with the adrenaline spike, but she had got away with it. Stay calm; take some more slow breaths. What to do now? Stay here? What about Jude? Where was he, and what was he hoping to achieve? The slope of the ground meant she could only be seen by someone standing at the French doors; she should be safe if she didn't move. Unless Jude got caught, then the first she'd know about it would be when Lavrov or his friend turned up. So it was practically madness to stay where she was. But where to move to? The last place they'd expect her would be down by the villa. It must be the adrenaline still flushing through her veins; this was a crazy plan. No, you just want an excuse to find out why Lavrov is here, and you aren't going to find that out hiding in a shrub. Elspeth crawled back from the bush and then headed through the trees to her right.

It was easy going through the open woods around the house, especially as she was heading down the slope to come out near the garage and the driveway. Even so, she could feel the tension building at the base of her neck. What if Jude had already headed back? Would he wait for her? She reached the garage. Her ears strained for any sounds to betray an ambush. Her heart racing, Elspeth crept forward. She winced at the sound her shoes made on the gravel driveway as she headed past the cars. A couple of travelling bags were stuffed into the passenger seat of the Hispano-Suiza. It looked like Volkov was about to go on his travels.

There was a side door to the main house. If Volkov had been packing ready to leave, there was a chance the door would be open. Why would you bother to walk the long way round to the garage if there was a shortcut through the villa? She turned the door handle, flinching as it squealed softly. Her pulse thumped in her throat as she kept the handle turned. Did she imagine the sound of footsteps heading toward the door? The breeze from the Bosphorus made the trees murmur; just do it! Elspeth opened the door. A corridor ran straight from it with no one standing at its end.

She stepped inside, pressing the door shut and letting

the tension in the handle unwind with as little sound as possible. If only the tension in her neck would do likewise. The corridor was dark, with wood-panelled walls and a wooden floor sucking up what little light there was. Three doors were on the left, and the last one was half open. The light from it spilt across the foot of a staircase opposite it. At the end of the corridor was a door. This place felt like it was the servant's area, with the door at the end probably leading into the main house. Elspeth slipped her shoes off and padded along the corridor.

She stopped by the open door and glanced inside. It was a scullery with a couple of sinks and an array of cupboards. Boots and coats clustered around an outside door; this must have been where Jude entered the house. So, where had he gone? A muffled thud followed by the squeal of furniture being dragged sounded from deeper in the building. Elspeth pressed her hand against the door leading into the rest of the house. What was beyond it? From the corridor's length, the room with the French doors must be close by. It was too risky to chance opening the door. Someone screamed. Elspeth pulled her hand away from the door as if its surface was scalding.

She stared at the door for several seconds and then hurried up the stairs. At the top, she paused and stuffed her shoes into her coat pockets. The landing mirrored the corridor below, although to her right was an opening rather than a door. She could hear voices. Barely breathing, Elspeth crept forward. The opening led to a gallery running around a large room. Elspeth crouched down and crawled to the bannisters.

The room below was in half-shadow. The shutters for the windows along its upper part were closed, and the only source of light came from the French doors and the windows on either side of them. In the centre of the room were two large leather couches with a low square table separating them. Against the far wall was a writing desk, its draws pulled open and their contents scattered around it. The desk's chair was set between the desk and the couches. A big man with shoulder-length dark hair was slumped in the chair, his arms behind him. His lank hair hung down, hiding his face. Around his feet, dark red splashes marked the polished floor. This must be Volkov. The man she'd seen outside with Lavrov was standing next to Volkov, rapping a riding crop into his gloved palm. Its slap sounded like a perverted clock, ticking away the time before the next inevitable slice of violence. Lavrov had his back to Elspeth. In his hand was a pistol which he pressed into the back of Jude's neck.

"Jude, would you go and sit next to Viktor? I find it tiresome asking questions behind your back instead of to your face."

Elspeth stifled her surprise; Lavrov's accent wouldn't have been out of place at a Buckingham Palace garden party. Jude limped over to Volkov, holding his left arm tight against himself. He winced as he struggled to sit on the floor. The man with the riding crop grinned.

"I'm sorry about your arm, Jude. Dmitry can be a little over-zealous, but you did surprise him." Lavrov's words were hardly dripping in sincerity; he could barely stop himself from laughing.

"So surprised that he tried to break my jaw as well?"

Jude's words were thick as if his tongue was too large for his mouth. Elspeth's stomach clenched. Even from her location, she could see the swelling on the left side of Jude's face and the spatter of blood down his shirt. Dmitry said something to Lavrov, who sniggered.

170

"Dmitry says he knows a good dentist, but he's in Leningrad."

Jude glared at Lavrov.

"Now, Viktor," said Lavrov, "shall we try again? Where is the girl?"

Viktor's head lifted slowly. His left eye was closed, and blood trickled from his nostril. His right eye blazed like a jewel. He spat on the floor and said something in Russian. Dmitry raised the riding crop to strike. Viktor kept his gaze fixed on Lavrov. Dmitry glanced at Lavrov, who shook his head. Dmitry's hand came back down to his side.

"Now, now, Viktor. Let's keep this in English so our friend here can join in."

Viktor turned his head to look at Jude and then let it drop forward again, his hair hanging down and hiding his face.

"Never met him. I don't know who he is," said Viktor.

Lavrov chuckled.

"Viktor, you're being uncharacteristically loyal. Isn't that heart-warming, Jude?"

Jude glared at Lavrov while Viktor just sagged against the cords binding him to his chair. A few more beads of blood spattered onto the floor around his feet.

"Shall I remind you, Viktor?" asked Lavrov. The seconds ticked by as Lavrov waited for a reply to his question. "This is Jude Faulkner, a British spy masquerading as a diplomat as well you know. He's the same man that pays you to smuggle enemies of the revolution into our motherland. Do you still call Russia our motherland, or have you spent so long selling her to anyone

171

who will pay that you no longer care?"

Lavrov spat the last sentence at Viktor. Elspeth could feel her stomach starting to screw itself tight. Lavrov scowled down at Viktor as he paced back and forth in front of him. Viktor's shoulders started a slow shake in time with a low rumble; he was laughing. Lavrov snatched the riding crop from Dmitry and forced it beneath Viktor's chin, making him look up at him.

"I'm so glad you find this funny. Maybe you will still find it amusing when we're finished with you?"

Viktor had stopped laughing, but his battered face still held a smile. Elspeth could see Lavrov's fist whitening around the handle of the riding crop.

"What girl?" It was Jude's voice. "What girl are you looking for?"

Lavrov straightened up and pulled the riding crop away. Viktor kept staring at Lavrov, his smile taunting him.

"The girl?" asked Lavrov. "Anna. Anna Kravchenko. She's one of Viktor's little projects. Snatched from the sewers and being trained to serve the cause. Isn't that so, Viktor?"

Lavrov was pacing once more, a slow, measured beat. Each thud of his boot in time with his words, every step part of the performance. Elspeth forced herself to breathe. She had to get help but wasn't Anna the name of the girl that Salome had mentioned? Lavrov looked at Viktor.

"You know who I mean, don't you, Viktor?" The smile had shrunk from Viktor's face. Lavrov stopped in front of Jude. "He's been working hard to get her some good papers so she can get to Paris. Join up with all the other traitors to Russia and do their best to destroy everything the Party has won for our glorious motherland."

Viktor mumbled something in Russian. The chair protested as Viktor struggled against his bonds. Lavrov tossed the riding crop to Dmitry, who brought it down across Viktor's back.

"Now, now, Viktor. You've done an excellent job of protecting her. It was a bit sloppy having all those letters and papers about her in your desk, but you never were that careful, were you? How many agents have you lost, I wonder? Who did you blame? I bet you always blamed them. Of course, it was never your fault, was it? They were the careless ones, or it was always some nasty little Bolshevik that blew their cover?"

Viktor snarled, then yelped as the riding crop came down across the side of his head. Lavrov turned to Jude.

"I thought he'd give up Anna the second I walked in here, but he thinks this one's special. Thinks she has something, something worth training and turning into a weapon to use against his enemies. Isn't that so, Viktor?" He still looked at Jude. "What he doesn't realise, but might be starting to cotton on, is that I trained her. Natalia Perskov, Alina Askenova, just a couple of the people she has been, and now she's Anna Kravchenko."

Lavrov walked over to Viktor. If will alone could kill, then Lavrov would be rotting in his grave, but all Viktor could do was spit on the floor in front of him.

"Would you like to know her real name, Viktor? It's Tamara Korovina. I know we shouldn't share our agent's names, but she is far more than that to me, which is why I need you to tell me where she is."

The only sounds in the room were Viktor's chair

protesting as he struggled against his bonds. Lavrov nodded at Dmitry. The riding crop landed across Viktor's shoulders again and again. Viktor's stifled grunts merged into a low moan as he sagged. The beating continued as Lavrov paced over to Jude.

"Jude, perhaps you'd like to fill me in on Tamara's whereabouts?"

Jude's head snapped round as Viktor's chair toppled to one side. Dmitry's riding crop didn't miss a beat as Viktor's moans morphed into a keening cry.

"Jude? I asked you a question. Where is Tamara Korovina, or maybe you prefer the name Anna Kravchenko?"

"I… I don't know. I've never heard of either of them."

Viktor screamed, and Jude jumped. Lavrov reached inside his jacket.

"I have Anna's passport here. It's French. You might recognise her photograph." He tossed the document at Jude. "It's a forgery, of course, but a very good one with all the latest stamps. Go on, take a look."

Jude winced as he leaned forward and picked up the passport, fumbling to open the pages with just his right hand. He shook his head slowly.

"I've never seen this woman."

The riding crop smacked down, and Viktor cried out.

"Please! You have to believe me!" said Jude.

"Then why are you here? Social call? Returning a book you borrowed?" Lavrov barked something in Russian at Dmitry, and the beating stopped. Now the only sound in the room was Viktor's whimpering. Elspeth could feel her heart hammering as Jude stared at the passport in his hand; what story would he be able to claw from its pages? She should get out of here now; there wasn't anything she could do to save him.

"We're trying to find the man behind that passport."

Elspeth smothered her shock. What the hell was Jude doing? Don't offer Lavrov anything! Lie! Act dumb! It's your only chance; the second he senses there's something to find out, he won't stop. She started inching back from the bannisters.

"We? Have you got an accomplice? Where is he?"

Elspeth froze as Lavrov spoke. Dmitry marched back to the French doors.

"No. It's just me."

"Then why did you say we?"

"I meant the Service, British Intelligence." Jude sighed. It was somewhere between a groan and a sob. "I came here alone."

Lavrov said something to Dmitry. He shook his head and continued his search outside the windows.

"Who is this man you're looking for?"

Elspeth's hands clenched into fists. Don't say it, don't say his name!

"Jasper Lewingdon."

A small smile flickered across Lavrov's face.

"Tell me about him. Why might Viktor know where he is?"

Elspeth shuffled back from her vantage point. She had to get Jude out of there or at least shut him up. He'd tried to cover his slip, but there was no way he'd hold up against Lavrov, and he was bound to tell him about her. Could she get far enough away before Jude inevitably gave her up to try and stave off the torture they had already served to Volkov?

There were several doors off the gallery. Elspeth stared at the doors. If she kept low, she shouldn't be seen by Dmitry or Lavrov, but it was anyone's guess as to where they led. No, it was too risky to go further into the house. She'd have to go back the way she'd come. Elspeth crawled back into the corridor at the top of the servant's staircase. Jude was talking again, but she couldn't make out his words. Lavrov laughed; hardly a good sign. No doubt some violence would be on its way to either Volkov or Jude.

Go now while you've got a chance; you can't help him. Elspeth grasped the handle of the door at the top of the stairs. Someone howled in pain; was it Volkov or Jude? It didn't matter. Elspeth opened the door. On the other side was a tidy bedroom. A bare mattress was propped on the single bed beside a dressing table. An oil lamp sat on a chest of drawers. Run or try and create a distraction? Another yell came from behind her. Elspeth picked up the lamp; it was half full. She pulled it apart and poured the kerosene over the mattress. Elspeth took a dog-eared book of matches from her coat pocket; there were just two matches in it. She tore a match out and struck it. As it flared into life, she threw it onto the oil-sodden mattress. The match's flame fluttered for a second, daring to die, but then it caught, a yellow frontier starting to consume the mattress. Elspeth headed down the staircase.

How long did she have before the flames took hold properly and Lavrov noticed? A minute? Two? Three?

When was the last time she'd tried to burn down a house? She looked in the room at the foot of the stairs. A few odd coats but no convenient can of petrol or oil lamp. She tried the next door; it was the kitchen. Elspeth grabbed a chair from the kitchen table. She carried it to the door leading to the main room, now doubling as Lavrov's temporary torture chamber, and wedged it under the door handle. That door wasn't going to open in a hurry. She headed back into the kitchen. On the table was a good-sized oil lamp with a full reservoir. Grabbing a couple of cloths and the lamp Elspeth went back to the barricaded door. She stuffed the rags against the door and doused them in kerosene.

Elspeth held her breath; this was her final match. It had to count. She struck the match and willed its flame to take. Then, crouching down, she held the match against the cloths. They immediately caught fire, the flame spreading onto the film of oil that had spread across the wooden floor. Now it was time to run.

Outside, a trace of smoke touched the back of her throat. No, that was just wishful thinking. She ran to the corner of the garage stifling the urge to swear as gravel tore at her stockinged feet. Pausing to pull her shoes back on, Elspeth glanced back at the villa. Smoke was starting to curl from the window of the bedroom she'd set fire to. She stopped in astonishment. It's a wooden house; what did you think was going to happen? She sprinted behind the garage, her heart thumping. This was a feeble hiding place, but Lavrov must know that something was happening, and there wasn't time to find anywhere better.

A sharp crack came from the house. Time froze as she waited. It had been a pistol shot. Jude or Volkov? Which one was next? Voices. Russian voices. It was Lavrov shouting at Dmitry. If only she had a weapon, anything. Footsteps crashed over gravel; they were heading this way.

If she ran now, could she make the treeline and escape? Lavrov was shouting again but was further away. Were they fanning out to cut off her escape? She reached down and picked up a stone. A pathetic hope, but she wouldn't give in without a fight. An engine rattled into life. A car door slammed, followed by the engine revving and a crunch of gears. Don't hope, not yet. Another car door slammed, and tyres scrabbled on gravel, getting ever more distant. Elspeth let the rock fall from her fingers.

Creeping around the side of the garage, Elspeth looked at the drive. Only Volkov's car was there. The burning bedroom was pushing a thick shaft of smoke into the sky. Someone was going to spot that before long and come and investigate. She had to get away before they did. But there had only been one gunshot. Elspeth ran for the back of the house. The French doors were open, a haze of smoke starting to creep past them.

Elspeth stopped at the doors. Inside, a shroud of smoke filled the top third of the room. The gallery was completely hidden. Already her eyes were starting to smart. Pulling her coat up around her mouth and nose, Elspeth dashed inside. A pulse of heat pressed down on her like a giant hand. She stooped lower but with no respite. Her eyes were streaming as she started to cough. Where was Jude? The crackle of flames was audible, even if she couldn't see them.

She stumbled forward into the table. Jude must be to her left. She could just make out Volkov's body still strapped to his chair, and just beyond was another figure. A pulse of heat pressed Elspeth to the ground. The smoke was thicker now and had almost reached the floor. She crawled to Jude's side. He was lying face down. Elspeth shoved him, but there was no response. The smoke scoured her lungs, and she started coughing, barely able to stop as she pulled Jude onto his back. He flopped over. The bullet hole in his forehead told her she was too late. He still had the passport in his hand. Elspeth took it.

A low rumble was followed by fizzing and cracking as dark orange flames flitted through the smoke hanging above her. Elspeth crawled as fast as she could towards the open doors, which now had a distant gauzy look. She screamed as something caught her leg. She kicked out at it, but it held on. It was Volkov; he was still alive! The rumble was getting louder and more urgent. Elspeth felt her way back to Volkov, trying to find the knots holding him to the chair. His grip failed. Should she just leave him? At last, her fingers found purchase, and the cords slipped free.

"Come on!" she yelled. "You have to help me!"

She heaved at Volkov's bulk, trying to drag him while crawling towards the doors. She could feel him half-dragging himself forward and half-pulling her backwards. A gout of flame erupted from the side of the room. That must have been the second fire she'd set. The French doors suddenly seemed so far away. Clarity started to force the panic away; she was going to die in the fire she'd started; well done, Elspeth! Then they were at the doors. She tumbled out into the almost fresh air dragging Volkov with her. She lay retching, the bulk of Volkov unmoving beside her. Thick flames were dancing like a seascape across the ceiling inside the room.

Elspeth staggered upright, grabbed Volkov by his shoulders and dragged him across the patio to the edge of the tennis court. She retched once more. Volkov groaned, then coughed. Elspeth wiped her mouth and looked at Volkov; he was watching her.

"Thank you," he said.

Flames burst through the shutters of the bedroom.

179

"We need to go before someone comes to find out what's happened," said Elspeth. "Can you walk?"

"Yes, I think so. It wasn't my legs they were hitting."

Volkov started to pull himself up against the tennis court wall. Elspeth grabbed his arm and helped him upright.

"We'll have to take your car," she said. Volkov nodded mutely as they shuffled forward. Volkov was wheezing like a clapped-out steam train, but he seemed to get stronger with each step. Even so, it seemed to be taking forever to reach the car. Above them, the flames were punching a plume of smoke into the sky. At the car, Volkov all but collapsed across the bonnet, a fit of coughing racking his body. Elspeth pulled the bags from the passenger's seat and tossed them onto the driveway.

"No!" said Volkov followed by another bout of hacking. "I need the small bag; the others we can leave."

Elspeth picked up the canvas travelling bag and shoved it into the passenger's footwell before helping Volkov get into the car. Once in, he seemed to almost collapse in on himself. Perhaps he wasn't going to last much longer. She pressed the starter. The engine kicked into life, the exhaust rasping in response to the throttle. Volkov barely reacted. She shoved the car into gear. Gravel spattered behind them as she let out the clutch and gunned the engine.

Where were they heading for? No, that wasn't the question for now. How far could they put between themselves and this house before someone came up the track from the village to find out what was on fire? That was the critical question. The Hispano-Suiza skittered as its tyres bit into the surface of the track. The car swept down the track, its suspension protesting at the occasional pothole or hump, but it couldn't be helped. Jude's Austin was still where they had left it, ready to be found and linked to a corpse in a burnt-out building. All the more reason to get as far away as possible.

Only about a hundred yards of the track left, and they'd be on the coast road. A couple of men were marching up the trail towards them. The oldest of the pair stopped in the middle of the track waving his arms; it looked like he recognised the car. Elspeth sounded the horn, but still, he stayed where he was. Fifty yards. Elspeth hit the horn, dropped a gear and pressed the accelerator down. The engine howled as the car leapt forward. The man on the track jumped to one side. Elspeth hauled at the steering wheel as they burst out onto the coastal road. The car's tyres screeched as the car's back end fish-tailed on the tarmac. Elspeth fought the steering but kept her foot pressed flat on the accelerator. More haste, less speed? Rubbish; give it all you've got. Someone knows that car and is heading for a murder scene. Whose description will the police get hold of in the next few hours?

They sped through the village. A few faces must have followed their flight. There can't have been that many bright-red Hispano-Suizas around here. But, at least they were now heading away. Elspeth glanced at Volkov. He was still slumped down in his seat, but his head was up, and his gaze fixed on the road ahead.

"I thought my last moments were going to be in that house. I was wrong. It's going to be in this bloody car!"

He started to laugh, but it quickly turned into another coughing fit. The tyres chirped as Elspeth coaxed the car through the next series of bends.

"If you don't like my driving, I can let you out."

Volkov's chuckle rumbled.

"No, no. You keep going. Where are we heading?"

"I haven't worked that out yet. If you have any suggestions, don't hold back."

Elspeth slewed the car through a couple of bends, barely lifting off before pressing on harder down the next straight.

"The two men on the track, do you know them?" she asked.

"Yes," said Volkov. "They help to look after the house. They'll have been going to find out what was happening and to deal with the fire."

"We'll have to get rid of this car; they'll know it's yours and must have recognised you." And have a description of me; the unspoken words felt heavy.

"Don't worry, I know where we can go." Volkov looked at her. "I'm sorry about your partner. Jude was a good man. This is a shitty business we're in, and not everybody gets out of it alive."

How true, thought Elspeth.

15.   Guilt

Jasper scrawled his signature and slid the paper across the desk to the clerk opposite him. It had been a while since he'd signed himself as Jasper Lewingdon. The letters felt awkward and strange to his hand; he'd spent too long inhabiting Max Bolton. How hard would it be to become Jasper once more? Had he ever stopped? He'd worked hard at being Max Bolton and tried to forget that Jasper had existed; he'd always been Max. Who else could he be? It was a lie he'd been telling himself for far too long.

The clerk was taking his time comparing the signature with the one Jasper had given when he'd first washed up in Istanbul. The clerk peered at him, his eyes narrowing as if trying to detect deceit. Jasper let an apologetic smile skip across his face before pulling out his passport and pushing it across the desk. The clerk picked it up but kept his gaze fixed on Jasper. Was the man just naturally cautious, or did he suspect something? What was there to question? He was Jasper Lewingdon, after all. The clerk stood up. The scrape of the chair on the floor put Jasper's teeth on edge.

"Where are you going?" asked Jasper

"I need to check something," said the clerk.

The clerk left, pulling the cubicle's curtain back in place and leaving Jasper alone.

Stay calm, don't lose it now; that would confirm everything he must be thinking right now. How do you look relaxed when you feel anything but relaxed? Try affronted? No, just sit tight. The signature was a bit rough, but the passport should have been the clincher. Had he seen that clerk before? He was pretty young. Maybe he'd seen him in one of the clubs on the Grande Rue or, more likely, one of the bars in the alleys leading off it. So what? He's seen your face before and doesn't think it tallies with the one in that passport. Perhaps you have worked too hard at being Max Bolton.

Voices seeped past the curtain that closed off the cubicle from prying eyes in the outer office. Jasper's ear dialled into them. One was the young clerk. From its timbre, he was stating his case; the barrister for this prosecution? Would the defence get a say? An older, deeper voice replied, its tone short and clipped. The presiding judge? All went quiet. No doubt the judge was examining the evidence. Worry was starting to work its way from the place where he'd tried to pin it. Had he seen that clerk before? A wild night at La Mouette, too much to drink, a stint on stage with the band. Was the clerk's face one from the crowd laughing as he took his bow?

The judge's voice cut through his musings. The summing up was terse. The prosecutor's reply was equally short as he was galvanised into action. Fast footsteps headed past the curtained cubicle. Jasper bit down the urge to swear. If he'd made some effort to learn Turkish instead of exploring the delights that backstreet Beyoğlu had to offer, he might have understood what had just happened. Was the clerk off to get his safe deposit box, or had he been sent to summon the nearest policeman? Jasper got up. If the coast was clear, he could make a dash for it. He reached for the curtain, but it flew back before his fingers could touch it. Jasper gasped, but his cry was swamped by the manager's screech. Jasper took a pace back into the cubicle.

"I'm so sorry, sir," said the manager steadying himself against the cubicle wall but blocking its exit. "I wasn't expecting…"

He breathed in heavily, a slight flush appearing around

his cheeks. Was he about to have a heart attack? He was a little flabby in the way Turkish wrestlers can be and was just as big. He still had one hand against the cubicle wall; it wouldn't be easy to barge past.

"Is there a problem?" asked Jasper.

"Problem? No, no problem." The manager pulled a handkerchief from his breast pocket and dabbed at his brow.

"Your assistant seemed concerned about something."

The manager shoved a smile onto his face.

"No, no. He's young." He laughed or at least tried to. "He finds secrets and mysteries around him all the time; I think he makes up these distractions to fill his head instead of getting on with his job. You know how these young lads are."

Jasper winced a smile in response. No, he didn't know what bored office clerks were like, but the manager was putting on a pretty convincing impression of someone stalling for time.

"Can I offer you a coffee while we wait? Or perhaps tea?" The manager's smile was starting to look brittle.

"No, thank you." Jasper checked his watch. "Look, I've other business to attend to. I'll come back tomorrow."

Jasper took half a step forward. The manager stepped back but not out of the way.

"I'm sure that Selim will be back soon." The manager dabbed his handkerchief across his forehead. "There is no need to leave."

Jasper could feel his jaw starting to clench. The twitch

in the manager's eye said he could see it too. If ever there was a need to leave, it was now. Kerim's pistol was in his pocket; that was one way to insist that he was leaving. A clatter from outside the cubicle snatched the manager's attention. Jasper's right hand slipped around the butt of Kerim's pistol. The manager snapped out a string of Turkish; the only word Jasper recognised was 'Selim'.The Turkish tirade continued as Selim came into view carrying a grey metal box. The manager looked at Jasper.

"I'm sorry, sir." He shook his head as he took the box from Selim and handed it to Jasper. "This boy will be the death of me."

Jasper's fingers uncurled from the pistol. He slid a smile on as he took the box from the manager.

"That's quite alright."

The cubicle's curtain swished shut as he put the box on the table. Would he have used Kerim's pistol? Curious, in his mind, it was still Kerim's pistol. Maybe if Kerim's pistol did the killing, it would make murder acceptable. Jasper listened. The manager was still berating Selim. No, murder was murder. No matter how you dressed it up and justified it to yourself. He put the key in the lock of the box. Just get what you came for and get out of here. Jasper turned the key and opened the box.

The lid clunked on the table's top. Jasper grabbed the bundles of dollars from the box. A dull clatter sounded as a gold wedding ring dropped back into the box. He swallowed. It was Ruby's. Why hadn't he given it back to her?

* * *

Albania, September 1928

Jasper walked up the track to the church. It was nearly two years since he had been here. Against the backdrop of the Albanian Alps, the building still looked little more than a part-plastered barn, grey shingles covering its roof. About the only thing that singled the building out as a church was the rough stone tower on one side holding a pair of bells to summon the faithful. The other was the black-robed priest standing in front of it.

Was it the same man? Jasper squinted. It looked like him, but he'd been too busy fleeing to study him in detail. Each step as Jasper drew closer seemed heavier; the path was steep but not that steep. The priest smiled as he got closer. He spoke. Albanian? Some northern Gheg dialect? It didn't matter; he couldn't understand either.

"I'm sorry, I don't understand," said Jasper. His Greek was weak at the best of times; he'd just have to hope it was enough. The priest frowned. Jasper repeated what he said, only slower. The priest nodded slowly in time with the rise and fall of his speech, and then a smile broke onto his face.

"You are Italian?"

Jasper shook his head.

"No, I'm English."

"Ah," the priest nodded, "you are a traveller? Seeing the sights?" He pointed towards the mountains.

"I'm looking…" What were the words he could use? "I'm looking for someone." The priest was concentrating hard. "I'm looking for a woman. Small, black hair to here." He motioned to indicate the length of Ruby's hair. The

187

priest was still frowning, shaking his head slowly. Was it that he didn't understand or something else? Jasper pointed up the slope to the track into the mountain pass.

"Two years ago," said Jasper holding up two fingers. "Men. Shooting." He mimed firing a rifle, making the sound of shots. The priest looked bemused. "English woman, up there!" He pointed towards the mountain pass. The priest followed the direction he was pointing. It didn't look like there was going to be a lightbulb moment. Why the hell hadn't he found a translator to come with him? Because this is private, and it hurts enough without telling everyone what you did. He'd come here and failed her just as he had two years ago. "The English girl, where is she?"

The priest looked at him.

"The English girl?"

Jasper nodded.

The priest pointed past the church to where a small orchard clung to the side of the slope.

"She's over there."

"Thank you."

Jasper shook the priest's hand and headed off towards the orchard. The ground was stony. Patches of grass hung on in places where the goats hadn't got to them yet. A low stone wall hemmed in the stunted trees, and a small mound of partly-grassed soil with a half-collapsed cross was next to it. As he reached the grave, Jasper took his hat off. He straightened the cross. It wasn't much of a memorial, but at least there was one. He knelt down at the graveside. What now? Say a prayer? Would anyone listen if he did? He took Ruby's wedding ring from his pocket and pressed it into the soil of the grave.

"I said I'd come back for you," said Jasper.

A shadow fell across him. He turned, shielding his eyes against the sun.

"I knew you would."

Jasper stared. A punch from a prize fighter couldn't have stunned him more. She was here. How could she be?

"But… you're…" The words could barely force themselves past his lips.

"Alive?" said Ruby, a half-smile flickered on her face. "Well, mostly alive." She looked pale, or at least paler than his memory of her. "Are you going to carry on grubbing with that grave, or shall we go somewhere I can sit down?"

Ruby turned and headed towards the church. Jasper stared for several seconds and then stood up. She was limping; it was slight but noticeable. Her face seemed thinner. She wasn't gaunt, but she'd never had that much weight she could lose it. It was hard to tell as her long grey coat swamped her figure. Jasper looked at the grave. Whose was it? It didn't matter; they couldn't hang on to Ruby's wedding ring. He pulled it from the soil and jogged after Ruby

His eyes took a couple of seconds to adjust to the light inside the church. The small, high windows did their best, but most of the light came from the open door. Ruby was lighting a candle. Jasper waited as she crossed herself.

"Who was the candle for?" he asked.

Ruby shrugged.

"I don't really know. It feels like the right thing to do in here." She let her gaze wander around the interior, pausing on the carving of Christ on the cross. "Maybe it's

189

just a thank you."

She limped down the aisle towards Jasper, wincing with every other pace. Jasper took a step forward.

"No. I'm alright." Ruby sagged into the pew next to her. She shoved a smile onto her face. "See, nothing that a short rest won't put right."

Jasper felt frozen. He could barely speak.

"What happened?"

"Oh, just the wound in my leg. It hurts when I walk too much. The quacks insist I keep using it to build up the strength—"

"Stop!" The word forced itself out, bright and bitter. "Just stop. You know what I meant."

Ruby looked at him, her lips pursed, the seconds ticking away as she studied him.

"Yes, I know what you meant. You meant, why aren't you dead? How did you survive? How long must I carry this guilt? I can probably answer the first two. The third? You'll have to find the answer to that."

"But I ran. I left you."

"I ordered you to. There's no blame, and there never was."

"If I'd stayed—"

"There would have been twice as many targets for them to shoot at. We had one crappy pistol between us, and let's face it, I'm better at shooting people than you are."

The casual dismissal of two years of blame and self-loathing didn't smother those feelings. He could feel his jaw tighten as the anger stewed. Why the hell was he cross with her? What the hell had she done for him to fling his anger at her? Perhaps because she was no longer the martyred saint he'd used to justify everything he'd done. That didn't change the fact that she'd still been shot, and he'd run.

"What happened? How did you survive?" He needed a distraction, a tall tale to drag him from his corrosive conscience. Would she supply it?

Ruby shrugged.

"I did my best to hold them up; hit one, maybe two. Then I ran out of bullets. Tried to hobble away but got shot twice more. After that, I don't remember much."

"Then how did you? I heard far more than two shots before..." before I escaped and left you behind.

"It was Gezim, the priest here. He heard the shooting and sent some men to investigate. Turns out they had a feud with the men of the village that were after you. What you heard was them settling it or at least moving it on to its next round. That grave you were whispering sweet nothings to is where they buried Bihar."

Bihar: a half-forgotten face who'd wanted him dead and was now a corpse. Did that change anything? Not really.

"And the priest nursed you back to health?"

"Not exactly. He gave me the last rites. Then, two days later, he was nagged into summoning a doctor when I was inconveniently still alive. That reminds me, I hope you've brought some cash as there are a few bills to pay, not least for the truck you stole making your escape."

Ruby was wearing her painted doll face radiating innocence. She could have just asked him to pay a taxi fare or collect some dry cleaning. Two years and near-death hadn't dimmed her self-assurance.

"You never doubted I'd come back here, did you?"

"I was counting on it."

"Doctor's bills?"

"Not exactly."

Jasper could feel a fist-sized lump forming in his chest.

"By not exactly, you mean not at all?"

"Where were you on your way to? Where has K banished you to?"

The lump now had the consistency of coal; there was an inevitability in the course of this conversation, and he'd have no control over it.

"Why do you think I was on my way to…"

Jasper sighed. What was the point of fencing with her when you always lost?

"Istanbul. K told me to disappear there. Somewhere far enough that I wasn't likely to bump into anyone I knew or might be looking for me." He shrugged. "Jasper Lewingdon is now a corpse fished out of the Thames."

Ruby smirked, then nodded.

"Istanbul. That could work."

"What could work? What have you been up to?"

"I guess I could give you the sob story of the woman all alone, with no money, desperate to make ends meet…"

Ruby sighed. She was studying his face. "No, I wouldn't buy that one either, although the alone and no money bit was true."

Jasper tried to keep his face flat, but the stab of shame was too sharp. The fleeting frown on Ruby's face said she'd spotted it.

"I'm sorry," said Ruby. "That wasn't a dig at you. You've nothing to blame yourself for." If only that were true. "I couldn't hang around here forever surviving on charity. Besides, I was in danger of a couple of the locals seeing me as the next Mrs Hoxha or some such nonsense."

Jasper pressed a grin onto his face. It covered the almost immediate reply that she was already married. Married to a leading communist spy that she thought had betrayed her and their entire network in Trieste. Reminding her of that would hardly have been bright.

"I'm sure you would have looked fetching in a milkmaid's costume. Perhaps I should start calling you Heidi." Ruby's eyes narrowed. "So what did you do?"

"I made contact with the Centre."

The grin slid from his face.

"The OGPU Centre! The Russian secret service? After all you've done! You know they have people out there ready to put a bullet in the back of your head. Are you mad?"

"No. I was bored."

"Bored! You were bored—"

Ruby held up her hand, cutting him off.

"I spent the best part of a year laying on my back,

barely able to walk. There's only so much time you can spend gossiping in pidgin Albanian with the priest's housekeeper." Her scowl softened. "I didn't just send a letter to the head of the OGPU saying remember me? I searched out some old contacts from my days in Trieste. Tested the ground and did my best to find out what politics hold sway amongst my old employers before making a move."

Jasper could feel the muscles of his jaw tightening. How could she be so rash? This wasn't like Ruby. Where was the caution, the forensic attention to planning and detail? A smile was starting to slink onto her face.

"Are you reading my mind?" he asked.

"No, just your face." The smile drifted away. "I didn't rush into anything. Remember, time has been on my side, and I took it. Besides, what about you?"

"What do you mean?"

"Your little vendetta spree in London? Striking a deal with my husband in Berlin? No wonder K has had to banish you to Istanbul."

Jasper swallowed. Ruby's face was opaque. He knew his had guilt written all over it.

"I...I thought you were dead. No one would listen, and no one would do anything. I couldn't just walk away from it."

The corners of Ruby's mouth twitched.

"That Galahad streak will get you killed one day, but thank you for trying to avenge my almost death."

The twitch had turned into a grin, wiping away whatever was left of the stew of anger he'd been feeling. A thought dripped into his head.

"Hang on, how do you know what I've been up to in London? How did you know about my deal with Marek? Oh…" The realisation sank in. "You've got in contact with him, haven't you?"

"Yes. Well, my darling ex-husband got in contact with me."

If she was in contact with Valentin Marek, how much had he told her?

"Ex-husband?"

"Ex in the eyes of the Communist Party and the OGPU. They still think I'm dead." She shrugged. "But not in the eyes of God and the Catholic church."

Sarcasm or a rare display of emotion? Her face was impenetrable.

"It must have been…" He was tiptoeing his way through this. How the hell to say this? Ruby was staring at him. A smirk was starting to pucker the corner of her mouth once more.

"Awkward? I think that might be the word you're looking for."

Yes, awkward was a suitable understatement. Awkward meeting a man when you'd spent the last two years with the certainty that he'd betrayed you and your comrades, leaving you all to be tortured and murdered. But he hadn't.

"You know he didn't betray the Trieste network, don't you?"

Ruby nodded.

"It was a casualty of internal OGPU politics. Jealousy

at Marek's success, our success. It had to be snuffed out, and his reputation killed with it."

"It didn't work."

"Not entirely. When you saw Marek in Berlin, his star was riding high. He'd turned the rumours of what happened to the Trieste network to his advantage. If a man was ruthless enough to snuff out his own network, what wouldn't he do in the service of the revolution? The Centre likes that sort of dedication."

"But?"

Ruby glanced away. The lump in his chest hardened. Her gaze flicked back to him. So this was the pitch; would it be the big lie wrapped around a slice of truth, or would she just lay out the situation and expect him to follow?

"Marek's star is falling. Stalin's paranoia shapes the politics of the OGPU, and the heady days of the international revolution are far in the past. Backstab and blame are the weapons of choice, and Marek knows it will only get worse. It's Trieste all over again but on a much grander scale."

"Is he looking for a way out?"

"No. Marek will never defect. He's a true believer and will die for the cause even if it's the cause that will kill him."

"So, what does he want?"

"He doesn't want another Trieste with him sitting on the sidelines watching his agents being butchered, only this time with OGPU officers doing the shooting. He wants to give his people the option to disappear when they're summoned to Moscow to discuss their futures."

"How does he intend to do that?"

Ruby leant forward, a smile inching onto her face.

"For all sorts of reasons, plenty of people are looking to start a new life. For that, they need a new identity. Not just a hard core of suspicious spooks running to save their necks, but many more whose faces and politics aren't sympathetic to their Soviet supervisors." Her smile inched up in intensity. "Marek wants us to set up a travel agency."

"Us? When did I become part of this scheme?"

"Marek was impressed with you."

"But a travel agency, are you serious? And what are we doing next? Offering a week's B&B in Clacton on Sea complete with a cast iron cover story?"

Ruby's lips tightened.

"I didn't mean a literal travel agency. More of a service to help those in need. Sort out papers and passports suited to destinations where they can have a chance to start again, disappear or whatever it is they want to do." She tilted her head, her face softening. "But we are doing something?"

"What? No."

A sigh escaped from Ruby's lips.

"In Albania, you said that when it was all over, you would be finished with this filthy life. Yet, here we are two years later, and you're still up to your elbows in it. So here's a chance to use your talents to help people, maybe even to slip away yourself."

"And help Marek get his agents fresh identities. I'd be working for the OGPU in all but name."

"K has cast you adrift. You've worked for Marek

before."

"But last time, he was giving me something I needed."

"This time, he's giving you a chance to appease your conscience."

Ruby's blue-eyed gaze held him. A small crease of concern furrowed her brow. Jasper burst out laughing.

"How the hell are you keeping a straight face with those lines?"

Ruby grinned back.

"Too much? I should have spun out the guilt angle a bit longer; it always used to work on you."

Jasper slouched back in the pew.

"So we're going to set up in Istanbul and source new identities for Marek's agents?"

"Actually, anyone that will pay us."

"Why anyone?"

"It puts distance between Marek and us. We set up as a pair of chancers fabricating legends for the desperate and dangerous fleeing the workers' paradise. Anyone using us gets a further layer of plausibility to their tale should anyone start to look at them too carefully."

"What's wrong with an identity manufactured in Moscow by the OGPU?"

"Nothing, apart from the fact the OGPU know exactly who is using it, and it's the OGPU they want to hide from."

Jasper let his gaze drift to a flaw in the stone slab beneath his feet. A breeze caused the door to creak; he glanced at it before looking at Ruby once more.

"I can't say I'm thrilled at the thought of helping OGPU agents."

"Most of those we help will be genuine refugees just looking for an escape route."

"Refugees with money."

Ruby briefly pursed her lips.

"Do I detect disapproval in your tone?" Jasper could feel his jaw tighten. She carried on before he could reply. "We'll need to make a living, and sadly it'll have to be on the backs of those that can afford to buy a new life."

"Isn't Marek bankrolling this little venture?"

Ruby shook her head.

"Would you take his money if he was offering it? Of course you wouldn't." Ruby stared at him. He knew he was frowning. He wanted to look away, but that would make him look like a sulky child. Pride, guilt, just emotions, but hard to reason with. "Marek knows he's watched; everyone in the OGPU is these days: those above you, those below. All of them looking for something to use when it's their head on the chopping block. That's why we need to distance ourselves from Marek; it keeps him safe, and it'll keep us alive."

Jasper pushed a smile onto his face; it took some effort.

"In Berlin, Marek said you weren't that easy to kill."

Ruby laughed.

"He's right! I'm not!"

Jasper forced a chuckle past his lips. Stillness settled

on Ruby's face.

"So, are we going to do this?" she asked.

K had told him to disappear in Istanbul, not set up an escape route for agents of the very person he'd been working against. But K thought Ruby was dead; didn't that change everything? Of course it didn't, but when hadn't he just clung on and tried to keep up with whatever scheme Ruby hatched? He nodded.

"Good. Are you still travelling on that passport we used for Albania?"

"Yes. Once more, I'm Max Bolton."

Ruby stood up.

"That's handy. I can travel as your wife on your passport. Mrs Edith Bolton at your service." She bobbed a small curtsy. "I don't suppose you managed to hold onto my wedding ring after all this time?"

"No, sorry." The lie leapt out before he could bite it back. He shrugged an apologetic half-smile onto his face. "I left London in a bit of a hurry. Actually, K made me leave in a hurry."

Ruby shrugged.

"Never mind, can't be helped."

* * *

The gold wedding band stared up at Jasper. He reached to pick it up and stopped. It had been a mean little act, and even now, he struggled to understand it. Why had he lied and held onto her ring? Petulance at being so easily manipulated? No, she'd always done that, and it had kept them alive. Jealous that Marek was back in her life? That was even more absurd. Marek had never left, and there'd never been anything like that between them. Maybe at some level, he'd just wanted to hold onto something. There wasn't any point in trying to understand it; she was dead, and it was too late to return the ring.

Jasper closed the lid of the box. Now he had to try and make a deal with a devil.

16.   Obligations

The narrow street magnified the sound of the car's
exhaust, the tall houses forming a canyon as Elspeth
threaded it up the hill. Boxed-in balconies jutted over the
road, almost cutting off a view of the sky. No faces
appeared at windows or on the balconies to examine this
intruder. The tight, prim frontages presented privacy; this
wasn't the kind of neighbourhood where you aired your
laundry over the street. Elspeth's hands gripped the steering
wheel tighter. Just because you didn't see the net curtain
twitch didn't mean that you weren't being watched.

"Turn left here," croaked Volkov.

A gap-toothed break in the genteel façade marked the
turning. It was almost too tight a turn for the Hispano-
Suiza, but Elspeth coaxed the car into the alley. Volkov
chuckled, although it was hard to discern between each
stifled cough and laboured wheeze.

"It takes practice to get the car round there. Thank you
for not scraping it on the corner."

Elspeth pressed her lips into a thin smile. The man was
half-dead, but still, he worried about his car, or perhaps it
was her driving; probably both. The alley ended in an open-
ended shed built against the side of the left-hand building;
this must be the journey's end. Elspeth pressed the clutch
down and let the car roll into the shed. The brakes squealed
softly as she brought the car to a halt and switched the
ignition off. The Hisapno-Suiza's engine shuddered to a
stop. Elspeth breathed out. The only sounds were the
tinkling of its exhaust pipes cooling and the wheeze of
Volkov's breathing. Judging from the oil cans and tools
hung on the end wall, this lean-to shed was meant to be a
garage. Elspeth flipped the lights off, and the details

disappeared into the shadows. Volkov dragged himself out of the car, wincing and cursing with every movement.

"You'll have to help me get this covered."

He groaned as he bent down to the rolled-up tarpaulin in front of the car. Elspeth got out and grabbed hold of it. Volkov leant against the car, his breathing ragged. Finally, after several deep breaths that sounded like he was going to expire, he nodded. The tarpaulin was awkward but not especially heavy. Judging by Volkov's difficulty dragging it over the car, he must be in a worse state than she thought.

"We'd better get you inside," said Elspeth.

"Wait, I need my bag."

Volkov sagged and then stared at Elspeth. She pulled the tarpaulin aside and grabbed his bag.

"I think you had better lean on me. Where are we going?"

Volkov gestured to the gate in the alley just outside the lean-to. Elspeth shouldered his bag, then put an arm around him. Volkov stumbled against her as he straightened himself up; his weight nearly flattened her against the garage wall.

"I hope we haven't got far to go."

"I'm sorry," he rumbled. "My apartment is on the third floor."

They half-hobbled their way to the gate, and Elspeth pushed it open. The entrance led to a small courtyard and garden sloping downhill towards the Golden Horn in the distance. The graceful garden looked well-tended, with fruit trees and neat bushes. The building's four floors looked out over the same admirable view, but most windows were shuttered tight.

"Who lives here?" asked Elspeth.

"Hardly anyone. It's somewhere you bring someone, and your wife pretends they don't exist. It's why I bought it."

"You're married?"

"No, but the other tenants are. They don't ask questions, and that's good enough for me." Volkov pulled a key from his pocket and unlocked the door to the building. He seemed to be taking his weight better, his breathing less laboured. "This way."

The walls of the passage leading to a staircase were panelled in light oak; the place smelt faintly of fresh polish. If this was the backstairs of the building, goodness knows what the front entrance was like. Volkov looked like he was doing alright for himself. He stopped halfway up, holding tightly to the bannister rail. Yes, he was doing alright if you ignored being recently tortured and left to burn to death. Another rattle of keys, and he led the way into his apartment. Despite the spring sunshine, the place was cold, the deep empty cold a building gets when it's been ignored for a while. Elspeth followed Volkov into the lounge.

"I'd better get the fire going."

There was already a fire laid in the grate of the fireplace. Volkov hissed as he bent down to apply a match to the paper and kindling. The flame caught in an instant, the fire crackling into life. Volkov stared at the flames for several moments before straightening up. His cough sounded like a Colt 45 going off. He clung to the side of the fireplace, almost retching as he fought to clear his lungs. Finally, he spat into the fire. The phlegm sizzled briefly and then was gone. He crumpled back against the wall, his eyes shut, and his breath laboured. Was he about to collapse?

"Are you alright?" asked Elspeth.

Volkov's eyes crawled open, and a smile crept onto his soot-smeared face.

"As well as can be expected for someone that has been beaten and burnt." He tried to chuckle; it quickly turned into another bout of coughing. Elspeth walked over to the apartment's window and looked outside. The view across the Golden Horn was exquisite. Any other time this would be a lovely place to be. Volkov's coughing subsided. Elspeth snapped the slats of the blinds shut.

"Are we safe here? How long before Lavrov comes looking for you?" she asked.

Volkov shrugged.

"With luck, he thinks I died in that fire."

"Except there's only one body in that building, and it has a bullet in its head."

Volkov combed his fingers through his beard, his gaze glued to the floor.

"A few days, a week at the most. However long it takes for the news to leak from the police." He straightened up, his face grave. "The police will come looking for me long before Lavrov does." He glared at the floor once more. "A dead British diplomat in a burnt-out house that I was renting will make them put down their coffee cups and hookah pipes." Viktor's stare swung back to Elspeth. "What about you? You were seen driving us away."

Us? Had circumstance tied her to this man? So far, she had only thought about getting away; what was she going to do when, or perhaps if, she got away?

"Go to a station and get on the first train heading to the border, any border."

"Where the guards will be checking papers carefully." He stared at her, his face still grim. "You are someone that will attract attention. Why not go to the consulate and report what happened to Jude? Tell them who killed him."

Was that an option? She could try and get a message through to K, but Jude was meant to be her contact here. Did the British Consul in Istanbul know what Jude was? Would he even want to be reminded if he did? She shook her head.

"I think I might be better off trying my chances with the trains. The sooner I leave, the better my chances will be."

"Jude's car was left behind. The police are probably at the house wondering what it is doing out there by a burning building. Can you move before they start looking for the man and woman seen fleeing from that place in my car?"

She couldn't fault his logic. Maybe he was right; she should go and find sanctuary at the consulate. What would be her cover story? She could hardly go there and blurt out that she was an agent for MI5 sent out to track down a man whose death the head of the Security Service had gone to a lot of effort to fake. Oh, and it looks like my fiancé is in cahoots with the man that murdered one of your diplomats. Do I have any proof? Not exactly; I had to burn down the house where he was murdered. No, that conversation was best left for when she got back to London; at any other time, it would result in her ending up in a Turkish prison. The only sounds in the room were the crackle from the fire and the wheeze of Volkov's breathing. Elspeth realised that

Volkov was staring at her.

"Thank you for saving my life," he said. Elspeth looked away. "I know you were trying to save Jude and not me, but thank you anyway."

"What happened? Why did they shoot him?" and not you? She didn't look at Volkov; she knew her face would betray the unspoken words.

"It was Lavrov's ape, Dmitry. I think he panicked when he realised the house was on fire. They didn't bother to waste any time killing me as I wasn't going anywhere. More fun to let me burn to death."

Elspeth looked at Volkov. An accidental execution caused by her actions. Would Jude still be alive if she hadn't started the fire? Volkov spoke.

"Don't blame yourself. If you hadn't started that fire as a distraction, they would have killed both of us anyway." Elspeth winced a smile at him; it masked the guilt. She'd only started that fire to cover her escape; rescuing Volkov had been an accident. "Why were you and Jude at my house?"

Alarm pirouetted through her mind. But she was too weary to respond, too tired to come up with a decent story. So the truth would have to do.

"The same as Lavrov." Surprise flitted across Volkov's face. He sighed, limped over to an armchair and slumped into it. "We were looking for someone and thought you might be able to help."

"Anna Kravchenko?"

"No. The couple you were using to get her a passport."

Volkov practically growled. His swift scowl sent

butterflies coursing through Elspeth's stomach; the half-closed eye crusted with blood just added to his menace.

"Her or him?" The distaste was plain to see on Volkov's face when he said 'him'; it looked like Jasper had made an impression.

"Him."

"That bastard murdered his partner and took my money!"

Elspeth stared at Volkov. His glare was impressive, even with a half-shut eye. The butterflies were refusing to settle, but she mustn't look away. The fire popped. Volkov harrumphed, pulled himself from his chair and went over to tend the fire.

"Why do you think he killed his partner?" Elspeth said the words to Volkov's back as he continued to fiddle with a fire that didn't need it. He grunted and stabbed the fire a couple more times before straightening up.

"He was seen running from the house where her body was found. Who else could have done it?"

"How about whoever it was he was running from?"

"The guilty don't run!"

"We've just run."

Volkov turned and looked at her; his glare faded.

"I know this man," said Elspeth. "If there's one person in this world he would never have laid a finger on, it was Ruby."

"So what about my money? He ran off with that."

This time the bluster didn't seem so emphatic. Elspeth

felt in her pocket and pulled out Anna Kravchenko's passport. She opened it, flicking through the pages. Several stamps combined with the occasional dog ear and stain told the story of a well-travelled woman; it didn't feel fake.

"I think your money went on this." She glanced at Volkov. The fight seemed to have seeped from him. Now he looked like what he was: a battered man in his fifties who had watched his world crumble. "Why use Ruby and Max to get hold of a new passport?"

Volkov sank back into his chair.

"They were the best."

The passport in her hand backed up Volkov's words, but she wouldn't have expected anything less from Ruby.

"How long have you known them?"

Volkov shrugged; his face was once more fixed on the floor.

"A few months, six at the most?"

"But you must have been in Istanbul, what? Five, six years?"

"Almost nine. I arrived with Wrangel's fleet in 1920. I've been here ever since."

"In nine years, there must have been others you could go to get passports, papers and fake identities?"

"To start with, yes. But now the bigger fish have snapped up all the small fry. The bigger fish pay their dues to the Emniyet, the OGPU, and anyone else that wants to know who is getting a new identity and where they might be heading."

"And Ruby could be trusted to be discreet? You trusted

her?"

"Yes. As much as you can trust anyone in this business."

Thank God Volkov didn't know about Ruby's past; probably best to lead him away from that. But Ruby had invariably charted her own path; maybe she had been trustworthy or at least more than anyone else from the underside of Istanbul.

"How did you meet her?"

A half-smile puckered the corner of Volkov's face.

"I heard some gossip. A former countess flaunting her new papers, soon to be heading for a new life in Paris. I…borrowed her new passport to see how good it was. I couldn't fault it, so I started asking around without any luck. One morning I come back here and find Ruby sitting in this chair as if she owns this place."

"And what about Max?"

"Yes, he was there too." He grunted. "Probably meant to frighten me."

The wrinkle of distaste ushered the half-smile away. Elspeth forced herself not to react. Of course Jasper would be there; he was Ruby's Burglar Bill, never the muscle. If Ruby wanted someone scared, she could do that herself, but that was rarely how she worked.

"No, you don't strike me as someone that frightens easily. So why didn't you throw them out?"

The half-smile was back.

"I was curious, and Ruby was pointing a pistol at my head. She looked like someone that didn't mind shooting people when she had to."

"What did she want?"

Yes, it would be what Ruby wanted, no one else.

"She set out her stall. Made it clear what she could do and how much it would cost. A business proposition."

"All carried out at gunpoint, no doubt."

"No, no. The pop guns went away quite quickly. She even sent Max off to fetch the vodka and glasses." Elspeth could feel her jaw tighten. Volkov's eyes creased in amusement. "You didn't like Ruby, did you?"

Bugger! She shouldn't have let her bitterness towards Ruby show. Too late now.

"But you did?" If in doubt, throw a question back to cover your own discomfort.

"Yes. She was a professional."

"If Ruby had been operating in Istanbul for six months, how come the bigger fish, as you put it, hadn't put her out of business?" Perhaps that's what happened to her, the reason Jasper was on the run now.

"I don't know. Maybe she wasn't big enough for them to care?" Volkov shrugged. "You only went to Ruby if you had the money to pay for top quality."

"Like you did for Anna Kravchenko?"

A frown flickered across Volkov's face.

"Yes." His response was half-lost in his beard.

"Why did Anna need..." Elspeth flicked through the passport again, stopping to stare at the picture in it. "Why

211

does she need to be a French citizen?"

The frown grew deeper, Volkov's silence almost a shout. Stand your ground, he owes you, and he knows it.

"I heard what Lavrov said about her," said Elspeth. "Who she's working for."

Volkov sighed; a final capitulation?

"If you're a foreigner in France, you can be booted out any time. If they decide they don't like your face, you go. If they don't like your politics, you go. So much for liberté, égalité and fraternité; that only comes with a French passport."

Elspeth looked at the picture staring back from the passport.

"She's rather pretty. Why wouldn't they like her face?"

The growl from Volkov barely registered. Elspeth kept her face glued to Anna's picture in the passport; it was the only way to keep the smirk off hers.

"It's her politics they won't like. I wanted Anna to work for Kutepov at the Russian All-Military Union. That's all that's left these days of Wrangel's army, our army, but we can still fight those Bolshevik bastards! So many in the French government cosy up to the Bolsheviks, make deals and do as their communist lords and masters tell them. Or take their roubles and look the other way. The Bolsheviks would love to get Kutepov kicked out of France, and if they can't do that, they'll kill him."

"And Anna is—"

"An assassin."

Elspeth looked at Volkov. Was that defiance on his

face? No, it was pride.

"But Lavrov said he'd trained her. Isn't she working for him?"

"Pah! Of course he would say that. He was playing with me, like the cat with a mouse before it kills it. Anna hates the Bolsheviks as much as I do."

But Lavrov's taunt had felt a lot more than that.

"How can you be so sure?"

"She has proved herself. The Bolsheviks send assassins around the world but think they are safe in their beds." A grin marched onto Volkov's face. "In Odessa, the head of the OGPU was a bastard called Liminov. He's behind several murders in Istanbul, and nobody lifted a finger because all the victims were Russian. White Russians. People like me." Volkov beat his fist against his chest, emphasising his point. "Now Liminov is dead; Anna killed him."

"You sent her there?"

"Yes. Jude and me."

Volkov was practically beaming. Elspeth let a smile slip onto her lips; her mind raced. What the hell had Jude been up to? Who the hell had authorised him to organise the murder of an OGPU Colonel on Soviet soil? Was Lavrov responding to a war that Jude had started? It explained why he was so keen to catch up with Anna.

"I knew Jude was sending people into Russia, but he didn't tell me what they were doing there."

"Yes, Jude was a good friend for our cause. He's going to be badly missed."

"What will happen to your people in Odessa? If Lavrov tracked you down to find Anna, doesn't that mean your network in Odessa is in danger?"

The glow on Volkov's face dimmed; the weight of middle age suddenly seemed heavy on him. His eyes dropped to the floor.

"I'm going back there."

"When?"

"Tomorrow." He nodded at the bag from the car. "That's where I was going when Lavrov and his ape caught up with me."

"Isn't it too risky for you to go, even if Lavrov thinks you're dead? You must have some other way to get in touch with them. What channels did Jude have?"

"There's a couple of groups that Jude had links with. They arranged cultural visits; state-managed propaganda on how wonderful life is in the Soviet Union. It was usually for the benefit of blinkered English intellectuals too deluded to look beyond the lies they were pedalled. Jude was tired of the pretence; he wanted to do something real. He found Anna." Volkov shrugged. "The people I have to deal with, I need to see them face to face. A postcard or a telegram is no good."

Volkov got up and went to the window. He opened the blinds a fraction, scowling at the world outside. Elspeth could feel her pulse; it wasn't fast, but each beat was like a goad. Anna Kravchenko was Jude's creature, and now she was clinging to Jasper. She needed to find out more, but she'd have to take it easy. No point in charging in and making Volkov suspicious.

"How did he find her?"

214

Volkov turned and stared at her. Sometimes there just wasn't the time to be subtle.

17.   Resentment and revenge

Baku, 14th September 1918

The smell of smoke was everywhere. Shells were bursting amongst the houses at the city's edge, but rifle shots were much closer than that. Tamara sprinted across the train tracks. The station looked deserted, but every building had the dead-eyed stare of a town about to be taken. Those that hadn't already fled were hiding. The staccato chatter of a machine gun was answered by several rifle shots. The start of a counterattack? No. Everyone knew the city was doomed. The British were holding on just long enough to get their people away; the Turks were already in the town. She had to get to the quayside and onboard the ship before it was too late. Where the hell was Nathan?

Twilight made the shadows long. The crump of shells was getting closer as Tamara pressed herself into the cover offered by an entrance alcove. The door's surface was cold against her back. She stiffened at the scuff of a boot nearby. Her right hand slid into the pocket of her long wool skirt. The cool feel of the service revolver was a comfort as her fingers curled around it. Nathan or someone else? Two more footsteps; how close? It was hard to tell. Her heart was starting to hammer. This was no time to lose control; she had to stay still. Someone was approaching, no two people. She pulled the pistol out; this wasn't Nathan.

Voices. Turkish? Maybe; it didn't matter as it wasn't Nathan. What had happened to him? He'd said to meet here before they headed to the SS Kruger and made their way out of Baku. More voices; it sounded like orders were being given. They were probably soldiers, but they could be looters. At times like these, they were usually the same thing. The crunch of boots said they were around the corner and getting closer. Run or hide? The pistol was in her hand,

216

lined up at head height for the first man to come into view. Her pulse slowed; any second now.

Why was she lying on the ground? Her head rang, and her back hurt, but the pistol was still in her hand. The ground was hard and gritty, just like the dust filling her mouth. Sound staggered back, sharp and bright. Someone was screaming. Tamara tried to move, but something held onto her. The corner of the station building was missing. The door was on top of her; it must have shielded her from the shell's blast. The screaming was coming from the other side of the rubble that pinned her.

Twisting and kicking, Tamara inched herself free. The end of the station building had been destroyed, but the buildings across the street looked untouched. She forced herself to stand. Warm wetness glued her hair to the side of her face. She pushed the hair behind her ear; her hand was slick with blood when she looked at it. The screaming rose in pitch. She had to get away, get to the boat before it left. Tripping, stumbling, she staggered across the street. The screaming waned to a whimper. Tamara looked back at the ruined station. Why was only the station hit? Why just one shell?

The machine gun started up again with longer and more urgent bursts. She had to move. Each step hurt, but each step got easier. Her right arm hung by her side, the pistol all but welded into her grip. The coppery tang of blood in her nose was displaced by the smell of the sea. Piles of sandbags flanked the road to the dockside; no signs of soldiers in them. Was she too late? Huddles of people were clustered at the end of a quay, a large steamer against the jetty. The steamer's whistle sounded. Tamara pushed herself forward through the desperate crush.

A man turned to snarl but practically leapt back at the

sight of her. Tamara pushed him aside and started to run. The lines from the stern of the steamer were being cast off. Her decks were crammed with people, soldiers and civilians taking a last look at the corpse of Baku. Tamara stopped; she was too late. The gap between the quayside and the steamer was growing. The pathetic puddles of people who'd failed to get aboard plodded past her. She stared up at the brimming decks. Nathan was staring back at her.

Tamara forced herself along the quayside. It felt as though a fist was pushing itself through her chest. On the ship, Nathan was fighting his way towards the stern. She yelled and waved. The steamer was pulling away from her; she couldn't keep pace with it. Finally, Nathan had reached the stern, his fists gripping the rail. Tamara stopped. There was nothing else she could do but watch him sail away from her. Nathan drew a pistol from inside his coat. Tamara stared, stuck to the spot, as he took aim at her. But, of course, it hadn't been a shell; you always liked your bombs, didn't you, Nathan? Her revolver hung heavy in her hand. What would be the point? Another corpse wouldn't wipe away the betrayal that had already happened.

A British officer lurched into Nathan. Nathan pushed his pistol inside his coat as the officer steadied himself against him, no doubt apologising for his clumsiness. Nathan turned and shoved his way through the press of people on the ship's stern. Tamara stared at the departing vessel. Without any lights, its outline was already getting dim against the pitch-black eastern sky. Now the pain from her head wound growled, competing with the anger stewing inside her.

What to do now? Try and find a boat, any boat and get away? The scattered crowd along the quayside suggested that was probably a poor plan, but it was the only one she

218

had. There were still a few small steamers at the eastern end of the docks, the occasional gunshot keeping the crowds at bay. Tamara glanced at her revolver; at least that would give her a little more bargaining power. She started walking.

The last glimmers of daylight etched the edges of the hills around the city into the skyline. Darkness had claimed the streets. The shelling had stopped, probably because the gunners could no longer see what they were trying to hit. A lot of shooting was coming from the west. The Turks must be inside the city now; with luck, they'd be too busy looting to push quickly towards the docks. She might have a bit more time to get aboard a boat.

"Tamara!"

Tamara stopped, the revolver ready to be brought up. A figure stepped from a side street onto the quayside. It was Cameron Lowe.

"Tamara, what on earth are you still doing here? Where's Nathan?"

"I…he's on the ship."

Cameron strode up to her. A group of men, several with rifles, bundled out of the side street. Cameron stared at her, his eyes scanning then fixing on the wound on her head.

"What happened? Why aren't you on that ship?"

"I had an accident… with an artillery shell." She tried to grin, but it turned into more of a grimace than a smile. "Nathan must have thought I'd been killed."

Why the hell was she covering for Nathan? Did Cameron have any idea that he had meant to kill her? Had they agreed on it? Cameron frowned and reached out to her scalp. She pulled away and then stopped. His fingers gently probed at the wound, and she winced with the pain.

"Sorry," said Cameron, his fingers jerking back. "It looks worse than it is. You'd better come with me; we've got a ship waiting." He glanced at his wristwatch. "We should just make it."

* * *

The shrill note of the ferry's whistle sent seagulls circling above. Tamara tracked them wheeling against the blue sky, white angel wings with hearts as black as soot. No, that was unfair. They were just birds following the winds looking for their next meal, much like the refugees crammed aboard the steamer fleeing Baku. Only people lied, betrayed, murdered and then justified it all to themselves: it is for the people; it is for your own good; it is for… What had it all been for?

She glanced at Max sitting beside her on the ferry's upper deck. His gaze was fixed on the eastern side of the Bosphorous. Judging how his hands were balled into fists, he expected a welcoming committee. The tall building of Haydarpasa railway station and its landing stage was clearly in sight, but it was too far to make out people's faces. Funny to think that back then, there had been a welcoming committee for that ship when it reached the far side of the Caspian Sea. Funny, if you weren't the ones they were waiting for.

"What do you know of the 26 Baku Commissars?"

Max almost jumped, forcing himself to break away from his vigil.

"What?"

"The 26 Baku Commissars. Have you heard of them?"

Max frowned as he looked at her; maybe he thought it was a trick question.

"Yes, I think so. Wasn't it some revolutionary unpleasantness at the end of the war?"

Tamara searched his face for any sign of a punchline. Strained bewilderment stared back at her. No, he was being genuine. So much for the heroic sacrifice of the revolutionaries who had been betrayed and murdered. That story was still being rewritten and retold. Now it was her turn to retell it.

"They were the leaders of the Baku commune, appointed by Lenin to control the revolution there. They were led by Stepan Shaumian, the Lenin of the Caucasus. When the Turks started closing in on Baku, there was a coup. Stepan and his comrades were arrested, and the British arrived to try and fight off the Turks."

Max angled his body towards her, his distant vigil of the shore forgotten for now.

"Is this to do with Cameron Lowe's deal with Lavrov?"

"Yes. It was Cameron that broke them out of prison as the city fell and got them onto a waiting ship."

"That sounds... extraordinary. Are you sure?"

"Yes. I was there."

Max was scrutinizing her face; there was nothing for him to find as she was telling the truth. His frown deepened.

"But Cameron is practically a fascist. I can't believe he is working for the Bolsheviks—"

"He isn't." Max's eyes widened a fraction. Tamara carried on. "Cameron Lowe only works for Cameron Lowe, but he'll deal with anyone."

"And this time, it was with the Bolsheviks?"

"No. He was dealing with Nathan and Nathan alone."

"Help Lavrov's friends escape from Baku?" Tamara stayed quiet. Don't answer; let him work it out. Max's frown returned as her silence grew. "It's a pity for them that the ship took them somewhere they weren't welcome. Didn't they end up being executed? There was some codswallop in the papers a couple of years back, the Soviet government accusing a British officer... oh."

No, he wasn't the idiot he made himself out to be.

"The deal wasn't to help Lavrov's friends escape, was it?"

"I'm not sure Nathan has any friends, just people he can use."

Tamara looked out to sea. She hadn't hidden the edge in her voice. It was never a good idea to let your true feelings surface, but it was unlikely to surprise Max; maybe it was best to let him see her as the bitter woman out for revenge.

"Why did he want Cameron to make sure his old comrades met an untimely end?"

"Just one comrade. Stepan Shaumian."

"The Lenin of the Caucasus as you described him." Tamara nodded. "A political rival?"

222

Tamara turned to look at Max.

"He was a political rival for somebody, but not Nathan's. Nathan saw an opportunity to gain favour and took it."

"And what did he promise Cameron for his help?"

"Nathan thought that he would be the natural successor to Shaumian, ready to rule over the Caucasus with its oil fields. Cameron was very keen to take advantage of all that oil."

"He was doing this on behalf of the British government?"

She could feel the thin smile seeping onto her face. It would be so easy to agree with him and add a little extra to the myths and legends built around the deaths of the Baku commissars, but others were busy doing that. Tamara shook her head.

"No, Cameron was doing this for himself. Make a deal to buy Soviet oil cheaply and sell it to make a profit. He was very pleased with himself."

Max's eyes narrowed.

"You said that Lavrov abandoned you in Baku. How did you get out?"

"Nathan tried to kill me; make sure I wouldn't share his secrets. But Cameron found me and took me with him."

Did he believe her? Sometimes it got hard to remember what was true and what was not. The three days aboard that ship would be hard to forget. Wondering what Nathan had shared with Cameron about her, would Cameron finish what Nathan had failed to do? She didn't know where the ship was heading. From the arguments between the ship's

223

captain, the crew, and the unexpected party of Bolsheviks, neither did they. She'd stayed in the background watching as Cameron charmed, bribed, and eventually threatened to make sure the ship went east to Krasnovodsk, sealing the fate of the 26 Baku Commissars. Cameron had told her what he was doing, and she'd said nothing. She knew they'd be arrested there. She'd told herself that Shaumian was too important to stay a prisoner; he'd be released and sent to Russia. She'd told herself … No, she'd lied to herself. She knew what awaited them and, by saying nothing, had become their executioner.

"I can see why Lavrov is so keen to find you. Besides you, Cameron, and Lavrov, who knows about this?"

"Just you."

Max chuckled.

"It doesn't fill me with happiness to know that another person has a reason to want me dead." His gaze drifted for a moment. "Although whoever Lavrov was doing the favour for must also know what was done, and Lavrov doesn't look like the king of the Caucasus that he hoped he'd become. What went wrong?"

"The 26 Baku Commissars became martyrs for the revolution. Nathan was supposed to leave them dead, buried, and forgotten. Instead, Trotsky used their deaths to build a cult around them. It's being taught to school children how the British murdered them."

"And now Trotsky is in exile in Istanbul."

"With Nathan acting as his jailer and bodyguard."

The ferry sounded its whistle as it approached the landing stage. Several passengers were already standing. The subtle scrabble to gain position to be the first off the boat and get clear of the pack had started. Max was studying the faces of the small crowd waiting for the ferry to dock. At least there wasn't a gunboat here demanding they drop anchor and prepare to be boarded. Max stood up.

"Come on, we'll slip through in the scrum."

Tamara scanned the waiting faces. Damn! She shouldn't have let her mind wander. Max wasn't a fool; what had he seen there? No, who had he seen there? She pressed up close to Max's side. Present that picture of the cosy couple; that way, people were less likely to try and get between them. The ferry bumped against the quayside, lines already being tied to hold it in place. The man behind stumbled against her. Her right hand gripped the blade in her pocket. A mumbled apology from the man. Just a stumble, nothing more. Her hand still clasped the knife.

"Did you see someone in the crowd?" asked Tamara.

"I'm not sure. I thought I saw one of Kimon Panakis' people. The sooner we can get off this crate, the better."

She couldn't disagree with him. The gangplank thumped into place. A deck hand called out, and the press of passengers started to move forward. Not much chance to hide in those five or six single-file paces across the gangplank to the quay. She stepped behind Max as he started up the gangway. He had his head down and was outwardly checking where he was walking. It was plausible playacting. The brim of his fedora would hide his face from anyone watching, and his clothes weren't what they might expect. Tamara studied the people ahead. No need to hide her face; it was Max that Panakis wanted, not her. Bored impatience was all she could see amongst the crowd on the quayside.

Stepping ashore Tamara took her place on Max's right,

her left hand looping through his arm. Outwardly, they were the cosy couple once more, but her right hand was welded around the knife's hilt.

"We'll head through the station. It'll give us a better chance of spotting anyone following us," said Max.

The towering edifice of Haydarpasa station was directly ahead. The ferry sounded its whistle, urging those not already aboard to get a move on. She felt Max's arm stiffen. Two men were running from the station; one carried a case, the other holding onto his hat. They weren't assassins, just running late. Tamara glanced around. No faces in the crowd were heading their way. The tension in Max's arm lessened as the pair pushed past. What if they had been after them? Would she leave Max to it? No, she needed him, at least for now. Worry about that when it happens.

They entered the station. The sun had started to dip, its rays stretching shadows across the concourse floor. The place was lively but not heaving. Tamara glanced at the rows of benches across the room facing the exit to the platforms. There were a dozen or more people dotted across the seating. Some must be waiting for a train to depart, others for an arrival. A train must have recently arrived, as passengers were still seeping into the station from the platform. An occasional head looked up to check a face and then returned to its newspaper. Nobody seemed in a hurry to head out. It didn't look like a departure was due any time soon.

"We have to move." Max was already angling them to the right and a side exit. Stay calm, and get ready. The knife was in her hand but held lightly. Don't get tense; that only slowed you down. It wasn't far to the door. Max had his head down. She let her hand drop from his arm and slipped

226

the knife clear of her pocket. Max pushed on into the revolving door, not missing a step. Tamara half-stumbled, then turned, the knife up and ready to… There was no one behind. She stepped into the revolving door, the blade back in her pocket and followed Max.

A half-dozen overly fast steps and she'd caught up, her heels clacking against the pavement.

"You're walking too fast. You look obvious."

Max carried on.

"Right now, we need distance between the station and us."

"No. Right now, we need to look like a blissful couple enjoying the view over the sea. There is no one on our tail. I checked."

Max stopped and made the pretence of staring across the waters of the Bosphorous.

"Sorry. I saw someone I knew. An enforcer who works for Panakis."

"Where?"

"He was in the third row of benches."

"Black hair, balding, brown jacket and a cream coat folded over the seat next to him?"

"Yes."

"He was still in his seat reading a newspaper as we left."

Max shrugged.

"How far to your place?" asked Max.

"Not far, fifteen, maybe twenty minutes." Max was still staring at the view, or at least his face was pointed at it. "It's only five if we march at your speed."

Max chuckled.

"Okay, point taken. We'd better get moving."

Despite the sun, the air was cool. There weren't many people about. Just a few couples taking the opportunity to stroll along the road by the station heading into Kadiköy. The occasional taxi chugged past. None of them slowed down on the off chance of a fare; probably better pickings amongst the ferry passengers.

"Why did we go into the station? You weren't trying to spot someone following us, were you?"

"No. I wanted to see if anyone was keeping an eye out for me there. I had half an idea of taking the train across Anatolia to Aleppo."

"But they have someone here?"

They walked on in silence, Max studying the pavement for several minutes.

"Yes, but maybe not for you. Once you're in Syria, you are effectively on French soil."

Was that the plan? Couldn't she have bought a train ticket by herself?

"How do I get across the border? I haven't got a passport, let alone a nice French one that won't raise an eyebrow from any gendarme that cares to look."

Max sighed.

"That's why we're here. I need you to sit tight while I get you a passport and make peace with Kimon Panakis."

Sit tight. Be a good little girl. Do as I tell you. Who the hell did he think he was to say that to her?

"And if you don't make your peace with Panakis? What then? Shall I sit a little tighter?"

She could see the muscles in his jaw tighten. They walked on another half dozen paces in silence with the occasional seabird passing commentary.

"If I'm not back by midnight, you're on your own. Take the first train to Izmir and find Elliot Dixon; he runs a business sailing wealthy people around the eastern Mediterranean. His office is at the northern end of the harbour, just past the breakwater. When you find him, tell him I sent you and give him this."

Max handed her a dark blue passport. She opened it and looked at the picture; it was Max, but the name said Jasper Lewingdon.

"Is this the name he knows you by?"

"Yes. It's my real one. Elliot is my cousin. You'll also need to give him this." He handed her a crisp bundle of U.S. dollars held together with a paper band from a bank. "You'll need the money to get him to sail you somewhere without papers or asking questions; his business isn't as watertight as it could be. You'll need the passport to convince him I'm still alive; that may surprise him as I think he attended my funeral."

18.   It's just business

The taxi crawled to a halt, its engine puttering gently. The pair of white-painted gate posts practically shone in the late afternoon sun. This was as far as the driver would go despite the open gates. He turned to look at Jasper.

"Do you want me to wait for you?"

Jasper suppressed a smile. It was flattering that the taxi driver had enough faith in him to think he might be coming back, let alone needing a taxi.

"No, thank you." He paid the driver, pressing a healthy tip into his hand. The man smiled. Maybe he'd raise a glass to that fare he'd dropped at the edge of the Panakis estate before he got on with his life. It was certainly better than letting one of the thugs that Panakis used get their hands on it. Jasper got out of the taxi and swung the door shut. As soon as the door clunked, the driver let the clutch out. No farewell, no good luck. Hardly surprising. No one sane wants to hang around Kimon Panakis' home and attract the attention of people they really didn't need to meet. The poor chap was probably thanking whatever saints he prayed to that he hadn't been asked to wait.

Jasper watched the taxi turn round and head back down the track through the Cypress-clad slopes. The view from up here was impressive; the Bosphorous and the whole European side of Istanbul laid out to be admired. A few steamers were making their way towards the Black Sea, another heading for the Mediterranean. Would Anna still be there when he got back? If he came back. If she had any sense, she'd already be on her way to Izmir and cousin Elliot. Good luck, Elliot; you'll be needing it.

Deep breath, best foot forward and all that. He

breathed in deeply, held it for a count of three and breathed out, sighing loudly. No half-arsed pep talk to yourself will make the blindest bit of difference to how this turns out. Jasper turned and headed through the gates. The gates to the Panakis estate were never shut. There was no point as the estate had no wall surrounding it; it didn't need one. The formal gateway made a statement. Don't come in if you know what's good for you. Most people who'd heard of Kimon Panakis did know, or at least knew what wasn't good for them and made sure they stayed away.

The gravel of the drive crunched beneath his brogues. His brogues, unlike the purloined suit he was wearing. It was a pity the brown leather didn't quite go with the charcoal grey of the suit, but your own shoes were always comfortable. It was a fine suit, though. Shut up! Concentrate! Think about what you're going to say. Have you got anything to say? He'd only been here once before, and that was with Ruby. She'd done the talking, charmed the man and struck a deal. What did he have to offer?

The house was in view through the trees. It was a bright-white art deco mansion, all edges and angles at odds with the softness of the cypress trees surrounding it. It looked like an Atlantic liner had ploughed into the hillside and been left there for all to admire. The squeals of small children playing drifted down from the terrace. Close on the heels of their laughter were a pair of goons heading straight down the drive towards him. They were well-dressed goons, but goons all the same. Jasper stopped holding his hands away from his sides.

Goon One marched up to him. Goon Two stood to the side studying proceedings; maybe he was the intellectual of the pair. Goon One did a quick but thorough pat-down for weapons. There was nothing there to be found. Kerim's automatic had been left with Anna for safekeeping; only a fool would bring a weapon up here. Only a fool would come up here full stop. Goon One extracted Jasper's wallet and the passport bearing his cover name of Max Bolton. He flicked through the wallet before handing it back. The passport was thoroughly examined before he gave it to Goon Two. Shrill shrieks and laughter sounded again, but closer this time.

"Follow me," ordered Goon Two and headed for the house.

Better do as the nice man says. Jasper headed after him with Goon One alongside for company. Nice that he handed his wallet back without filching any of the money; he must be a well-brought-up mobster. There again, he could always help himself later if things went badly. The path looped around to the right, closely-clipped bushes hiding it from anyone enjoying the late afternoon sun on the terrace. The Goons wouldn't want to disturb whatever party was taking place there, at least not until they'd had a chance to find out if he was worth the bother. If he didn't get to talk to Panakis directly, then this was all going to be a costly and possibly terminal adventure.

"Bang! Bang! You're dead!"

Goon One jumped, his hand speeding for his jacket's inside pocket before his self-control took over. Nikos stood at the side of the path, having leapt out from the tall shrubs shrouding the slopes to the side of the house. His forefinger was held out in front of him, ready to deliver a coup de grâce.

"You're dead! You're dead!" he cried with glee. Best to play along; who knows how long you had for real around here.

"Agh! You got me!" Jasper half-crumpled in mock

232

agony. Nikos shrieked with delight. The Goons were wearing matching frowns, Goon One moving to intercept the would-be assassin.

"Nikos! Nikos! Where are you?"

A small girl about the same age as Nikos pushed through the shrubs. Her dark hair and cream dress showed signs of losing their fight against the undergrowth, even if she did not. She stood at the path's edge with her hands on her hips, frowning at Nikos; everyone else was immaterial.

"You were meant to shoot them when I said!"

Nikos wilted under her glare. The Goons had taken an almost imperceptible step back, their frowns replaced by... what? Indecision? Who was this girl?

"Sofia, Nikos. There you are."

A short man in his late sixties, maybe early seventies, ambled up the path towards them. A broad smile cracked his tanned face. The thick mass of grey curls and cardigan just added to the air of the indulgent grandfather. The Goons might not realise it, but they were standing to attention. It might be wise to join in; this was Kimon Panakis.

"Grandfather, Nikos shot the man before I told him to. I'm supposed to be in charge!"

Panakis chuckled as he strolled up to Nikos and put his hand on the lad's shoulder. Nikos glared back at Sofia, his lower lip pushed out in defiance.

"So, who did you shoot, Nikos?"

Nikos snapped his glare into a smile as he looked at Panakis. Well done, lad. You know how to play the game.

"This is my friend Max! He owes me toffees."

Panakis straightened up and looked at Jasper. The smile was still in place, but the eyes were harder. Jasper could sense the ice in his guts; please, God, let that be all I feel today.

"Do you owe Nikos toffees? Some would consider that a reason to shoot a man."

From anyone other than Kimon Panakis, that would be a joke. Jasper smiled back.

"I'm afraid so. I suspect that my debt may have grown to two bags with interest. Assuming his mother allows it."

Panakis laughed.

"Yes, Maria, my daughter's maid, will put a tax on Nikos' ill-gotten gains." He looked at his granddaughter. "Sofia, your mother wants you to get ready for dinner. Take Nikos and go inside."

"But Grandfather—"

Panakis raised a finger, and Sofia went silent.

"Now, now. Do as I ask. Maria will bring Nikos tomorrow, so you can play then."

"Yes, Grandfather."

Sofia took Nikos' hand, and the pair ran off along the path and from view. Panakis watched them disappear, chuckling to himself. Had he ever read Great Expectations? The chuckling stopped, and the ice returned to Jasper's guts. Goon Two handed Panakis the passport. Panakis flicked through it, pausing to examine several stamps before giving it back to Jasper.

"Mr Max Bolton, you have become a very popular

person. So let's sit on the terrace and enjoy the view before my daughter demands that I dress for dinner."

The view from the terrace was worth enjoying. Tea was brought out to the table. Panakis poured out two cups. The Goons stood discreetly at the edge of the terrace but without tea.

"Would you like milk?" he asked.

"Yes, thank you."

Panakis handed him a cup and saucer.

"I would have had some cake sent out, but my daughter won't allow it so close to dinner. She says such things set a bad example to Sofia."

"Yes, it's important to set a good example."

Panakis looked at him but had no smile this time. Suddenly those words didn't feel quite so smart.

"Viktor Volkov is keen to talk to you."

"So I'd heard."

"You know why?"

"He thinks I murdered Ruby and stole the money he paid us."

Panakis sat back and sipped his tea. The whole time his deep brown eyes were fixed on Jasper's. It wasn't comfortable getting trapped in a staring contest, but he couldn't afford to back down, at least not yet.

"Viktor was very unhappy about it. He makes quite a case against you." Panakis placed his teacup on its saucer. He looked at Jasper and shrugged. "He's very sure of your guilt. He must be, given what he's doing in return for getting you." Panakis picked up his teacup and took a sip of tea. "Why did you kill her?"

"I didn't kill her." The words spat out. Stay calm, and stay in control. To hell with that! Tension twisted the muscles in his shoulders. "Why don't you ask your daughter's maid?" Goon Two stiffened, taking a pace closer. Panakis waved him away with a flick of a finger. The grandfatherly smile flickered, calming the situation. Was this a situation? No, it was a test.

"I know you didn't. The post-mortem says Ruby took an overdose of morphine. A regrettable accident—"

"It wasn't an accident. She was murdered."

Panakis' eyes widened a fraction. Was it in response to the interruption or the edge in his voice? It didn't matter; Goon Two was still looking twitchy.

"But not by you?"

"No."

"What about Viktor's money? What happened to that?"

"That money was a down payment. I gave it to Kerim Yazaroğlu to make a passport for one of Viktor's projects. I suspect that Kerim will have spent it by now."

Panakis chuckled.

"Ah, yes. Kerim's love of the latest fashion. His work was excellent. Too expensive for me; not enough profit in it. Pity that Kerim's dead. The police want to talk to you about it."

Shock, surprise, grief, what emotion would be appropriate to display right now? Probably guilt. It didn't come as much of a surprise that Kerim had been murdered.

236

No doubt his new Russian friends were tidying up loose threads. Anna would probably just shrug: think yourself lucky it was him and not you. But they'd only found Kerim because of him. Just like Ruby.

"I didn't kill Kerim either."

"You seem to be an unlucky man to be around. Perhaps I should watch my back, eh?" Panakis chuckled. "What happened to the passport?"

"Kerim's killers took it. Russians. Nathan Lavrov, to be specific. So if Viktor wants that passport, that's who he should go and ask for it."

Panakis looked amused rather than surprised; did he believe any of this?

"Are you sure it wasn't the British?"

Was he sure? What about the elusive Englishman?

"Why do you say that?"

"I talked to Nikos' mother. Someone from the consulate, Jude Faulkner, has been paying her a lot of attention recently. He was very interested in Ruby and you. Maria has been good enough to keep me informed. I think Mr Faulkner outbid your toffees."

"Does Maria know why he was interested in Ruby and me?"

"No. She didn't ask questions. Didn't want to put him off her."

Of course she didn't. Not when some junior official from the British Consulate had taken a shine to her after bumping into her at the bazaar. You have to hang onto such opportunities. It was also a pure coincidence that a maid working for Kimon Panakis' daughter had rooms in the same boarding house as Ruby. All this bitterness was starting to ruin a lovely cup of tea. Jasper gave Panakis a thin smile. But if Jude Faulkner was the Englishman haunting his footsteps, who in London had put him there? And what should he be doing about it?

"I want to make you an offer," said Jasper. Amusement flitted across Panakis' face, but he hadn't laughed aloud. "The French have changed all their stamps, visas, and forms. I can give you them. You'd have a three-month window, maybe more, to get anyone into France with no awkward questions asked. With no competition, you'd make a fortune."

Believe in what you're selling; it isn't the pathetic last-gasp offering of a soon-to-be-dead man.

"But I don't have Kerim. He's dead."

"Your man, Kristos, is more than capable, plus he'll have the real thing to work from. So there's no risk to you, just opportunity."

Panakis chuckled. He poured a little more tea into his cup and added a bit of milk, followed by a spoonful of sugar. His gaze drifted over Istanbul as he stirred his tea. He'd been calculating precisely what this could bring him down to a single penny or piastra.

"And what do you want in return, other than for me not to give you to Viktor?"

"A safe passage out of the city and Turkey for me and one other."

"Oh, who?"

"Viktor's project, Anna Kravchenko. Ruby and I

238

agreed to get her papers so she could get out of Turkey. This way, I can fulfil our agreement with Viktor even if he has only paid half the money. You might want to get the other half from him for the service you would be providing."

Panakis laughed. Not his customary chuckle but a full-on laugh. He dabbed at the corner of his eye and grew solemn. Jasper could feel the sun clouding over. The sudden drop in temperature wasn't just on his skin.

"It is a good offer, but it's not enough."

Jasper's guts twisted.

"How much more?"

He had nothing else. Would he beg? Is that what Panakis wanted to see?

"Two bags of toffees for Nikos!"

Panakis slapped his palm on the table, rattling the crockery as his laughter bellowed. Jasper forced a smile onto his face to match the one that Goon Two was wearing. God save us from dangerous men who thought they were funny. A woman's voice called from the house. Panakis stifled his laughter and turned to wave at whoever was calling him. He turned back to face Jasper and shrugged an apology.

"My daughter," he explained, "It's time for me to dress for dinner." He stood up, and Jasper followed suit. "We have a deal. Tomorrow morning, three o'clock, be on the dockside next to the Hasköy shipyard. The captain of the Paros will be expecting you. They're heading for Odessa but will call in at Constanta in Romania. I suggest you get off there." Pankais thrust his hand out and shook Jasper's. He nodded in the direction of Goon Two. "Yiannis will see

239

you out."

19.   The one you're looking for?

The sun had all but disappeared, taking the day's
warmth with it. Elspeth pulled her coat collar up. The drop
in temperature was a good excuse to take on the anonymous
silhouette of just another pedestrian hurrying home to a
warm fire. Hide amongst the passers-by. At least, that
would be the plan, if there were any. The narrow streets
near Volkov's apartment were deserted; the lack of street
lighting added to her uneasiness. Lavrov had tracked
Volkov to his villa. Who's to say one of his henchmen
hadn't staked out Volkov's apartment? Elspeth glanced over
her shoulder. Nothing there but shadows and shapes. She
followed the lane downhill. The sound of traffic, filtered
through the buildings, was coming from that direction. She
couldn't be that far from the Pera Palace, but she'd got lost
in Istanbul's backstreets before.

Would there be a reception committee waiting for her
at the hotel? Volkov had urged her not to go; why take the
risk when he could get her aboard the ship he was taking to
Odessa? The ship was calling at Constanta. He'd call in a
favour there, and she could get ashore with no questions
asked, let alone passports checked. From there, she could
take the train to Bucharest and throw herself on the charity
of the British embassy claiming her passport had been
stolen. Then, if the Turkish police were looking for her,
they would be too late, and she'd be free to return to
London.

Were the Turkish police looking for her? It seemed
likely. If only it were just the Turkish police, Volkov's plan
would be fine. What about Cameron? Cameron, who was in
league with Lavrov. Lavrov, who had murdered a man that
the Turkish police have probably linked her to. Not a good
mix, especially when it looked like her cover was blown.

241

All that meant she couldn't throw herself on the mercy of either the British Embassy in Bucharest or the consulate in Constanta. She had to be able to get back to London under her own steam to talk to K and only K. That meant travelling with a different identity.

The lane tumbled out onto the road leading from the ferry across the Golden Horn. Taxis and cars hooted at each other and pedestrians alike. Elspeth stopped, eyeing the moment to dash across the road and into the short-term safety of the street opposite. It would be ridiculous if she ended up in the hands of the Turkish police because of a road traffic accident. At least there were more people about. She followed another woman across the road; safety in numbers or at least two bodies might make a driver think twice or keener to brake.

The lights of the Pera Palace were visible at the top of the hill. The tall windows of its dining room could be glimpsed through the thin screen of trees that dotted the slope up to the Petits-Champs Park. Pity it was such a slog to reach it. Lights from hotel rooms dotted the five floors above the dining room. Thank God hers was on the first floor of guest rooms; she could use the stairs and avoid the lift. Her eye was drawn to a light winking into life at the first-floor corner. That was her room. Elspeth increased her pace, her eyes focusing on the square of light.

Who was in her room? Why were they in her room? Her heels cracked against the pavement underlining the questions in her head. Calm yourself. You don't know anything. It's just a light. It's probably the maid doing a final service before turning the bed down. But isn't it too early for that? Volkov was right; she should have stayed at his apartment until it was time to board the steamer and get out of this city. Heading back isn't an option. Volkov would already have left for another bolt hole to make sure she couldn't lead anyone back to him. So what now? Spend the next nine hours lurking in the backstreets of Beyoğlu? The main light in her room winked out. Maybe not.

Elspeth scanned the other windows on the same floor as hers. A couple of them had lights on, but the windows on the far corner were thankfully dark; that was Cameron's suite. It was almost as far as it could be from hers while still being on the same floor. Was that intentional, or just a coincidence? Didn't matter now; as long as Cameron was out, that was all that was important. She was at the corner of the hotel. Time to play a part. She almost laughed. She'd been playing a part for a very long time. Would she ever get the chance to stop?

There was a scrum of taxis and the cars of the well-to-do, dropping and picking up people. A mixture of evening suits and sparkly frocks vied with the uniforms of the harassed doormen, trying to corral and contain the confusion in front of the entrance. Suddenly her long, pale camel hair coat didn't seem quite so anonymous. She'd got the worst of the soot off it at Volkov's apartment. Thank goodness the dark blue felt of her hat hid the worst of the damage. Did she still smell of smoke? Blag it, girl; remember you belong here. Head up and barely acknowledging the chaos, she marched towards the entrance. She barely had to break step as a doorman pulled the door open for her. Elspeth flashed a smile of appreciation at him and continued straight to the front desk.

Despite the bustle in the foyer, a receptionist was waiting, ready to receive her instructions; it was an advantage of being 'someone', but right now, it felt like a curse.

"Can I have my room key, please?"

"Of course, Miss Stirling." He knew her face. He knew

243

her name. There was little chance he'd forget her when the police came looking for her. He placed the key on the counter. "Is there anything else, miss?"

"Is Mr Lowe back yet?"

The receptionist checked.

"I'm afraid not, miss. His key is still here."

"And there are no messages for me?"

"I'm afraid not. I checked when I saw you come in."

"Oh dear. It looks like I'm not as famous as I thought." The young chap smiled at her attempt at humour. "I'll probably be dining in my room this evening. Would you call me when Mr Lowe arrives?"

"Of course, miss."

The commotion died down. The well-dressed party had tramped through to the dining room or the grand hall. Elspeth headed up the short flight of steps separating the foyer from the interior. She felt she was being watched: a shaven-headed man in a rumpled suit sat at the side of the foyer. She had spotted him as soon as she'd come in. He looked out of place: in the hotel but not of the hotel. Police? OGPU? A driver waiting to pick someone up? He must have heard the receptionist say her name. She paused at the glass screen of the tea lounge peering inside. The reflection was poor, but she could make out Mr Rumple-Suit behind her; he'd gone back to staring at the entrance door. Stop messing about, woman, and get on with what you're here to do.

Elspeth headed to the main staircase. The hotel lift arrived and disgorged a couple dressed in their finest. There must be some event taking place at the hotel that night.

With luck, it would provide a distraction if she needed one. The bellhop looked expectantly at her. Elspeth smiled, shook her head and started to climb the stairs.

Was the man in the lobby innocent? Probably not, but that didn't mean he was looking for her. What about the lights going on in her room? It's probably just the maid, but that doesn't mean they aren't looking for you. Who are 'they' anyway? Does it matter? Get in, get what you need, and then get out. That's all that matters for now. The first floor had arrived all too soon. A ripple of laughter reverberated along the corridor. Evening dresses topped off with pearls were escorted by a dinner suit with white tie. The trio was clustered at the head of the stairs, waiting for the lift. Elspeth flashed a smile in their direction; one face held hers for a fraction too long.

"My word! Elspeth Stirling! It is, isn't it?" Elspeth's heart sank. She turned to look at the woman who'd spoken. Her face wasn't familiar, but her voice trumpeting her name was setting off alarm bells. "I do so love your column in the Chronicle. So witty, so daring, I can't believe some of the things you print."

"I have a very understanding editor." How on earth to escape? Where the hell was the lift?

"Can we expect anything in the paper about tonight's shindig?"

"I can pretty much guarantee it," said Elspeth through the most brittle of smiles. "Please excuse me. I must go and get ready."

"Don't forget your notebook and pencil," laughed the woman.

The lift rose into view, signalling an end to this private

245

little purgatory. The trio twittered their goodbyes to Elspeth's back as she walked down the short corridor to the door of her suite. She stopped and listened. The lift door clattered shut, followed by the soft whine of the motor as it descended. Elspeth counted to ten. Muted notes of music from downstairs drifted up to her. No voices were nearby. No bangs, thumps, or crashes signalling impending disaster. She was alone. Elspeth breathed out and opened the door.

The writing desk lamp was on, as was the standard lamp in the room's opposite corner. The subdued lighting gave the room a warm and welcoming ambience. It was precisely the opposite of what Elspeth was experiencing right now. She let her eyes scour every detail of the room. The papers on the desk were tidy and perfectly aligned. The collection of discarded emery boards and cosmetics had been cleared from the coffee table. The wastepaper basket was empty. The cushions on the chaise longue were arranged with military perfection, and the room carried a hint of polish. Even the flowers had been tidied in their vase. The room was nothing like she had left it, but given the mess that always seemed to trail her domestic arrangements, no self-respecting hotel would have left it that way. She pressed the door shut behind her as softly as she could. The room looked exactly as it did after the maid had been, even the choice of lighting.

Elspeth slipped her shoes off and padded over to the bedroom. She opened the door and flicked the light switch on. The bulb glowed into life. Elspeth stiffened. Her travelling trunk was sat in the middle of the floor, certainly not where she'd left it. Barely breathing, her chest tight, she opened its lid. All her clothes were still in it; she hadn't got around to unpacking. Her pulse was starting to throb. Please let it be there, please. She felt down the trunk's lining; it had been sliced open. Her heart sank. She felt inside. It wasn't there, but she knew it wouldn't be the second she'd seen her trunk had been taken from the closet.

She rocked back on her haunches. Her fake passport had gone. The one insurance policy she had and it was gone. Think, think. Don't panic, not yet. You still have your real one. You can use that. But won't they be looking for Elspeth Stirling at the border? Bound to be. Bribery? She knelt down and pushed her hand further into the trunk's lining. Her fingertips found the package where it should be. With a slight tug, she pulled it out. Two thousand US dollars. A fortune to anyone and enough to bribe your way across any border if you're careful. But whoever had taken her passport had left this. Careless, or didn't they care about the money?

A clunk sounded from the bathroom. Elspeth froze, her eyes fixed on the bathroom door. Maybe whoever had taken the passport hadn't had time to take the money? She stood up slowly, every sense stretching for further signs of the intruder. Her breathing was shallow, but now her pulse must be over a hundred. Run? No, she needed time to escape. Elspeth picked up the dressing table chair and tip-toed to the bathroom door. One, two, three… She rammed the back of the chair under the door handle and gave the chair leg a kick to wedge it home. Now, run!

A polite knock sounded from the bathroom door. She stared at it. The knock repeated.

"Elspeth." The voice was muffled by the door, but she knew it instantly. "You do realise this door opens inwards, don't you?"

To underline the observation, the door opened a few inches. The chair's back dropped away from the door handle. Elspeth's pulse was still racing, but the tension had sailed away; her nails dug into her palms as she fought the urge to yell.

"Jasper bloody Lewingdon!" The words squeezed themselves past her teeth. "What the hell are you doing here?"

"Stealing your passport?"

Elspeth stormed forward, pulling the chair out of the way and slamming the door open. Jasper jumped back.

"One more smart-arse comment, and I swear I'll shoot you!"

"No, you won't. You haven't got a gun; I checked."

She could feel the yell building deep inside her, trying to force itself out. Jasper looked alarmed. Was there something sharp to hand? The phone in the sitting room rang. A deluge of adrenalin purged the anger in an instant.

"That's Cameron. We have to go!"

"Pretend you're out."

"I can't. That call means he's on his way up. We haven't time to muck about!" Elspeth ran into the living room and grabbed her shoes. Jasper was right behind her. Was Cameron alone, or had he brought friends with him? She opened the door to the corridor and glanced out. "He'll be taking the lift."

Elspeth started to head away from the elevator and the main staircase. Jasper grabbed her hand.

"No. This way. There's a service lift and stairs for hotel staff. We'll have to be quick."

The lift's whine was unmistakable. Jasper pushed past and headed for the top of the staircase. Elspeth ran after him. The elevator was coming into view as they pelted past.

Was that Cameron in there? Too late to worry. Jasper shot down a passage to the side of the staircase. At the end was a service elevator.

"In here!" said Jasper as he pushed a door open into a small stairwell. Elspeth tumbled in after him. The door swung shut. Jasper pounded down ahead; she followed as fast as possible, her stockinged feet skidding on the steps. At the bottom, Jasper stopped, opening the door a fraction.

"Hang on," said Elspeth. She leaned against him and pulled her shoes on. "Okay."

"Through here is a service corridor from the kitchens," said Jasper. "There'll be some staff about, but hang on to me like you're an unfaithful wife sneaking out with her lover, and no one will pay the slightest attention."

"You say that like you've done this before."

Jasper gave her a lop-sided grin and opened the door. Head down and hanging onto him, they walked quickly along the service corridor. A couple of waiters swept past but were too busy to pay attention to them. The clatter from the kitchens followed them as they exited onto the street at the side of the hotel; she'd been here only a few minutes earlier.

"Have you got a backstreet dive or somewhere similar where we can hide out for a while?" asked Elspeth. "I think we need to talk." She could sense the grin even if she couldn't see it. "Don't make some stupid joke, or I really will stab you."

* * *

249

Weariness was eclipsing the adrenaline-driven strength that had kept her going since she'd fled the villa with Volkov. Elspeth looked at her latest refuge; it was cramped but hardly a dive. Jasper had guided them through backstreets and lanes to a tidy little bar near the port. Its clientele didn't shout 'sailor': too many sharp-dressed men with matching women. At least she didn't look out of place; that must have been the point of coming here. Jasper placed a brandy in front of her. A sandwich would be preferable, but don't be ungrateful.

Elspeth stared at Jasper. He stared back. Who was going to start first? She took a sip from her glass. Over to you, Jasper. The muscles in his jaw were twitching.

"How much do you know?" he asked.

It was a start, a cautious one, but a start. Didn't he trust her? He's been on the run for several days; of course he doesn't trust you.

"Let's start with Ruby. I know she's dead, as in recently dead. Not two years dead." He flinched at her words. "I'm sorry, that was blunt. It's been a bad day, and I don't think either of us has the time to spend it softening the truth."

"Does K know?"

"No. He should still be in the dark about her and your scheme of faking passports and identities."

"Should?"

"Unless his man out here, Jude Faulkner, reported his suspicions to him."

Jasper stiffened.

"He murdered Ruby."

"What makes you so sure?"

"He's been keeping tabs on Ruby and me." He broke eye contact and glared at the table. "I'm sure he was there when I found Ruby's body."

Certainty was stitched into Jasper's jawline. Would it help to try and persuade him that Jude was as much a victim as Ruby? Not yet.

"If you're thinking of taking revenge, you're too late." Jasper's head jerked up. "He got a bullet through his head this morning courtesy of an OGPU man called Nathan Lavrov."

Jasper's eyes narrowed.

"You were there?"

"Not exactly. I was hiding around the corner. As I said, it's been a bad day."

She took another sip of her brandy; it gave her an excuse to avoid Jasper's gaze.

"What were you doing? No. What are you doing in Istanbul? Why are you here? What's K up to?"

Which question to answer first, or should she answer something else and avoid the uncomfortable answers? She put her glass down; it bought a few moments to compose herself.

"K sent me to find you. Jude Faulkner was my contact in Istanbul; we were tracking down your old friend Viktor Volkov when we bumped into Lavrov. Lavrov had got to him first."

Jasper grimaced.

"Poor chap. Viktor may have had it in for me, but I

251

wouldn't wish him dead."

"Yes, you made quite an impression on him. He was hardly singing your praises when I left him."

"Viktor's alive?"

"Battered, but mostly in one piece."

A frown etched itself onto Jasper's face. Suspicion or curiosity?

"Why did you go to him?"

"Because of your new girlfriend, Anna Kravchenko." She studied his face for a reaction; nothing. "I assume she's why you were burgling my room." The wrinkles of a smile started to appear on Jasper's face. Elspeth tossed Anna Kravchenko's passport onto the table.

"I'll swap you this one for my spare."

Jasper's smile was instantly replaced with a silent 'oh'; a frown rapidly replaced it as he reached out and picked up the passport. He flicked through its pages before his eyes fixed on her face.

"How did you get this? I thought Lavrov had it."

"He left it behind in all the confusion of murder and burning buildings." Her words were flippant, but she couldn't help shuddering. Another brandy might take the edge off, but somehow she didn't think it would. Jasper's frown softened as he looked at her. She shrugged a smile on. "Brace yourself. Anna Kravchenko isn't her real name."

Jasper laughed.

"I think I'd have fallen off my chair if you'd said it was."

It was good to see him laugh. It felt like the tension between them had dwindled.

"Lavrov is desperate to find her."

"He has good reason to, and it involves your beau, Cameron Lowe." He paused. "By the way, congratulations on the engagement. I would have sent flowers, but I didn't have your current address." He glanced away, and the frown returned, furrowing his forehead. Then, his gaze swung back to her. "What on earth were you thinking? Were you really going to go through with it?"

"I…" Elspeth could feel her mouth moving, but no words were coming out. Anyway, what the hell had it do with Jasper? Why should she justify herself to him? She sighed. Don't fly off the handle, not yet. Besides, did you ever justify that decision to yourself? "His proposal caught me by surprise. I said yes to buy some time and work out a plan."

"What did K think?" The tightness in Jasper's jawline all but shouted what he thought.

Elspeth shrugged.

"He didn't try to dissuade me."

"That doesn't surprise me. He's happy to sacrifice his pawns to keep a game moving. What made him send you out here to find me?"

"He's worried that Cameron's business trip here is a front and that he's confirming suspicions that you're alive which means that my cover is well and truly blown."

Jasper's face softened.

"Instead of being out here, shouldn't you be running as fast as you can?"

A smirk flitted across her face.

"I am now."

"Why Cameron's sudden interest in me?"

"Lady Susan, your favourite ex-girlfriend, has been dripping poison into his ear since her brother was laid to rest. The burial of your stand-in corpse just intensified that lobbying." Jasper winced. "It turns out that she has a charitable side-line: helping those fleeing the Soviet socialist paradise of Russia."

"I don't think I'm going to like where this is going."

"Jude Faulkner had a private operation out here running agents in Odessa using Viktor Volkov as his go-between. From what Volkov told me, it looks like Lady Susan has been one of his financial backers. Probably the main one."

"And he had no idea who or what she really is?"

"No. Why would he? On the face of it, she's a leading light of the political right in Britain. Never short of invective about socialists, communists, or the Bolsheviks. She funds charitable works that oppose them—"

"And left in place by K to watch what she does next. I guess K didn't see fit to share with anyone that she's a communist spy?"

Jasper's frown was almost knitting his brows into one. Elspeth let him fume for a few moments before continuing.

"I think her aim, or her control's, is to frustrate Britain's attempts to build networks in the Soviet Union."

Jasper's brows unknitted a fraction.

"Marek was her control. He recruited her in Berlin. But

254

none of this sounds like his kind of operation. Ruby said that Marek had fallen out of favour with the OGPU Centre. I think that Lady Susan is someone else's creature these days."

"Well, she's upped her game. She pushed an assassin into Jude's path and asked him to get her to safety."

"Anna Kravchenko?"

"That's one name she goes by."

"To what end?"

"Looks like the OGPU wants to get a killer close to the remnants of the Russian opposition holed up in Paris. Everything she's been doing to date is her control's plan to build a plausible legend for Anna Kravchenko so she can get close to her target."

Jasper dropped his gaze to his lap. Elspeth studied him; he seemed to have deflated following her revelation about Anna Kravchenko. He looked back at her.

"What did Lavrov say about Anna? Did he say why he was looking for her?"

"No, he didn't say why, just that he trained her. I assume he's her control and presumably Lady Susan's."

A hint of a smile appeared on Jasper's face.

"The Anna Kravchenko I know is a killer, but she is genuinely running for her life. Lavrov may have trained her, but that was ten years ago. He needs to find her to protect a nasty little secret that he shares with Cameron."

"What secret?"

"You can ask her when you meet her."

"What? Are you mad? Why the hell do I need to meet your pet OGPU assassin?"

"I need you to hear her story. You're a professional journalist; being sceptical comes naturally to you. Test what she says like you would with any source for a big story. Believe me, this is a big story. K will listen to you. He'll just dismiss it if I tell him, and claim I was swayed by a pretty face."

"You think she has a pretty face, do you?"

20.   A meeting of minds

Jasper slowed down. In daylight, this lane was dispiriting. But in the early evening gloom, the place had all the appeal of a tomb. A wretched row of houses clung to the edge of a railway cutting. Gouts of spark-flecked smoke pulsed into the sky as a locomotive clawed its way along the cutting. Lost-soul screams from the train's wheels on the iron rails put Jasper's teeth on edge; welcome to hell. Elspeth coughed and pulled the collar of her coat across her face.

"I think I've had enough of breathing smoke and fumes to last me a lifetime!"

Jasper dragged a smile onto his face, but it took effort. How long would a lifetime be? At the time, persuading Elspeth to meet Anna seemed like a good idea. Right now, it was losing its appeal. There again, would Anna still be here? She was intelligent and resourceful, and he'd handed her a bundle of dollars. Would he still be hanging about if their positions were reversed? Probably not. It had been a stupid decision in a long line of stupid decisions. Why had he done it? Make her feel grateful? Make her feel obliged to wait for the sad little man to return and save her? You're an idiot, Lewingdon. When your neck is on the line, gratitude doesn't go far.

They were at the door to the safe house. Safe house; that description was a joke. It was a slum owned by Kimon Panakis and used by Viktor Volkov as a bolt hole. Just how safe was this place likely to be? Jasper pushed the door open. Elspeth was staring back down the lane.

"Did you see someone?" asked Jasper.

"No … I'm not sure."

Jasper peered into the shadows. They'd taken their time walking from the landing stage at Haydarpasa station, using every opportunity to make sure they hadn't been followed. He was sure they were clean, but Ruby had always said he was hopeless at spotting a tail. Was Elspeth any better? The rumble and clatter of the train wasn't helping.

"No," said Elspeth, "it was nothing. I'm just jumpy."

Jumpy was one way to describe how he felt. Shredded by the strain of the last few days would be more accurate.

"Let's get inside before it is something."

Narrow stairs climbed into darkness. No point in listening for any stray sounds that could give away an ambusher; the racket from the train made that impossible. On the plus side, anyone waiting for them wouldn't be able to hear much either.

"Wait here," said Jasper and jogged up the stairs, stopping by the door at the top. A would-be assassin wouldn't have heard him come up the stairs, but neither would Anna, and she had a gun. Jasper could feel his pulse thump as he turned the door knob. He let the door swing open. No bullets leapt from the darkness as he pulled his lighter from his coat pocket and flicked it into life. The room was empty. He sensed someone behind him.

"Has your little bird flown?" asked Elspeth.

Jasper walked into the room and lit the oil lamp on the table. The smoky glow from it shed the squalor of the place but didn't dispel his sense of defeat.

"It certainly looks that way. I can hardly blame her."

No, he couldn't blame her, just himself.

"Perhaps you should have told her she has a pretty face."

"Somehow, I don't think that would have made much difference."

The rumble from the railway was subsiding. Elspeth pushed the door shut and looked at him. She didn't say anything; she didn't have to. He was already asking himself the question that she was avoiding. What next? This had been his plan, and now it had run firmly into the buffers. He let his gaze drift around the room. Maybe he'd spot some hidden clue from Anna telling him where she had gone and where to meet her. Fat chance. That kind of thing only happened in Boy's Own thrillers. Elspeth was staring at him.

"I know," he said. "She's gone, and there's no point in hanging about here."

Elspeth checked her watch.

"We still have several hours to kill before my boat leaves."

Jasper winced. Several hours to kill or be killed in. But at least he had a way out on the Paros, assuming Panakis stuck to his side of the bargain. Ice-cold prickles clambered up his spine. The room was empty; had she taken them with her? If he turned up at the docks without the papers he'd promised Panakis... There wasn't much point in finishing that thought. Jasper walked to the small bed and pulled away the thin mattress and blanket. Nothing.

"What's up?" asked Elspeth.

Think, think! Anna must have stashed the papers. Why would she take them? They weren't of any use to her. Doubt was settling into certainty. The papers were no use to her, but she could always sell them on if she was in a tight spot, just like he had. He booted the bed. Its thud as it slammed into the wall made the lamp on the table shudder.

"Jasper! What the hell is going on?"

"I'm dead." He limped over to the table, dragged a chair from it and sat down. The ache in his foot suggested he'd broken a toe kicking out at the defenceless bed. Serves you right, you bloody idiot. "I made a deal, and now it's all screwed up. Ruby always said I was an idiot around women, and it looks like she was right."

"What deal?"

"Safe passage out of Istanbul in return for my recent acquisition of genuine French passports and visas. The trouble is, I left the papers with Anna for safekeeping, and she seems to have forgotten to leave them behind."

"Oh." Elspeth pulled the other chair out from the table and joined him. "I'm sure we can work something out. Volkov could get you aboard the ship with us; he owes me a favour for saving his life."

"What ship?"

An ember of hope started to glow.

"I think it was called the Parish or maybe the Perish. Something like that."

The ember dimmed, and then died in a drizzle of despair.

"It's called the Paros, and it belongs to Panakis. That's who I made my deal with."

Jasper slumped back into his chair.

"There has to be a way out of this," said Elspeth. "Get

out of Istanbul. Walk if you have to. Then, once you're clear, get a train or whatever to the border."

Jasper tried to smile, but he knew it was little more than a grimace. How far could he get before the bounty that Panakis would have on his head caught up with him? He couldn't even slip back into being Jasper Lewingdon, as Anna had his real passport. She was undoubtedly making her way to Izmir while he sat in this squalid room that was little better than a snare for the careless. The second the thought slipped into his head, his eyes swung to the door. Had he heard something? The rumble from the train had dropped to a mere murmur, but he was sure there had been something. Elspeth's mouth opened, her face already framing a question. Jasper held a finger to his lips. Another creak, and this time there was no doubt. They were trapped.

Jasper inched himself upright. A frown was forming on Elspeth's face. Maybe that creak had just been the house settling in response to the train's passing, but if it wasn't... He reached for the lamp. It was the only weapon he had, but if he threw it, he risked trapping them in a burning building. What was the alternative? Surrender.

The door handle turned. Jasper couldn't drag his eyes away as he hefted the lamp, ready to throw it. Elspeth pushed her chair back, its legs dragged at the rough floor. The door handle stopped turning, but Jasper's pulse hammered. They knew they were in here. The door would crash open any second, followed by someone's thugs. Whose, it didn't matter. He drew his arm back; it was now or never.

With a soft squeal, the door swung open: no mad rush of bodies and no shattering shots of gunfire followed. Anna stood in the doorway, the collar of her calf-length fur coat turned up and her hands thrust into its deep pockets. She looked at him, and then her gaze travelled from his face to his hand with the lamp in. The edge of an eyebrow flickered. It was impossible to judge whether it was in irritation or amusement, and suddenly the lamp felt very heavy. Jasper put it back on the table, which gave him an excuse to avoid her uncomfortable scrutiny. Anna marched to the table and pulled a packet from her pocket. She dropped it onto the table.

"I thought you would want those," she said.

It was the bundle of blank passports and documents that he had promised to Panakis.

"Thank you," said Jasper. "I thought you'd…"

Anna stared at him, no doubt waiting for him to finish that sentence. Could he finish it? Should he? She knew damn well what he'd been thinking. Anna shrugged and then stared at Elspeth.

"You've brought someone to see me."

The intonation in her voice was barely there. Maybe it was a statement, not a question, but Jasper could feel the pressure to respond. The unspoken part of that sentence asked him why?

"This is Elspeth Stirling—"

"You're Cameron Lowe's fiancé," said Anna ignoring him. Her eyes were fixed on Elspeth.

Elspeth smiled, or at least she pressed her lips together; there wasn't any warmth or welcome in it.

"And you're Tamara Korovina, an OGPU-trained assassin. Or do you prefer Anna?"

The tightening in Anna's shoulders was barely

noticeable, but it all but screamed at Elspeth's words. Jasper's mouth was paper dry. What the hell was Elspeth thinking? The two women were stuck in a staring contest, and nothing good could come from it. Anna's hand slid from her pocket, clutching Kerim's automatic. She glanced at Jasper and tossed the weapon to him.

"Max, go and keep watch. We have talking to do."

Anna sat down at the table, folded her arms, and continued her scrutiny of Elspeth. Jasper looked at Elspeth; she waved him away. What had just happened? Had he missed some part of the conversation? He walked to the room's door and took up a position to see the bottom of the stairs and stay in the room. There was no way he was leaving these two alone.

"Where did you get that name from?" asked Anna.

"Which one?" replied Elspeth.

"Tamara Korovina." Each syllable was accentuated as if being underlined in a letter.

"Your one-time lover, Nathan Lavrov."

Anna turned to glare at Jasper. He could feel an uncomfortable warmth clambering up his neck. Should he bluff it out? Pretend he hadn't said anything to Elspeth. What if Anna decided to shoot him? It'd be better than remaining under that stinging scrutiny. He shrugged an apology at Anna and returned to his vigil of the staircase. The creak of her chair suggested she'd switched her scowl back to Elspeth.

"And what else did Nathan tell you about me?"

Jasper let his attention swing back to Anna and Elspeth. With the oil lamp set midway between them, they looked like a sitting for an old master. Anna sat straight-backed in her chair, with her arms crossed tightly across her chest. Elspeth unfastened the top two buttons on her coat and removed her hat before shaking her hair free.

"Nothing. He was too busy torturing Viktor Volkov before putting a bullet through the head of a British diplomat." Elspeth shot a smile at Anna. "I didn't hang around to dig for any further details."

Anna let her gaze drift away from Elspeth, fixing for several seconds on a point on the wall. She sat back in her chair as she unfolded her arms.

"Is Viktor dead?"

"No, I got him out." Elspeth was studying Anna's face. God only knew what she could see there. As far as Jasper was concerned, Anna's expression was as solid as stone. "In case you're worried, he didn't believe what Lavrov said and didn't give you up. So as far as he's concerned, you're still a committed counter-revolutionary."

"And you don't think I am?"

"No."

"Why?"

"Lavrov was far too keen to taunt poor old Viktor. What he said had the ring of truth."

"That man is a liar. You cannot trust anything he says."

"You're right, of course. I suspect Lavrov's boast that he taught you everything you know was typical of the kind of drivel he is apt to spout." The room was starting to feel warm. Elspeth unbuttoned her coat and slipped it off. "Viktor told me about the assassination of Liminov in Odessa."

Anna's shoulders were tightening again.

"What more proof do you need that I'm an enemy of the Bolsheviks?"

"It was proof enough for Viktor and more importantly, for his backer, Jude Faulkner. By the way, it was Jude that Lavrov's man put a bullet through." Anna started to speak, but Elspeth held up a hand, cutting off her words before she could utter them. "Jude and Viktor didn't realise that the person funding their little scheme is herself a long-term OGPU agent. And she's probably much more than an agent: Lady Susan Linklater."

Jasper could see Anna's hands balling in her lap. It looked like Elspeth's words were having an effect. Which way would Anna jump?

"And you are here to tell me that you and Max cannot help me escape Istanbul because I am a Bolshevik?"

"No, far from it. We need you to stay alive." Elspeth pulled Anna's passport from her coat pocket and pushed it across the table. "I managed to rescue that. It's quite compelling."

Anna picked up the passport and flicked though a couple of pages before stopping at the page that held her picture. The seconds crept past, and Jasper held his breath. Finally, Anna closed the document and put it on the table, placing her hands over it; at least they were nowhere near her knife or gun. But, based on the number of corpses she'd left littering Istanbul, that distinction didn't really amount to much. Jasper breathed out.

"Why would you help me?" asked Anna.

"Self-interest, pure and simple," replied Elspeth. Anna's eyes narrowed a fraction, but Elspeth kept talking.

"Jasper filled me in about your past, especially the secret Lavrov and my soon-to-be ex-fiancé share."

"So what do you want me to do in return for your help? Do you want me to defect? Betray my country and my cause?"

Jasper tightened his grip on Kerim's automatic. The tension had returned to Anna's shoulders, but her hands hadn't moved. A silent prayer slipped into Jasper's mind that they stayed that way. Elspeth had her poker face on; where the hell was she going with this?

"Your mission is to get close to Kutepov in Paris. The murder of Liminov, and your escape using Viktor Volkov's services, were all planned to build your legend, just as Lady Susan intended. She has already been laying the groundwork for your acceptance in Paris. I don't really care what you get up to in Paris, but Jasper and I have previously been on the wrong end of her schemes, as I'm sure he has told you. The problem for you is that she is very close to Cameron Lowe, as indeed once were you."

Anna's stillness was unnerving. Jasper couldn't be sure, but she hadn't blinked for what seemed an age. Was she even breathing? There must be some calculation going on behind that steel façade. Elspeth hadn't spelt out the obvious threat to Anna from Cameron's link to Lavrov and Lady Susan; she didn't have to. What would be the result of the mental balance sheet in Anna's head?

"Can you promise that your masters will keep me safe in return for what I know?"

It looked like the balance sheet said it was time to jump.

"No, I can't," replied Elspeth. Jasper almost dropped

the automatic in surprise. "If I did, I'd be lying."

The corner of Anna's mouth twitched. It was barely a reaction, but at least Elspeth's words were having an effect, whatever it was. Elspeth carried on speaking.

"No doubt my lords and masters in London would want to keep you in place to eke out every last insight into Moscow's plans and thinking. That won't help you all the time that Lavrov knows you're alive."

"So, what is your plan for me?"

Anna's flat monotone hinted at sarcasm. Elspeth broke eye contact for several seconds and then looked back at Anna.

"My cover is well and truly blown, and Cameron knows I've been keeping watch on him and his friends on behalf of MI5." She glanced at her ring. "I suspect the ending of our engagement will be swiftly followed by my obituary in the paper I write for. So I need a reason for him to keep me alive, and that reason is—."

"The secret he shares with Nathan; their part in the execution of the Baku Commissars."

"Exactly. I think Cameron came out here so swiftly because Lavrov alerted him that their secret wasn't as safe as they thought."

"And now they both have a reason to kill me."

"Which is why we need insurance to ensure they put their murderous efforts into making sure you, and of course, I, remain very much alive."

"What kind of insurance?"

"The last thing anyone in this line of business wants is

publicity, which will be true for Lavrov and Cameron. Having the recent history of their affairs in Baku published in the papers wouldn't be welcomed by either."

The muscle in Anna's jaw tightened.

"Cameron owns newspapers. He's a powerful businessman. He'd be able to stop anything being published."

"That's true in Britain, and maybe Canada, but not in the U.S. He's got plenty of business rivals over there that wouldn't be sorry to take advantage of any misfortune he might suffer. And that goes for several influential editors that I know."

"Do you think the threat of publication if either of us has an accident will be enough?"

"Have you got anything better?"

Anna shrugged. Elspeth pulled a notebook and pencil from her coat pocket.

"In that case," said Elspeth, "let's get started. I will need everything, including dates and times, with as much detail as you can remember."

21. Setting sail

Jasper shivered. The dockside was cold, and the air felt damp. The lights of the old city glittered on the glassy surface of the Golden Horn, a mythical mirror world to the real one. He followed the outline of a steamer heading towards the gap in the Galata Bridge; only her navigation lights were visible in the pre-dawn gloom. Her wake ruined the reflections from the water's surface, spoiling the spell. He checked his watch: almost three. A couple of hours before the bridge shut, sealing all inside. The Istanbul rush hour decreed an early start for anyone wanting to sail from here. Still about four hours before sunrise. Jasper pulled himself further inside his coat, but it had little effect. He glanced at Elspeth. She wore Anna's coat, which was perfect for the chill: ankle length with a thick fur collar. Pity he couldn't abide fur, or he'd have offered to pretend to be Anna.

In contrast to the wraith-like steamer sailing past, the upper decks of the Paros were ablaze with lights. The putter of a diesel engine echoed around the steel sheds and workshops clustered by the dockside. A small crane swung a net bulging with bales of something over the ship. A crewman onboard the Paros shouted down commands to the crane's operator. It may be the small hours of the morning, but it looked like rush hour was already here. A man in a cap stood on the bridge wing of the Paros, smoking a cigarette. Was this the captain? A gangway gave access from the dock to the ship's deck just forward of her main superstructure. No one appeared to be taking names or checking passengers. There again, there didn't appear to be any other passengers.

"Come on." Elspeth's disembodied voice emanated from somewhere between the fur collar and her hat making him start.

"Are you sure?"

"No point in freezing to death out here. Better to get shot on board in the warm than out here. I can't believe I agreed to this crazy scheme."

"As I remember it, it was your idea."

Elspeth pulled the fur collar down far enough to shoot a scowl at him.

"Someone had to come up with a plan. You pointed out my similarity to Anna; that was your explanation for trying to steal my passport." The 'you' was very pointed.

"I didn't try. I succeeded. You're just irritated that I said she was pretty."

They were a few yards from the end of the gangway. The man in the cap looked down at them. Then, he flicked his cigarette over the side and headed into the wheelhouse.

"I think it's time for you to become Anna Kravchenko if anyone asks," said Jasper.

"Don't expect me to put on the accent."

Jasper trudged up the gangway. The music-hall comedy squabble was bravado; this felt like a bad idea. They were arriving at a place and time that the biggest crook in Istanbul knew about. Who else might he have let in on the secret? With luck, Anna should be in Ankara waiting to get a train to Aleppo. Jasper grimaced; Panakis' men would be looking for him and a woman. Not a woman travelling alone headed for Ankara. That left him and Elspeth to run interference playing the part of the decoy couple. Of course, if Panakis kept his end of the bargain, he and Elspeth would have a nice quiet cruise to Constanta. Jasper could feel his grimace deepen. If. They should be on a train heading anywhere, not here at three in the morning. But Elspeth was right; Anna was the only proof linking Lavrov and Cameron to the death of the 26 Baku Commissars. If K was going to be able to use it, then Anna had to survive. Would they be so lucky?

Jasper stepped onto the ship's deck. The hatch covers for the forward hold were pulled back. Several seamen were pulling on ropes to steer the bulging cargo net as it descended. The hand commands were getting more frequent, and the shouting more urgent. A door clanged open in the superstructure. The man from the bridge stepped out onto the deck; the dark blue jacket with gold braid around its cuffs marked him out as the captain or at least an officer on the ship. He walked a couple of paces toward Jasper, then stopped. His attention switched to the team dealing with the cargo swinging over the deck. He shouted a few short commands. The winching stopped. A tall man slouching against the ship's side ran forward to take hold of a rope and added his weight to it. The captain barked another order. The winch re-started, and the cargo slipped gracefully from view into the hold.

"Hello," said Jasper. "Mr Panakis said you'd be expecting us."

The captain watched the crewmen pulling the hatch covers into place. Several seconds passed before he let his attention be dragged away.

"Yes, Mr Bolton. You have something for him?"

"Of course."

Jasper unbuttoned his coat to get to the package of papers he'd pulled together. Elspeth edged closer to him. The captain looked at her, his eyes narrowing. Did he

271

suspect something?

"You must be the 'other'?" he said.

Elspeth returned his stare. She may have drawn the line at hacking her hair short to match Anna's, but her flat-faced stare had Anna down to a T. The captain seemed to recoil a fraction in response.

"Yes," said Jasper. "This is Anna Kravchenko. Do you need to see our papers?"

"Ah, no, that won't be necessary." His gaze wandered back to the sailors working on the hatch. "You don't have any luggage?"

"No, we're travelling light." Jasper handed the package to the captain. "Everything is there as agreed with Mr Panakis."

The captain took the package, seemingly weighing it in his hands; was he going to open it? Finally, he called out to someone, and a young lad ran over to him. He handed him the package, and the lad scampered off down the gangway.

"Will we be going soon?" asked Jasper.

"Yes, we will get underway as soon as we get the hatch cover fixed down."

Jasper's gaze followed the lad as he ran towards the row of sheds and buildings clustered along the side of the narrow dockside. A big man was limping towards the gangway. Jasper stared at him; it was Viktor Volkov.

"Are you expecting any other passengers?" asked Jasper.

"No. If you follow me, I will show you to your cabin."

The captain turned and headed for the open door in the

superstructure. Jasper felt Elspeth stiffen next to him. She dug an elbow in his side.

"The tall sailor at the side of the ship." Jasper let his gaze drift to the man leaning against the rails; his gaze was fixed on Elspeth. "That's Dmitry. Lavrov's pet killer."

"Run!" said Jasper.

Dmitry was already straightening up as Elspeth started for the gangway. He pulled a pistol from his jacket, his eyes tracking Elspeth as she pelted down the gangway.

"Viktor! Lavrov is here!" she yelled.

Jasper pulled Kerim's pathetic little automatic from his coat pocket. Dmitry's pistol was levelled. Please, God, let this be enough. The little automatic cracked three times and then was silent; it had jammed. Dmitry's gun barked as he dropped down. Had he hit him? Jasper worked his pistol's slide, trying to unjam it. Dmitry's head bobbed up. The automatic's slide wouldn't move; Jasper's pulse was galloping like a thoroughbred in the Grand National. Dmitry darted forward. A shot cracked out, and Dmitry fell to the deck as if he were a puppet whose strings had been cut.

Jasper looked around the deck. The captain was gone, and the deck crew were all cowering behind anything they could find. He got up and dashed down the gangway. He stopped as he saw Viktor levelling his pistol at him.

"No!" cried Elspeth. "That's Max." She grabbed Volkov's arm pulling him after her. They half-ran and half-hobbled into the cover of the nearest open-fronted shed. Two cars swung onto the dockside, shuddering to a halt. Jasper pelted after Elspeth and Volkov. Two pistol shots cracked out; the whine of a ricochet meant that the last one had been close. Shouts followed it, and the shooting stopped. He barrelled into the shadows inside the barn-like structure of the shed. Where the hell were Elspeth and Volkov?

After the lights on the Paros, the darkness inside the workshop seemed total. The open front gave him a good view across the dock and the Paros. Jasper slipped behind a block of machinery, the scent of oil and grease catching the back of his throat. He listened, straining to piece together what was going on. Outside the workshop, he could hear commands being given. A car rolled forward into view. Lavrov's men were using it as a shield, judging by the occasional head bobbing into view over its bonnet. How long before someone came to investigate the noise? Stupid question. This place belonged to Panakis; no one was coming unless he sent them.

Jasper popped the automatic's magazine out and worked the slide; at least he had something to defend himself with now. The thump of a large pistol reverberated around the shed. He heard the windscreen of the car shatter. That must mean Volkov was in here somewhere. Unfortunately, the way out from the docks was past the cars and Lavrov's men. Could they sneak past? Another shot thundered out. Jasper took a quick look. One vehicle was now sporting a hole in its radiator, a jet of steam venting from it. A clatter came from the right-hand end of the shed. Was Lavrov trying to drive them towards the other end of the shed and pin them against the end of the dock? What to do? Stay put and hope they missed him?

A couple of shadows shifted; his eyes must be getting used to the gloom. Jasper aimed the automatic at the leading figure, slowing his breathing. His finger tightened on the trigger. An engine revved, and the second car screeched past the first. Volkov's pistol let fly. In an instant, several shots came from the shadows. Jasper dropped flat. There was a yell, and Volkov stopped firing. The two figures ran forward. Keeping low, Jasper crawled towards the front of the shed and away from where Volkov must be.

Two men jumped from the second car heading for the shed. Jasper got on his feet and ran; he looked across the dock. Elspeth sprinted from her hiding place, her long coat flapping around her. One of the men saw her and stopped; he raised his pistol.

"No!" yelled Jasper running at him.

Elspeth glanced right, her eyes widening. The pistol cracked. Elspeth cried out and went over the side of the quay. Reality slowed, and silence swept away all sounds. No, no, no! Not again, not her! Jasper ran to the edge of the dock. The glossy black surface of the water was still. Jasper crumpled to his knees; Elspeth was dead.

The thud of running feet forced its way into his consciousness. A boot kicked him flat onto the ground, and another kicked the automatic from his hand. He stared at the old city's dancing reflections on the water as a pistol pressed against his head.

"No! She needs him alive and undamaged."

The words meant nothing; Elspeth was dead.

22.   An unwelcome reunion

Jasper stretched. The OGPU thug glanced up from his newspaper. Three days had passed since… Since. Three days of being cooped up in a single room with an OGPU minder. Never alone. Not allowed to the toilet without being watched. A meal was brought in once a day. Otherwise, he was ignored; no beatings, no threats. Boredom had long supplanted fear as his principal emotion; even guilt had taken a back seat. Jasper's guts twisted. Yes, boredom was in the front seat, but guilt was still the back seat driver. Distract yourself, don't dwell on it. How could he not dwell on it? It: a pronoun used to represent an inanimate thing… It. Is that what Elspeth had become? No, that's what you've made her.

"Hey!"

The OGPU man looked at him. A crease of irritation furrowed his forehead. He was one of three that were taking turns to keep an eye on him.

"So what happens now?" demanded Jasper. The OGPU man shook his head. Did that mean he didn't understand, or he didn't know? The newspaper he was reading was in English. Maybe he'd been ordered not to talk to him. Who ordered him? Lavrov?

"Can I have your paper when you've finished?"

The OGPU man shrugged and let his attention return to his newspaper. Jasper sighed and lay back on the thin bed. None of his babysitters had responded to any attempt to get them to react. Each of them was the size of a door. The threats didn't need to be verbalised; the scars and lumps on these men spoke for themselves.

How much longer would Lavrov keep him here? He'd

been searched at the docks. Lavrov's men had taken the automatic and his lockpicks but handed everything else back, including his passports. They hadn't even stolen the money from his wallet. So why was Lavrov holding on to him? It looked like he had a plan for him, which couldn't be a good thing. But it had to be better than a bullet in the head. Bitter bile brewed at the back of his throat. Coward. Face it; you're too frightened to try and escape this little canary cage.

A nearby door rattled, and footsteps sounded on the stairs leading to this floor. Jasper checked his watch. It was almost midnight. Way past mealtime, and his latest babysitter must have at least five hours left on his shift. Jasper could feel his chest tighten; perhaps that bullet was closer than he'd been telling himself. The OGPU man was staring at him. Jasper couldn't keep his eyes from the man's hands that were rolling his newspaper into a baton. It might not be steel, but in the hands of a professional, it was as good as. Finally, the footsteps halted outside the door. The doorknob rattled. Bile pushed itself into Jasper's mouth.

The door opened. A tall man with a near-shaven head stood there. Jasper hadn't seen Lavrov before, but Anna had described him perfectly. Jasper swallowed the bile, trying to suppress a grimace as he did so. A smirk crossed Lavrov's face as he studied Jasper. The OGPU man stood up, his makeshift baton clamped in his fist. Lavrov's smirk transformed into a smile; it had all the warmth of an icepick.

"Jasper Lewingdon, I've been looking for you for what seems like an age."

Anna had told him Lavrov's mother was English and that he'd been schooled there, but his clipped English accent was still a surprise. Finally, the mystery Englishman that had been stalking him was revealed.

"You should have sent a note to my club inviting me to supper," said Jasper.

Lavrov chuckled.

"Ah yes, I was warned that when cornered, you resort to sarcasm."

Cornered. That's exactly what he was, but what to do next? Keep silent or play along with the role of the comedy side-kick to Lavrov's leading man? Maybe he could get Lavrov to reveal what was happening and why. But who had told Lavrov about him? That mattered more.

"And what do you resort to when cornered?" asked Jasper. Play along it was then. A cold smile remained on Lavrov's face.

"I don't know. I've never been cornered."

That wasn't how Anna had described what had happened in Baku, but maybe Lavrov had been in control the whole time. In control until events had made a mockery of that notion. The OGPU minder stood up. He signalled for Jasper to get up. No doubt who was in control here.

"Are we off to the opera? Only I don't think I'm really dressed for it."

Lavrov's smile faded. Jasper got up and spent several seconds brushing some specks of imaginary fluff from his trousers. The minder hadn't moved a muscle. They'd shot Elspeth without a second thought, but so far, they hadn't laid a finger on him. How far could he push them? Jasper checked his fingernails, then looked at Lavrov.

"Have you got a comb? I feel that my hair must be a frightful mess."

The OGPU minder moved closer. Time to stop baiting the bear and comply with its wishes.

"Come on," said Lavrov. "You can make yourself look respectable in the car. There is someone that needs to talk to you."

Lavrov walked out of the room. The OGPU minder jabbed Jasper between his shoulder blades with the rolled-up newspaper. It wouldn't leave a bruise, but a second stab would be unwelcome. Jasper followed Lavrov outside. In the alley were the other two minders and a large black sedan. The car was a step up in luxury compared to the bullet-riddled wreck he had been brought here in. Lavrov got into the front; Jasper was wedged into the back between two OGPU men.

"I feel honoured," said Jasper. "It's not every day someone sends their chauffeur-driven limousine to pick me up. So, who are we going to see?"

"My control. They have a small job they require you to undertake for them."

A small job. What was it going to cost him? Why him? Jasper glanced at the streets and buildings they passed. He'd been held somewhere on the outskirts of Pera or Galata. Now, they were heading into the backstreets of Beyoğlu. Everywhere was starting to look uncomfortably familiar.

"What happened to Viktor?" asked Jasper. "What did you do with his body?"

"I left it for Panakis' people to clear up. So why do you care what happened to that traitor?"

"And the girl? Was she a traitor?"

Lavrov stared. The shadows inside the car made it hard to read his expression. Who did he think his men had executed?

"An unfortunate accident."

An accident. How right Lavrov was. He'd accidentally murdered the wrong woman. Lavrov was probably feeling comfortable that his secret was safe. Hardly a consolation to Elspeth wherever she was now. Another corpse floating in the waters of the Bosphorous? Or perhaps her body was already waiting to be claimed from the Istanbul morgue. Would Cameron be the one to do that, or would he send some flunky to do it for him? Who would write her obituary? His fingernails were gouging the back of his hand. Don't react, not now. If Lavrov gets a hint that Anna isn't dead, he's going wonder what she told you, and pretty soon, you'll be dead too.

The car slowed. They were turning into a narrow street. A couple of bars were open, with people clustered on the pavement outside, laughing and drinking. The driver nudged the car past the party-goers bringing it to a halt outside an open doorway with a flashing neon sign above it. They were outside La Mouette; stifled sounds of music wafted into the car. Jasper's heart sank.

"We're here," said Lavrov.

Of course they were; where else would they be? But the choice of La Mouette as a meeting place made this very personal. The OGPU man on his left got out and held the door open for him. Jasper started to move, then realised Lavrov was staying put, as were the other two thugs in the car.

"Aren't you coming in?" asked Jasper.

280

"No. Do you want someone to hold your hand?"

Jasper got out of the car. Lavrov opened his window.

"How will I recognise your control?" asked Jasper.

Lavrov grinned.

"You'll recognise them. I have no doubt about that."

"What if I run?"

"You won't." Lavrov's smug smile was grating. "Anatoly will make sure you get inside without any adventures. We'll be waiting here for you when my control has finished briefing you."

Lavrov wound his window shut; time to go. Jasper walked through the entrance of La Mouette. Ekrem sat at a small table to one side with a cash box and a lit cigarette hanging from his lip. Ekrem glanced up. The clump of ash on his cigarette gave up its battle against gravity, spattering down the front of his shirt. Jasper felt Anatolly prod him forward, ignoring Ekrem's curses as he brushed the ash from his otherwise pristine shirt. They must be expected if Ekrem wasn't chasing after them for payment. Did that mean Oktan and Ekrem were in on this, whatever this was?

Applause petered out as Jasper reached the swing door to the club's dance floor and bar. He pushed it open. A drum roll started as he stepped inside with Anatoly at his shoulder. A pair of cornets joined in with the snare drum. The centre of the room was awash with stage lights, the tables around it in shadow. The club was packed; the faces of the crowd focused on the stage at the centre of the room. All except one, and hers was fixed on him.

Jasper walked the dozen steps to the table as if his legs belonged to someone else. Lady Susan Linklater poured out two glasses of champagne. She picked one up and took a sip from it. Around them, the crowd started cheering as two dancers strutted onto the stage.

"You look well for someone who was buried six months ago," said Lady Susan.

Jasper sat down.

"Is this for me?" he asked, nodding at the champagne glass.

"I always try to be a good hostess," said Lady Susan. She took a cigarette from a gold cigarette case. "Would you?"

Lady Susan leaned forward. Jasper pulled his lighter from his pocket and coaxed it into life. The flame flickered; was that a draught or was it the tremble in his arm? Lady Susan's fingers encircled his hand, keeping it captive as she lit her cigarette. A stream of smoke jetted towards the ceiling as she exhaled, her perfume apparent in the tobacco smoke-laden atmosphere. How did this scene appear to anyone watching? A lover's tryst with him as the lucky man at the centre of this glamorous woman's world? Lady Susan let go of his hand, her nails gliding down to his wrist as she leant back into her seat. Jasper subdued the shudder that shot down his spine.

"It always amused me that you carry a lighter but don't smoke," said Lady Susan.

"You never know when it might come in useful."

Jasper slipped the lighter into his jacket pocket. Lady Susan toyed with the strands of her gold necklace. How much were that necklace and the matching earrings worth? They hardly seemed fitting for a Bolshevik spy, but all the best covers deflected attention away from the reality.

"Aren't you drinking?" asked Lady Susan.

"I thought it might be poisoned."

Lady Susan laughed.

"What a foolish notion. Why would I kill you when I have so much for you to do?"

"Your errand boy mentioned something about that when he brought me here."

"I don't think Nathan would appreciate being called an errand boy. After all, he is a diplomat of the Soviet Union."

"Who takes his orders from you."

"We all have to take orders from someone. So who gave you the order to murder my brother? Elspeth? No…" Lady Susan's eyes narrowed. "She probably just passed on the command."

"Would it make any difference if I told you I didn't kill Sir Nicholas?"

Lady Susan's face hardened.

"No." She took a drag from her cigarette, holding the smoke for a few seconds before breathing out and letting her gaze swing to the dance floor. "You're going to do a job for me."

"What if I refuse?"

Jasper followed Lady Susan's gaze to the stage. Cecile and Salome were almost through their opening set, and the crowd loved every second of the performance. Despite her stage-seasoned smiles and laughter, Jasper could tell that Salome had spotted him, but Cecile hadn't.

"You might be reckless with your own life but not so

quick to sacrifice one with a pretty face."

The band hit its climax. Salome and Cecile nailed the end of their routine, and the crowd whooped their applause. Salome and Cecile bowed. Cecile waved and blew kisses at their loving audience. Salome's eyes settled for a second on Jasper before she and her sister left the stage.

"Which one means the most to you, Jasper?" asked Lady Susan. "Is it the pretty one with the blond curls? I bet she laughs at your jokes, no matter how feeble they are. Makes you feel good about yourself. She'd follow you forever like the dutiful little wife she wants to be."

Lady Susan stubbed out her cigarette, grinding it into oblivion.

"No, it's not her, is it, Jasper? It's the dark-haired one with the anger in her eyes."

"Did you just bring me here to taunt me? I thought you had some pressing need for my skills. Whatever it is you want, let's get on with it."

"Oh, have I touched a nerve?"

One of Oktan's second-string singers had started warbling along to a tired tune the club's band were pedalling to a largely disinterested audience. This was the interval in the show. An all too brief pause to allow Salome and Cecile time to change costumes before their much-anticipated finale. How the hell could he get a message to Salome? He needed to warn her and give her and Cecile a chance to get out. Lady Susan chuckled.

"Your face is such a picture." She flipped open her cigarette case. "The only way you can save her is to do as I ask. You couldn't save your partner in that doss house, but you can save this one."

The buzz of the band grew distant. As Lady Susan selected a cigarette, Jasper's attention was fixed on her fingers. Every sparkle of light from a perfectly polished fingernail pinned his gaze in place. She'd been there when Ruby had died. Finally, he dragged his attention from her hand and forced himself to stare at her face.

"You killed her."

The words were barely louder than a whisper, but it felt like he'd screamed. Lady Susan's cigarette stopped on its journey to her lips. Her eyes narrowed. Thinking of something suitably vicious to toss back at him?

"No. She killed herself."

"You expect me to believe that?"

Lady Susan smirked and put the cigarette in her mouth. The smirk remained as she tore a match from a matchbook and lit her cigarette. She dropped the dying match into the ashtray. Jasper willed the tension from his jaw, but it was no good; every emotion was there for her to dissect.

"It's true," said Lady Susan. "She was smart. She knew I would use her to get to you, so she sold me a story about needing an injection. Would you like to know her last words to you?"

Careful, careful. Don't show too much, not yet. Ruby always said to wrap the big lie around a slice of truth.

"She wouldn't have said a thing."

Lady Susan took a short drag on her cigarette, her eyes flicking to the singer on stage.

"It's lucky that we still have Elspeth. Did you know she's in Istanbul looking for you?"

Jasper lunged forward, grabbing Lady Susan's arm.

"Leave Elspeth out of this."

Lady Susan's gaze dropped to his hand before fixing on something behind him, probably Anatoly. Jasper let go of her arm and slumped back into his seat. He could feel the sinews of his neck twanging. Lady Susan tapped the ash from her cigarette.

"You never tried the rough stuff when we were an item. Who knows where that might have led." She took another short drag. "If you don't want Elspeth to end up like your partner, I suggest you do exactly as I say."

Jasper didn't fight to stifle the scowl. She wants to torture you; let her see it working. Give her what she wants to see. Every hateful thought, every vicious idea, he dredged them up, let them flow across his face. She didn't know about Elspeth. It wasn't much, but it gave him an edge. He snatched the glass of champagne from the table and emptied it in a near-single gulp.

"Let's hear it. What is it you want me to do?"

If you wanted a dictionary definition of triumph, then Lady Susan's face was the place to look for it. How long would she eke this out for? She refilled Jasper's glass before topping up her own. If she had her way, she'd make this torture last an eternity.

"You're going to assassinate Leon Trotsky."

Jasper recognised all the words in her statement, but none of it made sense. Lady Susan took a sip of champagne. She held the glass up, watching the light from the stage scatter from the bubbles before putting the glass on the table.

"This champagne is quite tolerable, but I recommend you sip it instead of chugging it back if you want to get the best out of it," said Lady Susan.

Jasper shook his head. Had he heard her correctly?

"Have you gone mad?" he said. "You want me to kill Trotsky?"

"Yes." Lady Susan beamed at him as if he'd just proposed marriage. "And you'll do it tonight."

"And how the hell do you expect me to do that? Why would you want me to?"

Lady Susan opened her clutch bag taking out a key and slip of paper. She slid them across the table to Jasper.

"That's the key to my room at the Hotel Tokatlian. It's on the floor directly below Trotsky's suite. The number of his suite is on that slip of paper. Next to the bed in my room is a cigar box; it's a bomb set to explode at four o'clock in the morning. Put it next to the traitor's bed before it goes off. He's a heavy sleeper but goes to bed late."

The urge to empty the second glass of champagne was almost overwhelming; maybe the first one had been drugged. Bombs, Trotsky, assassination; this wasn't spontaneous. How long had he been in the frame as the scapegoat?

"Did you come up with this little scheme all on your own?"

"I had some help from Nathan."

"Like the bomb?"

"He does have an over-fondness of such things. Anyway, it will suit you better. I know you get squeamish

287

about shooting people." Her eyes hardened. "Even if you think nothing of smothering them in their sleep."

"And you'd have to give me a gun."

"I can't risk you getting some foolish notion in your head that you can shoot your way out of this."

Polite applause signalled that the singer had finished. The band's tempo changed; a ripple of anticipation travelled through the audience. The snare drum chattered out a drumroll. The crowd whistled and whooped their appreciation as Salome and Cecile sashayed back on stage. Jasper picked up the key and the paper. A cornet hit a wailing note as Salome and Cecile started their finale. Jasper stood up.

"I bet this was your errand boy's idea."

"What do you mean?"

"Accelerating the wheels of revolutionary justice to do someone a favour; he's got previous for that. If I was you, I'd ask him how it turned out last time."

Jasper headed for the exit with his heart rate matching the band's tempo. Salome and Cecile were hitting the hottest part of their routine. Like the rest of the crowd, Anatoly's attention was glued to the dancers; good. Jasper was halfway to the door. Maybe if he ran now, he could get away. That might just work. Anatoly's head turned. He had a thin smile on his face. Jasper's heart sank. The moment was lost, and so was he. Anatoly fell into step with him as they headed out of the club. Behind them, the audience burst into applause as Salome and Cecile finished their performance.

23.   Things that go bang in the night

Lavrov's car pulled over. The Hotel Tokatlian was about fifty yards further up the Grande Rue, hidden by the bend in the road.

"Time for you to get out, Mr Lewingdon," said Lavrov.

"What? No door-to-door service?" said Jasper. "Or are you worried about this car being remembered in the morning?"

Lavrov tapped his watch.

"Time is ticking, Mr Lewingdon, and there is more than your neck at stake."

Jasper got out of the car.

"So what happens after I've delivered your package?"

Lavrov smiled.

"Don't you worry about that. We'll be in touch."

The driver revved the car's engine and pulled away from the kerb. Jasper watched its tail lights as it disappeared around the corner. So what was the plan? Did he even have one? Beyond carrying out his orders from Lady Susan, no. Jasper trudged up to the bend. Even at one in the morning, the lights of the Grande Rue glittered like Blackpool at Christmas, the Hotel Tokatlian a singular jewel at their centre. The place wasn't busy, but the doormen were awake and alert. If he strolled in the front door, they'd remember his face. How about slipping down the next side street and see if he could get in through the kitchens? No, Trotsky's minders were bound to have that staked out. With each step he took, the heavier the sinker in

289

his stomach became. Ten yards to go.

The nearest doorman rubbed his hands together. The night-time air was cool, and even with his thick coat and gloves, the bite of the breeze was hard to ignore. A car was heading towards the hotel. The doorman looked towards it, his colleague already taking a step forward as it neared the kerb. Jasper squinted as the car's headlights swept across him; it was Lavrov's car. The driver braked sharply, and the car's tyres protested as it graunched to a halt. The rear passenger window dropped down, followed by a stream of Turkish that Jasper couldn't follow. The doorman bent closer as the words were repeated. He shook his head and then beckoned to his colleague. Jasper walked behind the pair and into the hotel.

The lobby was near-deserted. The soft sounds of a piano mixed with laughter wafted through an open door from the hotel's cocktail bar. It looked like the barman would be working a very late shift. A rumpled suit sat snoring gently in an armchair in the corner of the room. Judging from his threadbare style, this must be one of Trotsky's official OGPU minders; nothing but the best for a disgraced leader of the soviet socialist empire. A movement caught Jasper's eye; the night porter tidied something behind the front desk. Jasper pulled Lady Susan's room key from his pocket and headed to the lift before the man could try and be helpful. The bellhop slid the lift's lattice-work door open; its clatter made Jasper wince.

"Which floor, sir?" asked the Bellhop.

"The second," replied Jasper.

The door rattled shut, and the lift hummed into life. Jasper glanced at the dishevelled OGPU minder. He was awake and glaring at the lift; was that because someone had interrupted his night-time nap or that he'd just missed someone coming into the hotel? With luck, he'd see the lift stop safely at the second floor and head back to the land of nod. The lobby slid from sight.

The distraction with the car outside meant that Lavrov was keeping an eye on him after all. Perhaps he didn't think Lady Susan's threats would hold him to this task. It would have been helpful if Lavrov had told him what security was in place to keep unwanted visitors from bothering Trotsky. The lift sighed to a halt, and the bellhop slid the door open with a little less gusto than when he'd shut it. Jasper pressed a tip into the lad's hand and strode into the corridor. Look like you belong here; never mind that you've no idea where Lady Susan's room is. The thoughts circled in his head as he walked ahead, counting the seconds until the lift door shut and it descended. The clatter from behind, followed by the wine of the lift, told him he was alone now. Jasper checked the number on the nearest door; Lady Susan's room would be just around the corner.

The plush carpet softened his tread as he turned the corner. The place was empty, with only the barest background hum to suggest that there was anyone in the building. The key sounded unnaturally loud as he opened the door. Jasper's pulse was drumming, and his throat was dry. The room was empty, and a single lamp on the desk was the only illumination. It would have been a relief if someone had been waiting for him.

There, on the bedside table, was the cigar box. Jasper picked it up. The package was heavier than he expected, a pound in weight, maybe more. The lid was taped shut. Peeking inside wasn't an option, even if he had wanted to. How much damage could be done by something so small? Enough. What if it went off while he was carrying it? Would there be much left for anyone to recognise him? It didn't matter. As far as the world was concerned, Jasper

Lewingdon died half a year ago, and no one gave a damn about Max Bolton. If he failed, would Lady Susan go through with her implied threats against Salome and Cecile? Of course she would; she was that kind of a woman. He put the box back on the table.

How to get into Trotsky's room? Could he bluff his way in? What would be the excuse, and why was he carrying an overly-heavy box of cigars? No. That way wasn't an option, even if he had the time to plan it. Jasper walked to the window and pulled the drapes back. French doors opened onto a thin balcony. Beyond the rooftops, the lights of the old city of Istanbul glittered; the view would be charming if he wasn't sharing it with a bomb set to explode in a couple of hours.

Jasper opened the doors and stepped onto the balcony. The street below was silent, and thankfully the windows of the adjacent rooms were dark. No loafers or hotel staff taking a quick break. No one to witness what he was about to do or his untimely and no doubt spectacular death if it went wrong. Jasper leant back and looked up at the rooms of Trotsky's suite. The room directly above had a balcony matching this one. So that would have to be the way in. No convenient drainpipe running up the wall to cling to, just the joints between each course of stonework to hang onto. Jasper forced his fingers into the masonry joints and pulled himself up a couple of inches. This was going to be a tough climb, but it was doable if nothing went wrong. If.

Peeling his coat off and discarding his jacket, Jasper returned to the room and picked up the box. Somehow it felt better to think of this as just a cigar box and not to dwell on what it was. How on earth to carry it and clamber up the wall to the next balcony? Push it down the back of your trousers and hope for the best? No. Jasper pulled the sheets from the bed and tore them into strips using the letter

292

opener from the desk. It was a pity to ruin such lovely bedsheets, but even the best hotel rooms don't come with a length of rope, and calling room service for one wasn't an option. With the cigar box attached to one end of the improvised rope and the other secured to his belt, he returned to the balcony.

Jasper shivered. Was that just the breeze or his reaction to what he was about to do? Get on with it; your time is running out. He put the box on the balcony's floor and paid out his improvised rope. Hopefully, he'd judged the length correctly, and the rope was long enough; the last thing he wanted was to have the box swinging around beneath him while he climbed. Jasper checked his lock picks were secure in his pocket and then clambered onto the stone rail around the balcony. It wasn't much but at least that shortened the distance to climb. Reaching up, he dug the tips of his fingers into the gap between two blocks and pulled. He pressed the toe of his shoe into the nearest joint. It was just wide enough for the edge of his shoe's sole to get a purchase; at least something was going right. Deep breath, and don't look down.

The cool stone was rough but dry: good. Ignore that sting in the knuckles and the shriek from your tendons. It's someone else, not you. Focus, focus. Keep pulling. Kick that toe in place. Another pull, another inch. Not far now. Don't think about distance; just reach for the next hold. There is no pain; it's someone else suffering. Keep going. The bottom of the balcony was within reach. One last stretch. The fingers of his right hand grazed the balcony's concrete edge. Get higher? Fingers slipping. No! Lunge. Grab. Pray.

His feet were swinging free, but his fingers were welded to the edge of the balcony's floor. Don't look down, don't look down. Slowly, carefully, get your left hand into that crevice. Good. Now pull, pull! He shoved his right hand forward and grabbed onto a railing. Safe. Jasper hung for several breaths, then hauled himself onto the balcony. Come on, stay in control, slow that breathing, and calm yourself. Keeping close to the edge, Jasper looked down. The bedsheet rope was at full stretch, and the cigar box was starting to skitter across the balcony below. Time to pull it up before something terrible happened, something more terrible than what was already taking place. With the box safely with him, he untied the rope and fixed an end to the balustrade, letting the other drop free. It should make the descent a bit easier. Now for the hard part.

The room's drapes were shut, but no light bled through from inside the room. Was Trotsky already tucked up in bed? A low light glimmered from an adjacent window. Maybe a desk lamp. That would fit with what Lavrov had said about Trotsky's habits. There again, it might be another minder trying to stay awake. Whoever, or whatever it was, it meant he'd have to be damn quiet getting the lock open. Jasper stared at the French doors. There wasn't a keyhole for the lock on the outside. Shit! Don't panic now. You have to think this through. Why would you need to lock these doors from the outside when you were three floors up? Think, think. He grasped the door handle. Maybe that same logic would make you lazy about locking the doors from the inside. His heart rate hammered, but the handle turned.

Jasper opened the door half an inch. The breeze pushed at the drape, starting to make it billow. He stopped. His pulse still rattled, but he could hardly breathe. A sound was coming from inside. Was that the sound of someone snoring softly? The breeze dropped, and Jasper opened the door fully and pushed the drape aside. A mound of bedclothes outlined a figure in the bed. Take a good look; that's who you've come here to murder. The snoring stuttered as the

294

sleeper shifted; maybe he knew what was coming. Jasper gently pressed the door shut behind him.

Murder. Dress it up however you like; that's what you're here to commit. Ruby would tell you to get on with it, but they murdered her. If you don't get on with it, that's what will happen to Salome and Cecile. Jasper crept closer to the bed. Where to put the box? Beneath the bed, on the bedside table? Who cares? The victim, that's who. But isn't Trotsky a mass murderer? This would be justice for all his victims. Good try, Jasper, but that won't erase your guilt. They're forcing me to do this; I don't have a choice. But it's still you doing it; they're just accessories to the crime. Shut up, shut up! Jasper dug his nails deep into his palm. The pointed prickle of pain drove the circling voices from his head. It was time to get on with it.

Three soft steps, and he was next to the bed. Trotsky rolled onto his side. Jasper counted the seconds as he waited for Trotsky's breathing to slow and deepen. He crouched down and slid the cigar box beneath the bed; it was done. A cough sounded from the next room. Trotsky shifted in his sleep. Move, move, you need to get out of here. Slowly, oh so slowly, Jasper crept away. Don't wake your victim. Let him die in his sleep; it's the kindest thing to do. No, this is wrong. You can't do this. You can't commit murder.

Jasper stopped. If he couldn't kill the man he had been sent here to murder, what could he do? The bomb was going to explode in two hours. Don't try and fool yourself into thinking you can defuse it. Put it back in Lady Susan's room? That would buy him two hours to get back to the club and figure a way to get Salome and Cecile away. The confusion when it detonated might give him a bit more time. He went back to Trotsky's bedside. The sleeper seemed blissfully unaware. Jasper knelt down and reached

295

for the cigar box. The mattress springs creaked and groaned, and Jasper's fingers froze as their tips touched the box; Trotsky was awake.

"Leon?"

It was a woman's voice. Shit, shit, shit. It wasn't Trotsky in the bed; it was his wife, Natalia. The bed springs creaked once more. She must be sitting up now.

"Leon." Her voice was louder and more urgent.

What now? Hide under the bed clutching a bomb while Mr and Mrs Trotsky padded around the room in their pyjamas? The bedclothes were being pulled back. Any second now … The bedside lamp drenched the room in light. Jasper scrabbled to his feet. Natalia screamed as he fought with the drapes. Why the hell was he still holding the sodding bomb? A vase smashed against the wall next to his head. He kicked the French Doors open and dashed onto the balcony dropping the cigar box. Voices and clatter sounded from the adjoining room. Would that bedsheet rope hold him? No time to think. Just do it.

Jasper swung his legs over the balustrade. Deep breath, deep breath, don't look down. He grasped the improvised rope and swung into space. Could he hear the sound of tearing? Stop it! Come on, hand over hand. Quicker, quicker; you haven't time to worry. A shout from above. Jasper glanced up. Natalia was pointing at him and shouting to someone behind her. His foot touched the top of the balcony's balustrade just as the bedsheet rope seemed to slip. Jasper tried to hook his foot over the barrier and pull himself in. The sheets shifted again; it was giving up its fight against gravity. He looked up. Natalia was sawing away at his lifeline. The sheets parted as Jasper grabbed for the top of the balustrade.

Feet swaying free above the street, Jasper hung from the edge of the balcony. Natalia shouted at him; he couldn't translate the words, but their sentiment was clear. The cow! Didn't she realise he'd just saved her life? Of course not; she knows you were there to take it. Jasper dragged himself over the stone rail and flopped onto the balcony. Come on, come on, you don't have time to rest: move! He struggled upright and staggered through Lady Susan's room, grabbing his jacket and coat.

He needed to get away, and every sense in his body screamed at him to run. The sounds from the room above him said that the hounds were already on the loose. Run, but which way? He opened the door and peered into the corridor. All was quiet. A running man would attract attention, and he needed to deflect it. Jasper padded along the corridor, heading away from the lift. There had to be a set of service stairs somewhere. But wouldn't the OGPU apes be hurtling down them right now?

Jasper felt inside his trouser pocket. The lock picks were still there. What have you got to lose? Face it, you're already as good as caught. He slipped the tension bar into the lock of the nearest room, followed by the pick. What was the chance that this room was unoccupied? Judging by tonight's escapade, it must be close to zero. A door slammed open around the corner. Well, that solved the mystery as to where the service stairs were. The bedroom's lock turned, and Jasper opened the door and stepped inside. Before he pressed the door shut, the snatch of light showed an empty bed. Jasper leant back against the door as feet thudded past in the corridor.

How long did he have before someone started beating on this door? The room was empty; could he bluff it out and lay low? No. Any time now, Lavrov would know the plan to plant the bomb had failed, and there would be nothing to protect Salome and Cecile from Lady Susan's spite. Jasper went to the window. No balconies on this side of the hotel. He opened the window and leant out. No balconies but a drainpipe within reach. Thank you, God, for cheap rooms next to the utilities. The alley below was empty. Jasper heaved himself through the window and grasped the drainpipe. Just two floors to the ground. Hand over hand, he shinned down the pipe as fast as he could. Old flaking paint scratched at his palms, but the drainpipe held firm. Jasper jumped the last five feet and then stood still, waiting for the hue and cry to start.

Start walking, don't look back; there's nothing to see here. Ahead, the alley opened onto the Grande Rue. The glitter of its lights sharpened the shadows in the passage. Jasper turned his collar up. Well done, what a disguise; no one will recognise you now. He trudged ahead as his stomach screwed tighter. Was that a figure at the corner? A silhouette, no, it was more than that. The outline was that of a policeman. He turned to look towards Jasper. Keep moving, keep moving, and don't react. Jasper stepped onto the pavement of the Grande Rue. The policeman glanced at him and turned back to study the controlled chaos in front of the Hotel Tokatlian. A large black car was parked at an angle across the kerb in front of the entrance. A few men in suits were arguing with the doormen, and one of them was the OGPU minder from the foyer. Had he looked this way? Jasper crossed the Grande Rue. A convenient alleyway was beckoning him. The urge to look behind was overwhelming, and the screw in his stomach tightened with each step. Any second now, someone would shout.

A figure emerged from the alleyway blocking that escape route. Jasper stepped onto the pavement and turned left to head away from the hotel. Ahead of him, cutting across the road, was the policeman angling to head him off.

298

A car crunched to a halt behind, the sound of its doors opening reaching him almost before it had stopped. Jasper halted. What was the point in running now? He turned. Two Turkish policemen pinned his arms behind him and snapped a pair of handcuffs on him. From across the street, the OGPU minder glared at him.

24.   The journey's end

Jasper shuffled along the corridor, escorted by a policeman. Walking while trying to hold your trousers up when your wrists are handcuffed together is a challenge. Unlike his most recent jailers from the OGPU, the Turkish police had taken his belt, shoelaces, and tie along with his wallet. But so far, no one had threatened to shoot him. Finally, they halted outside a door. The policeman rapped twice on the door before opening it.

A large mahogany desk cut the room in two. To the right of the desk was a leather armchair. Its occupant reclined reading a newspaper, with his highly polished boots perched on the edge of the desk. The man's uniform marked him out as a colonel in the Turkish police force. He glanced up from his paper, a frown flitting across his face at the interruption. His white hair and moustache suggested he was in his sixties; his eyes seemed older. Jasper stifled a gasp. It wasn't the colonel that was the surprise but the photograph on the newspaper's front page.

The picture didn't flatter her, but the photographer had caught something of Lady Susan's personality. Her snarl was perfectly framed as a policeman pushed her into the back of a Black Mariah. A crowd of loafers and onlookers pressed forward to get a better look. The neon sign of La Mouette's front entrance hung like a banner over the image; Oktan would be loving the publicity. Jasper squinted to read the date. It was this morning's edition, so the photograph must have been taken last night. What the hell had happened?

The headline shrieked: English Aristocrat Arrested. Jasper snatched the smirk from his face; he'd have added an exclamation mark to the headline. No doubt the editor was too professional to allow such nonsense. The colonel folded the paper away, removing the opportunity to find out what the article thought she'd been arrested for. He stood up, walked to his desk, and beckoned Jasper to come in. The policeman nudged him in the centre of his back, propelling him toward the desk.

The colonel selected a cigarette from an ornate box and lit it. He took a long drag on the cigarette. The end glowed brightly as the cigarette's black paper turned to ash. The colonel breathed out a stream of cigarette smoke, making his outline momentarily hazy. All the while, he stared at Jasper. No, that wasn't quite correct; he was examining him. What for? Weakness? An as yet untold lie? The colonel placed the glowing cigarette on the edge of an ashtray and sat down. He steepled his fingers and stared at Jasper. This had a horribly familiar feel to it. Change the location from Istanbul to London, and change the unidentified Turkish colonel for an unnamed officer of MI5 or MI6, and it was the same.

"Please sit down," said the colonel.

Jasper shuffled forward to the desk. In front of the colonel were Jasper's passports. The colonel straightened the left-hand one; Jasper couldn't detect an apparent difference, but no doubt it was important to the man.

"Why am I being held?" asked Jasper. He might as well go on the attack; after all, what was there to lose?

"Someone broke into the hotel room of Leon Trotsky and left a bomb behind before escaping via the window." The colonel stared at Jasper. He didn't need to add that he was sure it was Jasper, and no doubt Natalia would identify him. The colonel cleared his throat before continuing. "And I'm looking for someone to hang for the murder of Kerim Yazaroğlu."

301

The surprise was like a slap.

"But I didn't …" It was too late to unsay those words, and there was no point in trying. "I didn't kill Kerim."

"Did I accuse you of his murder?"

Was that a rhetorical question? A device to get him to talk and incriminate himself further? Jasper glanced at the passports on the desk. How could he incriminate himself any further?

"Ah yes," said the colonel as he picked up the left-hand passport. "This says you are Max Bolton." He tossed it back onto the desk. "The other claims you are Jasper Lewingdon. Which is it, please?"

Jasper could feel his pulse starting to rattle. The question hung in the air. He might be doing that before long if he didn't cooperate.

"Jasper Lewingdon. Your officer didn't tell me who you are."

"I am Colonel Göçek." He nodded at the policeman who'd brought Jasper from his cell. The policeman saluted and left. The room didn't conform to Jasper's expectations of what an interrogation cell should look like. The bookcases and watercolours of local landscapes didn't project an air of menace. They didn't need to; the smiling old man opposite him was more than capable of achieving that by himself.

"According to the British Consulate in Istanbul, Jasper Lewingdon was certified dead six months ago." Colonel Göçek opened a slim folder and scanned its contents. "According to my sources, Max Bolton has been in Istanbul around the same time. Why did you fake your death and hide here with a false identity?"

Colonel Göçek picked up a pen ready to record, what, his confession? How much did he know? Can you lie your way out of a hangman's noose? Possibly, but you can certainly put yourself there with the wrong lies.

"What did Lady Susan say?"

Wrinkles of amusement creased the corners of Colonel Göçek's eyes.

"Not much. The British Consul did most of her talking for her. But she said enough to identify you as a British agent sent to assassinate Leon Trotsky."

Jasper could almost feel the rough hemp of the noose tightening around his throat.

"It must have slipped her mind that she is the one behind that plot."

"You admit that you were here to commit murder?"

Colonel Göçek's pen hovered over a typed sheet of paper. Shut up, say nothing. Too late for that; you've already said enough. Lady Susan has set you up. That was her plan all along, and you've waltzed right into it. Salome had called on the saints to protect him, and he was going to need them.

"No. I was escaping from Lady Susan and the people she works for." Colonel Göçek put his pen down. Was that in disbelief or encouragement? "I doubt she mentioned that she works for the OGPU. Their plan, or rather Lady Susan's, was to kill Trotsky and to pin the blame on the British secret service."

"But you work for the British secret services."

"No. I'm just an idiot fall guy that Lady Susan wants to see hang for it all."

Colonel Göçek sat back in his chair, steepling his fingers once more. Why the hell would he believe him? But why had Lady Susan been arrested? He must think that she was a British agent. It made sense; her cover had fooled most people.

"You should ask Lady Susan about the murder of my partner, Ruby Stevens," said Jasper. "Or ask her about her dealings with Nathan Lavrov. He's one of her agents."

"Mr Lavrov is a respected member of the Soviet diplomatic—"

"He's a psychopath and murdered Jude Faulkner, Elspeth Stirling, and Kerim Yazaroğlu."

"That's three murders you are accusing him of. Do you have any proof to back up your accusation?"

The steel of the handcuffs dug into Jasper's wrists; the thump of his pulse seemed to make them vibrate. What evidence did he have? Elspeth was the only witness to Jude's death, and Lavrov had removed her even if he hadn't meant to. Had Elspeth's body been found, would Cameron have reported her missing? His own face was firmly in the frame for Kerim's murder, and he couldn't see that changing anytime soon. He was going to hang, and nothing he said would make any difference. Colonel Göçek picked up his cigarette.

"I'll take that silence as a no." Colonel Göçek took a short drag from his cigarette. "Tell me about your partner." He glanced at the file on his desk before fixing Jasper with his stare. "My records say she was a prostitute who killed herself with an overdose of morphine."

Jasper felt an uptick in his heart rate.

"Ruby didn't kill herself. She was murdered."

Colonel Göçek took another drag from his cigarette, holding the smoke for several seconds before breathing out through his nose. Was this all part of his performance, or was he just taking time to think?

"You didn't refute the accusation that she was a prostitute. Why?"

"It was too absurd to acknowledge. If you seriously thought she was a prostitute and I was her pimp, you wouldn't be wasting your time interrogating me."

Göçek hid a sliver of a smile behind another intake of nicotine from his cigarette. Jasper dug the steel of the handcuffs into his wrist. The prickle of pain was sharp, quelling the fizz of anger. It had been an obvious gibe: blacken Ruby's reputation and see what his reaction was, but it had stung all the same. Well, if Göçek could put on a performance, he'd have to respond with one of his own.

"If she wasn't a prostitute, what was she doing here?" asked Göçek.

What tale to tell? Are you trying to save your neck or Ruby's reputation? She'd tell you not to be a bloody fool. Say whatever it takes to get out of here, and save your own skin no matter the cost. Once you're dead, it's too late, no matter how noble your intentions are. Noble intentions; there hadn't been much he'd done that was noble for the last few years.

"We came here to help refugees."

Göçek smiled.

"Refugees like the former countess Sophia Pokrovskaya? How much did you make her pay for her new papers?"

The title of countess painted a picture of some austere aristocrat dripping with diamonds and pearls, but the reality had been different. Jasper remembered a small, scared woman pressing a pair of thin gold bangles into his hands and asking him to go and get a good price for them. She'd paid with all she had, and her gratitude had left him feeling like a louse. Did it make any difference that the money had kept him and Ruby in business and helped get several others out of Istanbul? No. He was a parasite, and that wouldn't change no matter how much he rewrote the arguments in his head. Jasper could feel the muscles in his jaw clamping tighter. He deserved to hang.

"A guilty conscience?" Göçek's smile sharpened. "Is that why you were helping Anna Kravchenko?"

How much did Göçek know? Was her name all he had, or was she sitting in a nearby cell? There didn't seem much point in holding out, but why had he dragged up Sophia? Suspicion was starting to solidify. Göçek was trying to make him think he knew more than he did.

"Viktor Volkov asked us to get her some papers so she could get into France. He had contacts there that would look after her."

"Ah yes, his friends like Kutepov and fellow dreamers in Paris who plot to overthrow the Soviet state. I'm curious as to why you would help an OGPU assassin get close to her obvious target in Paris."

Bile forced itself into Jasper's mouth. He swallowed, trying to keep the bitterness from his face. It looked like the question about Sophia had been a ploy. Göçek knew what he and Ruby had been doing in Istanbul all along. So why had he helped Anna even when he knew she was an OGPU agent? Elspeth had known Anna's value, but he'd helped her because he could. If it helped derail what Lavrov was up to, then it was worth it.

"I'd like to speak to the British Consul," said Jasper.

Göçek laughed, but the apparent good humour didn't generate any warmth.

"Why would you want to do that?"

"I'm a British citizen, and he's supposed to protect my interests."

It was a feeble defence, and Göçek's continued chuckling confirmed it.

"As far as your consul is concerned, Jasper Lewingdon is dead, and Max Bolton doesn't exist. He has his hands full shepherding your mutual friend Lady Susan out of my country to some place where she can't cause too much trouble." He stubbed his cigarette out. "A small-time people smuggler and a failed assassin is not sufficiently eminent to trouble the Consul with."

"And what about Elspeth Stirling? Is she sufficiently eminent to be worth the trouble of bothering the British Consul with?" The small smouldering coal of anger in his guts was now burning bright. "Lavrov murdered her, and I saw her die. Have you pulled her body from the Bosphorous? Have you even bothered to look for her?"

"Why would I do that?" asked Colonel Göçek. "I think you should have a look at that."

He pushed the newspaper across the desk. Jasper's eyes skipped past the headline and picture to fix on the by-line; it was written by Elspeth Stirling.

"But ... I saw her die."

"Apparently not. Miss Stirling must be a strong

swimmer, even with a bullet hole in her arm. She warned me about Mr Lavrov and what he has been trying to do."

Jasper felt his chest tighten. Colonel Göçek stared at him.

"No, I haven't arrested... what shall I call her? Your client, Anna Kravchenko," said Colonel Göçek. "That's a pity, as I would have significantly more leverage over Mr Lavrov if she were in my custody."

Jasper closed his eyes. Elspeth was alive, and for the time being, Anna was free; didn't that count for something?

"I think," said Colonel Göçek, "it is time for Jasper Lewingdon to leave Istanbul, never to return."

"What about Elspeth?"

"She intends to remain in Istanbul. She has taken a job writing for our English language newspaper. I doubt her ex-fiancé and former employer would be overly pleased to see her anytime soon."

Jasper smiled. All Elspeth had ever wanted was, as she put it, 'to be a proper journalist'; all she had had to do was get shot to achieve it.

"However," said Colonel Göçek, "I still need someone to hang for Kerim Yazaroğlu's murder." He pushed Jasper's passports across the desk. "Who will it be?"

* * *

Keys rattled in the lock of the cell door. Jasper checked his watch; it was running fast, but it was approaching eleven. Execution time at the Sultanahmet jail. He got to his feet as the door opened. The warder beckoned him forward.

No point in disobeying as this was the end, and there was nothing else he could do. Two more warders stood on the landing. The shouts and jeers that usually echoed around the prison were absent; the inmates knew the significance of the time and the meaning of a single cell door being opened.

Jasper stepped out onto the landing and put his hands behind him. A pair of handcuffs were snapped into place. Firm but not too tight. He almost smiled to himself. You wouldn't want to hurt someone on their final journey, would you? The first warder spoke to him and then turned on his heel, starting a slow march along the prison landing. The almost gentle nudge in his back told him he had to follow.

As he fell into step with the warder, the man called out as if starting to recite the call to prayer. Another ten paces and the warder called out again, only this time it was answered by the clang of a tin mug or plate banged against a cell door. More bangs started to fill the space marking time with his steps and the warder's calls. A last farewell to someone leaving this world from his unseen fellow inmates. Ahead was the door that led to the execution chamber.

Two paces from the door, the warder halted. Sudden silence swamped the place. It looked like the locals here had had a lot of practice timing the length of the walk from the condemned cell to the execution chamber. Jasper swallowed or at least tried to, but his mouth was dry. Until now, it had all seemed like a dream, but the reality was starting to bite. Then, the keys rattled once more, and the warder beckoned him into the room.

His steps echoed on the wooden floor, reminding him of the drop directly below. A man in a long coat stepped forward and ushered him onto the trapdoor before strapping his ankles together. This was the executioner. He'd weighed and measured him yesterday to ensure everything went according to plan. There was something in the man's manner that reminded him of a tailor in Jermyn Street. At least he wouldn't have to worry about any unpaid bills. The hangman stood up and turned Jasper to his left.

In front was the audience. At least Colonel Göçek had the politeness to look sombre, but the man beside him looked bored. No doubt that would be the representative sent from the British Consulate to ensure he was correctly hanged. Had the consul insisted, or was this man here at K's insistence to make sure that an embarrassing episode had reached its conclusion? The hangman pulled a hood over Jasper's head.

Against the cloth of the hood, Jasper could feel how hot his breath was. Next the noose; tight but not too tight. His pulse was now at the gallop. His watch had been fast, but how long would he wait? The hangman stepped away, his footsteps quick and loud. Breathe, breathe while you still can. Weightless.

His scream turned into the shriek of the train's whistle. Jasper shuddered awake, sucking air into his lungs. Surely in time, the memory of that moment would lessen. Surely. He stood up and pulled the window down in the train carriage to lean out. The clock on the platform of Sirkeci Station clicked round to eleven. The guard's whistle screeched, signalling the train's departure. Max Bolton was dead. Jasper Lewingdon had a lot of living to catch up on.

The End

310

Printed in Great Britain
by Amazon

38589633R00175